the *one* in *my* heart

USA Today Bestselling Author

SHERRY THOMAS

This is a work of fiction. Names, characters, places, and incidents are the product of the author's imagination or are used fictitiously. Any resemblance to actual events, locales, or persons, living or dead, is purely coincidental.

Edited by Tiffany Yates Martin

Print Edition 1.0

To New York City and Middle-earth

Chapter 1

THE LAST THING I EXPECTED on that miserable August evening was a one-night stand. I expected even less that my accidental lover would swoop back into my life, metaphoric guns blazing. Though what really did me in was our subsequent fake relationship, which turned everything upside down even before the nude scandal erupted.

But it all began, for me at least, on the back lanes of Cos Cob, Connecticut.

A shower fell steadily. My hair was plastered to my skull, dripping water down my neck. My stomach had given up sending polite signals of hunger and was moodily folding in on itself. It must be nearly midnight. Had I eaten anything today? Had I eaten anything at all since I found Zelda four days ago in the grips of a major manic upswing?

A gust blew. I shivered, the chill of my drenched clothes sinking deep beneath my skin. But I kept walking. The lane wound between houses on heavily wooded lots, some hidden behind impenetrable tall hedges, others set apart by low stone walls. Was I tired enough yet? How much farther did I need to go, before I could sink into a dreamless sleep?

The bright headlights of an oncoming car startled me. I hurried to the edge of the narrow lane, my tired toes digging into waterlogged and slippery flip-flops.

As it passed, the low-slung, sporty model slowed to a crawl. Probably someone who lived in the area, coming back from a Friday-night party and wondering why a woman was out by herself in this weather, at this time of the night.

Come on. Keep moving. I didn't want any neighborly concern.

The car stopped, aerodynamic curves gleaming faintly, windows completely dark. It reversed a good fifteen, twenty feet. Now it faced me again, its headlights flooding the rain-slicked asphalt between us.

Alarm jolted me. What if I *wasn't* about to deal with neighborly concern? What if…I yanked out my phone, swiped to unlock the screen, and tapped 911.

The driver-side door opened and out came a large umbrella, followed by a man. Instinctively I stepped back—directly into the bulk of a low stone wall. My pulse hammered.

The man straightened, closed the car door, and didn't move for a few seconds, as if he too had second thoughts about the situation. Or was he merely figuring out the best way to overpower me?

He started toward me. I groped blindly for a weapon, my fingers closing around a loose rock from the top of the wall.

Stop. Stop right now.

He stopped six feet away. His face was in shadows, but against the flood of light from the car he seemed the size of a linebacker. "Evangeline, right?" he asked, his voice low yet clear against the percussion of rain on his umbrella.

I blinked, caught between hope and even greater suspicion. "Yes?"

"I'm Bennett. I took care of Collette Woolworth's dog for you this week."

"Oh," I said, my death grip around the rock unclenching a little.

I was in the neighborhood for the summer because Collette, Zelda's good friend, was overseas on a work assignment, and needed someone to keep an eye on Biscuit, her rat terrier. When Zelda's mania swung into high gear and I didn't want to leave her alone, I'd called a list of emergency contacts Collette had left me. Everyone was out of town except Bennett, who had sounded harried, but had agreed to look after Biscuit.

"Thanks for helping me out," I added.

"You are welcome," he answered.

I said nothing else. Had I met him in broad daylight, my gratitude might have been more effusive—in fact, I meant to get him a nice thank-you present. But it was the middle of the night, we were on a deserted lane, and a man who was nice to a dog could still commit a crime of opportunity.

After a moment he turned to look at his car, as if longing for its safety. As if he, rather than me, were the exposed and vulnerable one here.

As he did so, the headlights illuminated enough of his features for recognition to kick me in the chest. His name had meant nothing when I called, but I'd come across him a few times when I was out walking Biscuit. He was usually on a bicycle, though I'd also seen him running, fast and with a beautiful gait.

Once he stopped his bike, pushed his aviators up, and asked me the time. His demeanor was courteous, but not interested. In fact, he seemed wary, as if he suspected that the clock on my phone might be fifteen minutes off.

Yet I'd vibrated afterward, unable to stop thinking of his deep-set green eyes.

But just because I found a man attractive didn't mean I should trust him.

He looked back at me, his face once again in shadows. "People keep telling me this neighborhood is really safe. But it's late. Is there some-one I can call for you?"

The last thing I wanted was to alert anyone that I was wandering about the middle of the night, drowning in rain. "Thanks, but I'm okay."

"What if I gave you the key to my car? You can drive yourself home."

My eyes widened. I glanced at the sleek vehicle, a Tesla Roadster. "You're willing to let a stranger drive your car? Aren't you breaking some sacred man commandment?"

"I'll risk it."

He lobbed the key my way. I somehow managed to catch it between my wrists, while still holding on to both phone and rock. "But I'll get your car all wet!"

"It's an old car. It'll survive," he answered from over his shoulder, already walking away.

And kept walking away, with no backward glances for me or the fate of his car. I stared at him, and then down at the car key. He wasn't kid-ding—he'd really left me his car.

And I thought I was pretty deranged for stumbling about in the dark, even after it started to rain.

Not knowing what else to do, I got into the Roadster, wincing in apology as my soaked clothes squelched against the leather seat. Thank goodness I hadn't actually dialed 911, or I'd have to shamefacedly explain that not only hadn't the man assaulted me, but that I was now in possession of his vehicle.

I slowed as I approached Bennett, who was headed in the same direction as me. It wouldn't feel quite right to drive past him in his car, but I still hesitated, the adrenaline from my earlier scare not completely dissipated yet. What if he was running a long con? What if he meant to gain my trust and then pounce on me?

Shaking my head at my cynicism—nobody ran this kind of long con on a random stranger—I stopped a bit past him and lowered the window two inches on the passenger side. "Hey, people keep telling me this neighborhood is really safe. But it's late. Can I drop you off at home?"

He braced a hand on the top of the car and leaned down. "No. Grandma told me I'm too pretty to get into cars with strangers."

My lips twitched. "Grandma was lying through her teeth. You're just average."

"What? But I had plans for becoming a Park Avenue trophy husband."

I felt a smile spreading across my face, a lovely sensation. "Forget about sleeping your way to the top. You'll have to get to Park Avenue by exploiting the masses like everyone else—or not at all. Now get in the car before I give it back to you."

He shook his head, collapsed his umbrella, and got in. "When did it become so hard to be a Good Samaritan? You give up your ride to a woman in need and she calls you ugly."

"That'll teach you to give your ride to women in need. I could have fenced the car overnight."

He pulled on the seat belt. "You'll make me cry into my tiramisu."

I slowly eased my foot down on the accelerator—the engine was much more powerful than I'd expected. "Don't tell me you actually have tiramisu at home."

I *had* eaten earlier, now that I thought about it, but an apple and two scrambled eggs were not enough for an entire day. A huge serving of something sweet and dense would send me into a food stupor, and a food stupor might be exactly what I needed for a full night's sleep, which I hadn't had since the beginning of Zelda's episode.

"I never lie about food," said Bennett.

Then what do *you lie about?* "Lucky you."

"At least I can stuff my face on the night I find out I'm not pretty. You know, take it like a man."

I smiled again—there was something rather irresistible about him.

He gave me directions, and we arrived at a center-hall colonial with a circular driveway in front. As the Roadster came to a stop, he picked up a messenger bag from the floor of the car and looked inside.

"So what do you do to pass time while you're waiting to become a Park Avenue trophy husband?" I heard myself ask.

He mock-glared at me, his cheekbones remarkable in the exterior lights of the house that had come on when we pulled up. "You mean what do I do when I'm waiting to never become a Park Avenue trophy husband?"

"Don't let some hater step on your dream. But yeah, that."

He shook his head a little, smiling. "I'm a surgeon."

I looked him up and down. I'd have pegged him as a lawyer, one of those young, assertive, high-powered breed. Or a restaurateur, the shrewd kind who rehabbed derelict spaces into hole-in-the-wall eateries that had lines going around the block. I could even, in a pinch, imagine him as a Silicon Alley executive with a million frequent-flier miles accumulated from trips to San Jose and Austin.

But I wouldn't have guessed him to be a doctor, let alone the kind who worked with scalpels. "So, you're tired of cutting people open?"

"Sick of it—blood and guts every day. But someday my princess will come, and she'll carry me away from all this drudgery."

I couldn't help it—I laughed aloud. He laughed too, though more quietly.

In the wake of our mirth, a small silence fell. He closed the flap of the messenger bag and I was suddenly speaking again. "I've seen you around a few times."

He glanced at me. "Last time I saw you, you wore a shirt that said, 'To err is human; to really screw things up requires a computer programmer.'"

"Nerd humor." The shirt had been given to me by my friend Carolyn, who was in corporate IT security.

"Do you know your age in binary?"

I'd minored in computer science, so I did happen to know it. "One hundred thousand."

"I *have* been known to like an older woman," he replied, deadpan.

I chortled, feeling…elated, almost.

"That's thirty-two, right?" he asked.

"Yeah. You?"

"I'll be thirty-two in a few months."

So I really was an older woman here. Hmm.

He leaned back an inch. "I'll see you around, Evangeline. Thanks for the ride."

He already had his fingers on the door handle, but I wasn't ready to let him go—since he appeared, I hadn't freaked out about Zelda at all. "Umm…It was really nice of me to give you a ride. Do you think you can share some of your tiramisu with me?"

He considered. "That depends."

I was already smiling again from his mock-pompous tone. "On what?"

"On whether you are a secret princess."

"Of course I am."

"How would I know that?"

"There's a picture of me online in a diamond tiara and a ball gown." Which was not a lie. "I'm the real deal."

Something flickered in his eyes before he gave me a look to let me know he was reserving judgment. "Okay, then. You can come and have some tiramisu."

A thrill leaped through me. We got out of the car. Bennett dealt with the house's security system. I, waiting behind him, happened to glance down at myself—and barely managed to suppress a yelp.

Wherever my wet white T-shirt clung to my skin, I was practically naked. The flesh-tone cotton bra I wore underneath didn't appear to have turned as transparent, but it was thin, and Bennett would have to be blind not to see the outline of my cold-hardened nipples.

Hastily I crossed my arms over my chest. Without turning around, he asked, "Do you want me to find you a bathrobe or something like that to wear?"

My other choice would be to go back to Collette's house. But the closer I came to tiramisu, the more reluctant I was to give it up. "Yeah, sure. Thanks."

He showed me bathroom to the left of the front door. I ducked inside, nearly squealing again at my reflection. Then I covered my mouth and tried not to giggle. What a mess I was tonight.

But tiramisu was going to make everything better.

I stripped off my clothes, glad to be rid of their sodden weight. Bennett delivered a fluffy white towel and a blue lightweight bathrobe. When I came out of the bathroom, he was waiting for me.

"I can put your clothes in the dryer," he told me.

He was back a moment later to lead me down the central passage toward the back. The house was an *Architectural Digest* editor's dream come true. But I didn't give a second glance to the console table that would make an *Antiques Roadshow* appraiser jump for joy, or the paintings on the walls that were probably American Impressionist originals, by artists who had once thrived right here in Cos Cob.

Instead I took in the man in front of me, the soft-looking olive-green Henley shirt, the jeans that hung just right on his hips, the sexy gait, his strides long and easy, his footsteps almost silent on the gleaming wood floor. My adrenaline-soaked perception had lied to me earlier: He wasn't at all built like a linebacker, but along far more lithe and sinewy lines—kind of like his car, actually.

His kitchen was high ceilinged, with exposed beams and three exposed brick walls. Neat stacks of bowls and plates sat on open shelves. He took two plates and two spoons and placed them on the central island, shifting aside a bowl of red Bartlett pears and a vase of yellow daisies.

Now he pulled open a refrigerated drawer set beneath the counter of the island and took out a dish of—no kidding—honest-to-goodness tiramisu, with a thick dusting of cocoa powder and generous sprinkles of chocolate shavings.

I sucked in a breath.

"You look like an ER patient, the kind who comes in jonesing for a fix," he said.

I sat down on a bar stool opposite him. "Well, prescribe me my drug of choice, Doctor."

He handed me a heaping serving. The tiramisu was fresh and not too sweet, with just enough espresso and dark chocolate to cut the decadence of mascarpone cheese and whipped cream. I devoured it.

"Where'd you get this? It's so good."

"My housekeeper made it," he said, watching me.

Something in his gaze made my heart thump. Had I thought he wasn't interested in me? That indifference was nowhere to be seen now.

"So…what kind of surgeon are you?"

A kettle trilled. He poured hot water into a mug and pushed it toward me, along with a box of assorted teabags. "Cardiothoracic. But I'm still doing my fellowship."

"What's that?" I asked, gratefully wrapping my still-cold fingers around the mug.

"Extra training after residency."

"To take your God complex to the next level?"

He chortled softly. "Nah, I was born with a full-fledged God complex. In fact, I'll have you all fixed up by the time you leave, princess."

That made me grin. I couldn't believe it—from pure misery to this lightness of heart in mere minutes. I felt like…a princess, one who found herself under an unexpected enchantment.

Bennett studied me a moment, the corners of his lips lifting. My heart thudded again.

Black hair, great angles, and those mesmerizing eyes—he was drop-dead gorgeous.

"What do *you* do," he asked, "when you are not wearing a diamond tiara and a ball gown?"

"I'm an assistant professor of materials science."

"That's a mash-up of physics, chemistry, and engineering, right?"

"Close enough."

He whistled. "Beauty *and* brains—I'm not sure I can handle the two together."

"At this point it's mostly just beauty. My brain was confiscated in grad school and never given back."

He laughed. He had a great laugh.

Our eyes met. He didn't look away. I somehow couldn't.

It was late. We were alone. And I was already naked beneath the soft, warm robe that smelled faintly of sunshine and freshly mowed grass.

All this had been true since I stepped into his kitchen. But the possibilities that had only lurked in the depths of my subconscious mind now broke surface and created huge ripples.

I looked away, finished the last bite of my tiramisu, and asked, "Were you at the hospital when I called about Biscuit?"

He rolled up his sleeves. "Uh-hmm."

His forearms were lean and strong—and since when did I pay attention to a man's forearms? "Is your hospital in Greenwich?"

"It's in the city," he answered, giving his dishes a quick but expert wash.

Manhattan, he meant, thirty miles away. I was surprised. "Do you commute every day?"

"Usually I only come up on weekends, when I'm not on call."

"I hope you didn't have to come all this way for Biscuit."

It was fifty minutes by train—one way. Taking care of Biscuit had been a lot of trouble for him.

I remembered my T-shirt. *To err is human* was printed on the front. To know the rest, he would have had to turn around and watch me from behind.

He reached for a pear from the bowl on the island. "I did."

My gaze was riveted to his hand, the loose yet secure hold he had on the pear.

"You didn't ask your housekeeper to do it?"

"She was out most of the week. Just came back this afternoon."

I looked down at the smudges on my plate—all that remained of my dessert. A hot thrill had zigzagged through me when I'd thought that he'd made the trips because he'd wanted to. But now it seemed he'd done it only because he had to…

"That's really nice of you," I said, trying not to sound as deflated as I felt. "I hope it didn't interfere with your schedule."

He bit into the pear. "I traded an overnight shift with a colleague."

His shirt stretched with the movement, revealing a braided cord around his neck, which dipped with the weight of an unseen pendant. It shocked me how badly I wanted to know the shape and material of that pendant. "When do you have to take that overnight shift?"

"Tomorrow."

Tomorrow was Saturday. I turned my spoon over. "Did I ruin your weekend?"

"Effectively. I was going to sleep for thirty hours straight. Now I'll have to work for thirty hours straight."

"I'm so sorry."

He shook his head. "Don't be. I can't let a dog starve. Besides, I didn't help entirely out of altruism—Biscuit was going to be my introduction to this really beautiful woman."

I licked the back of my teeth. Finally, an expression of unambiguous interest on his part. But what exactly was the nature of this interest? "Well, introductions are done."

"So they are," he said softly.

Our gazes held again. The fridge hummed. Rain pounded on the skylight. My breath echoed in my head, all erratic agitation.

"Would you like some more?" He broke the silence, pointing at the tiramisu dish with the half-eaten pear in his hand.

"No, thank you. It was delicious, though."

He took my spoon and plate to the sink. I stared at his back. The shirt was a perfect fit across his shoulders, hinting at the lean, graceful build underneath.

"If I understand you correctly, you are the stereotypical workaholic, looking for some no-strings-attached sex."

Shit. Did I say that?

Or should I instead be surprised that it had taken me this long to get to this point, I who had invited myself to his house after midnight on the flimsiest of excuses?

It was never tiramisu that I wanted, was it?

He turned around and considered me. The flare of heat on my skin—as if someone had aimed a blowtorch at my throat and cheeks. "I wouldn't say no-strings-attached literally—sometimes it's fun to be tied up in bed. But yes, a metric ton of sex is right near the top of my Christmas wish list."

He bit into the pear again. The sight of his teeth sinking into the firm flesh of the fruit caused a jolt of lust in me such as I hadn't felt in years, perhaps ever.

Everything about our encounter was out of the ordinary. I couldn't tell whether I wasn't quite myself—or whether I was more myself than I'd ever been anywhere, with anyone.

The rain let up all of a sudden, its steady drumming softening to a pitter-patter on the roof. The fridge, too, fell quiet. But my heart continued to rattle my rib cage, its fast, hard slams thunderous in my ears.

He lowered his gaze for a moment, then looked back at me from underneath his eyelashes. "Is silence consent?"

Yes.

I wanted him to come closer. I wanted him to touch me. I wanted him to take whatever sorcery he was working with and enfold me securely inside.

My hand settled around my throat. My skin was hot, my pulse a rapid staccato. "Not to a metric ton of sex. Maybe once, tonight. I'm saving myself for marriage."

"So am I, but you can lead me astray anytime."

It was the sexiest thing anyone had said to me in a while, so much so that I had to clear my throat before I could speak again. "You're sure you want to do this? I mean, I *was* wandering around in the rain. Next thing you know I could be boiling your bunny."

"I'll send my bunny into protective custody first thing tomorrow morning." He put away the remainder of the tiramisu without taking his eyes off me. "Don't underestimate the desperation of a chronically underlaid man."

The intent in his gaze...I bit a corner of my lower lip. "Then we'd better get to it. You'll need to sleep soon so you don't kill patients tomorrow."

Did he swallow? The very handsome column of his neck moved in a way that made my heart beat even faster. "In that case, would you mind standing against that wall?"

I glanced in the direction he gestured. Unlike the other walls in the kitchen, this one didn't have exposed bricks, but was smoothly plastered. I hopped off the stool on wobbly knees and set my shoulder blades against the wall. "Like this?"

His gaze pinned me in place. I didn't feel as if I were leading anyone astray. Quite the opposite—I felt as if I were a girl from a convent school, secretly meeting a boy from a motorcycle gang.

He rounded the island and came up to me. Dipping his head close to my still-wet hair, he said softly, "So this is what rain smells like on a woman."

I couldn't quite breathe. Sex should be exciting, of course, but my reaction seemed to have shot right past excitement to land somewhere near trembling anticipation.

He loosened the sash and pushed the robe off my shoulders. I was entirely exposed, my heart pounding.

He sucked in a breath. I spread my fingers against the wall, trying to hold on to something—anything. His eyes dipped low, then lower, before they met mine again.

I panted, the sound primal. Animal.

He pulled his shirt over his head and tossed it aside, revealing a runner's build: strong shoulders, slim waist, beautifully cut abdomen.

I closed my eyes for a moment, overcome by lust. When I opened them again, it was to the sight of my hand on his upper arm. And then I did something that surprised me: I leaned in and nipped his shoulder.

He grunted. I found myself pressed hard against the wall, his hand between my thighs. For a moment I thought he'd be rough, but he touched me lightly, delicious little caresses at just the right places.

"Yes," I whimpered. "Yes."

He kept on with those clever fingers, finding all my most sensitive spots, stroking and teasing me, making my toes curl and my thighs weak.

I didn't want him to ever stop. Then all at once I wanted more—skin, contact, the heat of our bodies pressed together. I unbuckled his belt, unzipped his jeans, and touched him through his boxers. And almost yanked my hand back in shock—if a man had to pay tax according to the size of his endowment, Bennett would owe the government a lot of money.

"Do you have a condom?"

He extracted a foil packet from his pocket and spoke into my ear. "Very unprincessy of you, Evangeline. I expected to work much harder."

"Take off your clothes," I rasped.

He did. Then he opened the packet and rolled on the condom, his motion swift and efficient.

I stared. He caught me staring. "Like what you see?"

On the tail end of those words, he pushed into me. I expelled a lungful of air. God, that felt good. I wrapped my legs around him; he drove so deep my breath shook. He lifted me higher and licked my nipple. Pleasure rippled through me.

The next moment something else rippled through me: incredulity, as if I'd just woken up and realized what I was doing. I'd been entirely seduced by this man, in a way that had never happened to me before.

He braced one hand under my bottom. With his other hand he touched me again between my legs. Sensations flooded my nerve endings, drowning out everything in my head except a raging need for more.

More of the deftness of his fingers, more of the strength of his hold, more of the thorough penetration of his body into mine.

More of this very grown-up enchantment—a separate reality altogether. I didn't want it to end. I didn't want to leave its soft cocoon. I didn't want to head out to the night, back to my own reality.

Or my actual self.

But already I was crying out, throaty, desperate sounds. Already my sensations were gathering and cresting. I plunged my fingers into his hair, buried my face in his shoulder, and held on as my orgasm steamrolled over me, leaving me trembling in its wake.

Bennett was nearing his own peak, his thrusts hard and forceful. His breath caught. His teeth sank into my shoulder. And suddenly I was coming again, a climax that picked me up like a rogue wave and crashed over me just as violently.

MODERN ENCHANTMENTS WERE BROKEN NOT by the strike of midnight, but the wallop of ferocious orgasms.

I loved standing in Bennett's embrace afterward, listening to the sound of his breath slowly returning to normal. I loved the small drop kisses he left on my jaw, my neck, and my shoulder. I loved the way he sighed, cupped my face with one hand, and murmured, his lips brushing the shell of my ear, "Sweetheart, you blew my mind."

But I already knew our time was at an end.

His scent was that of the night—cool rain and summer foliage. I trailed my fingers up the musculature of his arm. My other hand I laid against his heart, feeling its strong and still-wild beat.

He kissed me on my temple. "Can I get you something? More tiramisu? A smoke?"

I played with his pendant. It was a glasswork semiabstract sea turtle about an inch across—the sort of souvenir one might bring back from Hawaii for a teenager. Not at all what I'd expected.

Which only made me more curious. "You smoke?"

"Officially not anymore, but I have a secret stash—you can't be a doctor unless you are a hypocrite about your own health."

I wanted to see that secret stash of cigarettes. I wanted to hear the story behind his pendant. I wanted to know whether he could still make me laugh when the sun was high in the sky.

"I should go," I said quietly. "You have to work tomorrow. You need your sleep."

He pulled back and traced a finger along my brow, a tender gesture, yet with a hint of melancholy. "True. You don't want to be subpoenaed to testify at my malpractice trial because you kept me up all night and caused me to remove the wrong lung from Mrs. Johnson."

That wrung a small smile from me.

We fell silent. Not an awkward silence, more like the kind that comes when two friends watch a spectacular sunset together. And then he broke away, disposed of the condom, and pulled on his clothes, giving me a view of his taut gluteal muscles.

When he was dressed, he picked up the bathrobe from where it had landed on the floor and handed it back to me—I realized only then that I hadn't moved at all. "Let me go check on your clothes," he said.

My clothes were warm and dry. I put them on. We walked out and got back into the Roadster, this time with him driving.

The rain had stopped. The clouds were parting—who knew there was a full moon tonight? Moonlight shimmered on wet leaves and glistened on the dark asphalt path. It limned Bennett's chiseled features, making my breath catch.

Collette's house was barely a quarter mile from his. All too soon he pulled into her driveway. "I'll watch you from here."

I let myself remain where I was a moment longer than necessary before I leaned in and kissed him on the cheek. "Thanks for showing me a great time."

"You're very welcome," he said. Then, after a pause, "I hope whatever was bothering you earlier won't look so bad when the sun rises."

Chapter 2

THE NEXT MORNING, WHEN THE sun rose, I was already packing. At noon Collette walked in—she'd canceled the vacation she'd planned to tack onto the end of her assignment and returned early, so I could go back to Manhattan. An hour later I was on the train, phone in hand, scrolling through the brief backlog of texts between Bennett and me.

I'd first called him on Monday, five days ago. And he'd texted me that evening. *Biscuit walked and fed. House key back under the sundial. Do you need me again tomorrow?*

I'd just spent a couple of difficult hours with Zelda, getting shouted at. I knew it had been the mania talking—Zelda was in a place where she could do no wrong, and anyone who stood in her way became a source of immense frustration. All the same, by the time she finally fell asleep I'd been shaking. Bennett's offer had brought a surge of relief: At least I didn't have to think about Biscuit for another day. *If you don't mind, I'd be ever so grateful.*

Consider it done.

We had similar exchanges until Thursday evening—Zelda had come down from her hypomanic state and I needed to go back to Cos Cob anyway for the handover of house and dog back to Collette. *I can take it from here. Thank you for everything.*

No problem.

They were the texts of a busy man who took his responsibilities seriously. But I couldn't have imagined that he would also be...beguiling.

This morning, after I finished packing, I'd taken Biscuit for a long walk. Twice we'd passed his house. It was set back quite a bit from the road, but built on a small incline, so I could still see the second story, with its white walls and green trim.

I didn't run into him. And he didn't call or text. A good thing—what happened between us should be an event in stark isolation. The perfection of a leaf preserved in amber.

Last night, after I reached Collette's front door, I'd turned around to wave good-bye. I expected to see the Roadster reverse and drive away. But it didn't. As seconds ticked by, it sat in place, a muscular, palpable presence.

I took a step toward him, my mind racing with possibilities. The hell with Mrs. Johnson's lung. If Bennett turned off the car and came out, I *would* keep him up all night—*and* make him late for his shift.

He reversed and drove away. I stood a long time, my hand braced on a pillar of the porch, watching the direction in which he'd disappeared.

ZELDA AND I LIVED ON the Upper West Side, a stone's throw from Central Park, in a narrow, four-story stone-and-stucco town house. Some people believed the house to be part of my late father's inheritance, and he'd never disabused anyone of the idea. But he'd bought it for a pittance in the early eighties, when Manhattan's real estate market hit rock-bottom. Second-best investment he'd ever made, he used to say, after the Andy Warhol original that he'd picked up for two thousand dollars and a used dining room set.

Inside it was comfortable and slightly shabby, full of books, records, and Middle-earth memorabilia. Zelda thought the place resembled a hobbit hole. To me it looked more like Wallace and Gromit's house—old-fashioned, but with a sense of whimsy.

Zelda sat in the living room, a pair of jeans in her lap, a heaping laundry basket on the coffee table before her. Her fully grey hair, usually in a stylish layered cut that reached her shoulders, was tied up in a messy ponytail. "Hello, darling," she murmured, as I bent down to kiss her on her cheek.

Those two words formed part of my oldest memory: that of the first time we met. *Eva, this is your new mother*, my father had said. My new mother's eyes had twinkled with curiosity and a zest for life. She'd brought me a teddy bear dressed up like a Buckingham Palace guardsman. And when she'd crouched down, offered me her hand to shake, and said, *Hello, darling*, in her cut-crystal English accent, she'd instantly become the love of my life.

I sat down next to Zelda and pulled a couple of T-shirts out of the laundry basket.

"I'm back."

A few beats passed before she answered, "How are you?"

I could never know how difficult it was for her to respond—could only guess by the vast difference between her usual bubbly self and this subdued...prisoner. "Fine, busy as usual."

To keep up the appearance of a normal conversation, I prattled about what I still had to do to get ready for the fall semester. By the time I ran through my checklist, she'd finally finished folding the pair of jeans in her lap and was staring at the laundry basket, willing herself to reach out and take another item.

The undertow of hopelessness, the most insidious part of depression, sometimes made the simplest tasks seem as daunting as setting out across the Sahara Desert with no compass and no supplies. I couldn't bear to watch her struggle. Mumbling something, I went to the kitchen and filled two glasses of water. But when I came back she'd succeeded—she had a pair of my pajama bottoms in her hands.

Tears filled my eyes—from immense pride...and a raging sense of injustice. Zelda had always worked diligently to manage her illness—she saw her therapist twice a week and took her meds faithfully. But sometimes she developed adverse reactions to those meds; sometimes other prescription drugs disrupted their effectiveness.

I went back to the kitchen and wiped away my tears before I returned to the living room. "Don't discount that victory," I told her as I sat down.

"Oh, darling," she said after a minute, "every day without snogging random strangers is a victory."

I almost chuckled. She'd told me that when she was eighteen, in a fit of mania, she'd kissed three different boys at a pub one night, and had to be dragged home by her girlfriends.

Yet the mania, for all its evils, made Zelda feel great—confident, energetic, practically invincible. Depression, on the other hand, turned her into a husk filled with nothing but despair and self-loathing.

Depression scared me.

When I was in fifth grade, a classmate's older brother committed suicide—he'd been suffering from a crushing depression and one day he couldn't take it anymore. I had nightmares for weeks. I never wanted to believe Zelda would give up. But whenever her illness reawakened, the same old fear would sink its claws into my spine. And I'd once more turn into the little girl who was petrified that something terrible would happen to her wonderful new mother.

Zelda was staring at the laundry basket again. This time she did not pull anything out.

Tears came back into my eyes. I sped up and finished sorting everything. "All done. I'll go put them up."

"Darling," she murmured as I reached the hallway.

I poked my head back into the living room. "Yes?"

She sat with her profile to me, the lines at the corners of her eyes deeply etched. "'I wish it need not have happened in my time.'"

What Frodo had said when he found out that the One Ring had come to him.

I first heard Zelda speak those words not long after my classmate's brother committed suicide. I'd gone to my room, closed the door, and sat on the floor for a long time, shaking. Then I flipped through *The Fellowship of the Ring* until I found the line, lugged the book downstairs, and read Gandalf's response to her.

After that, it became something of a ritual between us.

I put aside the clothes I was carrying, went back to her, and took her hands in mine. "'So do I, and so do all who live to see such times. But that is not for them to decide. All we have to decide is what to do with the time that is given us.'"

I RETURNED MOST OF ZELDA'S clothes to her closet, and put the rest in her chest of drawers.

The top of the chest of drawers was thick with framed photographs. Zelda and I in the first picture we ever took together, at Central Park

Zoo, my arms around a resigned-looking small white goat. Zelda holding aloft her Grammy for songwriting, surrounded by her musician friends. Zelda and I at the New Zealand premiere of *The Return of the King*, both of us laughing uproariously. Zelda with her cousins, hiking the southwest coast of England. Zelda and Mrs. Asquith, her godmother, the two of them holding up floral teacups with wildly exaggerated expressions of primness and decorum.

I loved looking through this pictorial record of Zelda's existence, of her living a full life despite all the obstacles that had been thrown her way. But today my attention was immediately drawn to a photo at the very back, the biggest and most elaborately framed of them all.

The one I'd told Bennett about: of me in a ball gown and a diamond tiara.

My father, Hoyt Canterbury, was born to old money, but that money ran out before he could do anything about it. My mother was the product of a quiet, unexceptional suburb, but she had a moment in the late disco era when she became an "it" girl, a fixture on the Manhattan social circuit, her style copied, her pictures splashed across glossy magazines.

The one who had the most family connections, however, was Zelda, whose bloodline was mingled with those of half a dozen aristocratic families. But the way she explained it, she'd never been more than a poor relation—not that some of the earls and viscounts she was related to weren't just as impoverished.

Pater—from *paterfamilias*, Latin for "father of the family," because he refused to be called anything as pedestrian as "Dad"—had been a highly respected art dealer, but had always looked down on himself for having a profession, for being what he considered a glorified shopkeeper. What he had truly wanted was the life of a proper gentleman of leisure, to serve on the board of directors of major museums and civic organizations, and rule fashionable society with a velvet-gloved iron fist.

Since that hadn't been in the cards for him, he'd turned his hopes of social prominence to a succession of women. But my mother left him early on, and Zelda was far happier working in her studio than entertaining. I had been his last, best chance. The fringes of high society were where some of the most influential hostesses launched from. And if I should turn out to be a girl with my mother's "it" factor and his polish and ambition...

But from the moment Zelda brought home a block of dry ice for our Halloween party when I was seven years old, it had been the sciences for me, rather than the social register. Pater watched with constipated incredulity as my projects won science fair after science fair, regional, state, national.

He wasn't reactionary enough to forbid me a life in goggles and lab coats, but he did draw a line in the sand: I had to have a proper debut when I was eighteen. And he set his sights high—the international Bal des Debutantes held at the Hotel Crillon in Paris.

He considered himself an American aristocrat; I harbored no such delusions. Yet to my shock, I was chosen. He, Zelda, and I flew to Paris. And since fashion was the reason the ball came into being in the first place, we went for a fitting as soon as we landed.

I was given a fashion-forward, slightly goth gown with a black net bodice over a sprawling black silk skirt. Pater whipped out a tiara that had been couriered from England, a loan from Mrs. Asquith, and placed it on my head. The designer's assistant clicked his camera and an unlikely fashion photograph was born, one that had since taken on a life of its own.

The young girl in the image, caught in profile, bore only a tenuous resemblance to me. An ethereal, almost otherworldly creature, she gazed to her right, beyond the edge of the frame. Her raised hand extended in the same direction, as if to beckon a young man toward her.

Except romance had been the last thing on my mind. Instead I'd been reaching toward Zelda, who had been displaying signs of hypomania. I'd been desperately hoping it wasn't the case, and Zelda had kept reassuring me it was only the excitement of being in Paris again.

But two days later, at the rehearsal, when the young man who had been designated my official escort for the ball failed to show up, Pater and I had to physically restrain her from jumping into the first taxi and rushing to the airport. Zelda, in the grip of mania, was one hundred percent confident that she would be able to drag the boy to my side in time for the ball, never mind that she didn't know where he had gone to, or even what he looked like.

In the following days we had to restrain her from many other not-entirely-sane impulses. And when she came down from that awful high, she fell into a most brutal depression.

Six months later, she asked Pater for a divorce.

In the long aftermath of those unhappy days, it became my fantasy, my escape, to imagine how things might have been different had my escort arrived exactly on time.

The truth of the matter was that had he been there, nothing would have been any different. Nothing. But that was what fantasies were for, wasn't it, to be as thoroughly divorced from reality as necessary? And so a faceless, nameless, and entirely ordinary boy became a magical Prince Charming, one whose mere presence was enough to save us from all future anguish and heartbreak.

I loved my Prince Charming, but only as a literary device, so I could tell myself the one story that lulled me to sleep on the longest, darkest nights. In fact, had I not run into Bennett, it was what I would have done when I eventually returned to Collette's house: rewind time back to that moment almost fourteen years ago and weave an alternate history where Zelda, Pater, and I were still together, a somewhat dysfunctional family, but a family nevertheless.

Next to my "princess" photo was one of the three of us together at my first national science fair, when I was fifteen. I had won the grand prize and Zelda and I had been captured in a tight embrace, Zelda's expression rapturous with pride. Pater stood a little to the side, looking bemused and resigned, whether at my victory or our closeness I would never know. Perhaps both.

I removed my hand from the frame of the picture, picked up the laundry basket, and carried on with my chores.

BY SUNDAY NIGHT BENNETT STILL hadn't called or texted.

I was in bed, the lights turned off—and unable to sleep. I missed how I'd felt when I'd been with him—safe and at ease, always on the verge of smiling.

If only…

Zelda suffered from a mental illness, but I was the one who was messed up: My preferred method for dealing with everything that frightened, saddened, or unsettled me was to never speak of or even acknowledge it.

In other words, I was incapable of emotional intimacy. Even with Zelda, as close as we were, I'd never brought myself to admit my fear. The opposite, in fact. In front of her I kept my despair locked down the tightest.

I would have made an awful girlfriend for Bennett.

But he'd given no indication that he wanted a relationship. Sex, that was what he wanted. We could hook up for delicious sex and nothing else.

I picked up my phone from the nightstand, considered it, and set it down again. I liked him too much. If we saw each other only when he felt horny, I would be crushed.

And I didn't need any more uncertainties in my life.

It was the correct decision, but not a happy one. The restlessness in my heart...I almost wished I had pouring rain and miles of deserted country lanes.

So I made up a new fantasy.

Bennett hadn't contacted me because he'd been called away all of a sudden by...Doctors Without Borders would be good here. That would easily put him on the opposite side of the globe from me. And when he arrived at his remote destination, while trying to get a new phone that worked locally, something would happen to his SIM card. So he couldn't call me, because he'd lost my number.

But we weren't destined to be parted forever. Instead, we'd run into each other at a most unexpected time and place. Perfect, I had a symposium in Munich next February. And he, on his way back from say, Tajikistan, would be staying at the exact same hotel.

I could already tell this was going to be a really, really good fantasy.

Chapter 3

ZELDA'S DEPRESSIVE EPISODE, MUCH TO my relief and gratitude, turned out to be relatively short. Her doctors arrived at a good new combination of meds, and life began to reapproach normal.

In the meanwhile, students returned to the university. I did most of my teaching in the fall, so I could concentrate on research the rest of the year. And teaching that many sections took up a huge amount of time, even without faculty meetings, my work with grad students, and the hours I needed to put in on my own papers.

Before I knew it, midterms were already over. One Friday afternoon Zelda and I went to the botanical garden to see the foliage, walking arm in arm on paths strewn with sweet gum and scarlet oak leaves.

Zelda had resumed working a while ago—she had accepted a commission to score a feature film, an exciting new venture after a successful career in songwriting and commercial music. We talked about her work and mine, and she told me that her therapist thought it would be fine for her to go on the Turquoise Coast walking trip that her English cousins had organized.

An older couple with a combined age well north of one hundred and fifty walked past us, hands held, nodding as they went. I gazed at them wistfully. I didn't envy my friends their fresh new love affairs, but a faithful yet mellow companionship that came of a lifetime spent together? That never failed to make my heart pinch with longing.

"Oh, I almost forgot," said Zelda. "I got an e-mail from the Somerset boy this morning."

"What Somerset boy?"

"You know, the one who ditched us in Paris."

I blinked. Was she talking about my Prince Charming?

One reason my alternate history had worked so well over the years was that the boy, who must now be a man in his early thirties, had simply disappeared. I never knew much about him to begin with, and I'd since remained happily ignorant.

Anonymity was key to Prince Charming's success as a fantasy figure. It really wouldn't be the same if the actual person was a divorced derivatives trader with a pending SEC investigation hanging over his head.

"How did he get hold of your e-mail address?"

"Oh, he's on marvelous terms with Mrs. Asquith—used to spend a lot of time at her place when he was in England."

I vaguely remembered now that my escort had been in England at the time, and was supposed to hop over to Paris for the weekend of the ball.

"And how does he know Mrs. Asquith?"

I'd never met Zelda's godmother, but I couldn't imagine her hanging out with American teenagers.

"His mother is English, and her aunt is a very close school friend of Mrs. Asquith's."

"Hmm," I said.

Granted, I hadn't had to lean on Prince Charming much lately—it had been all about Bennett and me in Munich. But I was loath to give up my workhorse of a fantasy. What if "the Somerset boy" had contacted Zelda to recruit her for a Ponzi scheme? That would totally limit Prince Charming's future utility.

"Anyway," said Zelda, "he e-mailed to apologize for ditching us all those years ago, and it was a very sincere apology."

That I did not expect. "Why? I mean why now, after all these years?"

"I rang up his mother the moment I read his e-mail, and I told her, 'I think the boy is finally ready to come home.'"

I didn't understand what she was talking about. "From where?"

"Don't you remember? His family disowned him after the ball."

The Somerset boy could have set himself on fire in the days after the ball and I, completely preoccupied with Zelda, wouldn't have known. "Not literally?"

"Literally. Wrote him out of their will. Cut off contact. Everything."

I gaped. "Because he was a no-show?"

Which had been a dick move, but hardly an offense of that stature.

"Oh, no, there were loads of things going on at the same time. He was absolutely impossible. And there were whispers of a most unsuitable older woman. Now, where was I? Oh, the e-mail. When I mentioned the e-mail, Frances said she hoped to God I was right. The boy came back in grand style, bought an apartment on Park Avenue and all that. In the beginning she was on pins and needles waiting for him to get in touch. But now she's wondering whether he didn't plant himself in the middle of Manhattan to rub his success in their faces."

My head spun with this overload of information. But at least there was no indictment. So maybe all was not lost.

"Frances would probably have taken the initiative to get in touch with him, if it were just her. But the real rupture was between the boy and his father. And she took her husband's side in the matter, so…"

Zelda sighed. "Families can be so complicated."

LATE THAT NIGHT I LAY in bed, still unable to process the fact that "the Somerset boy" lived on Park Avenue, not even a mile away.

Too close for comfort.

But thinking about Park Avenue also made me remember Bennett's "ambition" for becoming a Park Avenue trophy husband—and that never failed to bring a smile to my face.

Followed by a pang of melancholy.

The more I played back our encounter, the more improbable it seemed. How was it that I'd felt so comfortable with him, when he had seen me in a state of absolute vulnerability? One would think, given how adamant I was about keeping my pains and fears locked down and out of sight, that I'd want to get away from him as soon as possible.

And yet I'd done the exact opposite.

I snuggled more deeply under the covers and allowed myself to escape to Munich. The real-life me was scheduled to present a paper at the symposium. After my talk, the fantasy me would head out to Munich's famed Englischer Garten, warmly bundled, for a nice, long walk to unwind.

It would start to snow; the garden would be silent and lovely. And then, when I returned to the hotel, who should get in the elevator with me but the man I couldn't stop thinking about.

In some iterations of this fantasy, we could barely wait until we were in his room to rip off each other's clothes. But tonight I went for the ultradeluxe version, in which we shared coffee, dinner, after-dinner drinks, and even a few minutes outdoors on the hotel's observation deck, as that very romantic snow continued to fall, enveloping us in one of nature's most perfect crystalline forms.

I haven't stopped thinking about you since the night we met, said the fictional version of Bennett, pulling me toward him, a dusting of fresh snow on the shoulders of his coat.

I should believe that when I haven't heard from you for six months? I'd retort.

Yes, you should, he'd reply, looking into my eyes, *because it's true.*

And then he would kiss me at last.

EARLY IN DECEMBER, I TAUGHT my last class for the semester.

I ended the lecture fifteen minutes early, so the students could fill out evaluation forms, which my grad student would collect. But as I left the classroom, a student named Keeley followed me out.

"Dr. Canterbury, excuse me, can I ask you a question?"

"Sure."

"Savitha and I have a bet. I say this is you."

I knew exactly what I'd see even before she held out her phone toward me—she wasn't the first student to have stumbled across my "princess" photo, which had turned into a bit of an Internet meme. The last time a student asked me this question, the dress had been Photoshopped to a tutu pink, with a caption that read, *Someday my prince will come.* This time the couture gown had been swapped out altogether in favor of an Elvish robe. My hand was held out toward none other than Aragorn. And between us were the words, *Someday my king will return.*

I laughed. "No," I told Keeley, "it's not me. But can you send me the image? My stepmom is a huge Tolkien fan and she'll love this."

Back at home, as soon as I'd sat down on the living room couch, Zelda poked in her head and said, "I had lunch with the Somerset boy today."

"What? Just like that?"

"He rang. I asked him if he'd like to meet in person instead. He told me to name the time and the place."

Zelda flitted into the kitchen and came back with cups of tea and a plate of cheese crisps for us. "And guess what we talked about at lunch?"

"His intentions toward his parents?"

"No, he was quite guarded about that. We talked about you, mostly."

The idea of my gloriously anonymous Prince Charming not only acquiring a definite identity but holding a conversation about me…What the hell was going on?

"He knows all about you," Zelda went on. "Well, everything that can be Googled, in any case: the genius grant, your patents—and even that conference in Germany you're going to in February."

I gulped down some tea. "He's been cyberstalking me?"

"Well, why not? You are the point at which his life could have taken a very different turn—if he'd come to Paris. Why wouldn't he Google you? And once he saw what you look like, why wouldn't he want to know everything about you?" Zelda grinned. "I rubbed it in—told him he blew it by ditching us in Paris. And guess what he said to that?"

"Something about his Park Avenue apartment and how successful he's been without us?"

"No, he asked me whether you were seeing anyone."

I was speechless.

Zelda leaned forward. "I think you'll like him. He's splendid-looking. Very personable too. According to Frances, he made an absolute fortune out west. Not to mention he's a Somerset—your father would have been tickled."

Pater would indeed have enjoyed being connected to the Somersets, who were English aristocracy transplanted to New York. I gave Zelda a sideways glance. "You're not hearing wedding bells, are you? That would really be putting the cart before the horse."

"A little, I'll admit. But I get the sense the boy is seriously interested in you."

And the boy could take his serious interest and shove it. A man should know his place, and this man belonged firmly in fiction.

"Maybe I'll meet him after I get tenure, but not before."

And maybe after I was offered tenure, I'd find some other excuse to not meet the Somerset boy.

I pulled out my phone and brought up the image of Aragorn and me, together in one frame. "Now come here. I've got something that'll blow your mind."

TEN DAYS LATER, ZELDA LEFT for her trip to the Turquoise Coast of Turkey. I worked more or less day and night, Christmas Eve and Christmas Day included. The day after Christmas I woke up late, did laundry and dishes, and went for a walk in the afternoon.

It was a bright, crisp day, almost not cold under the sun. Central Park was crowded with tourists who wanted the Christmas-in-New York experience. I smiled at couples taking selfies together, and bundled-up toddlers riding on their fathers' shoulders—and wished Zelda were already back.

On the other side of the park was Fifth Avenue. The moment I set foot on it, someone called my name. "Dr. Canterbury!"

I looked across the street and couldn't speak for a moment. It was none other than Bennett, in a beautifully cut grey overcoat worn over jeans, a blue scarf around his neck, too stylish and gorgeous for someone not fronting an advertising campaign for a major Italian fashion house.

"Hey!" I found my voice somewhere.

It wasn't Munich. But I'd take it. I'd totally take it.

He crossed to my side and kissed me on my cheek. "You look almost too pretty."

I had on head-to-toe black and no makeup. His compliment stoked my vanity in all the best ways. I couldn't help smiling. "You, on the other hand, look only regular pretty."

"Medical school sucked all the hot out of me."

I laughed. "How are you? And what are you doing here?"

"Out for a walk. I live around the corner."

From where we stood, Park Avenue was only two blocks away. I raised a brow. "Don't tell me you've succeeded in becoming a Park Avenue trophy husband."

"No, I had to buy my own apartment on Park Avenue. But the maintenance fees are atrocious, so I'm still looking for a sugar mommy."

I'd figured he probably had independent wealth of some sort—the house in Cos Cob couldn't have come cheap—but an apartment on this stretch of Park Avenue too? A teasing question was on my lips about whether he worked at a mob hospital and knew where all the bodies were buried, when gears started turning in the back of my head.

The boy came back in grand style, bought an apartment on Park Avenue and all that.

Park Avenue apartment. Check.

According to Frances, he made an absolute fortune out west.

The area code of Bennett's cell phone number was 510. Berkeley, California—I'd looked it up.

And there were whispers of a most unsuitable older woman.

What had Bennett said to me when I told him that my age in binary was exactly one hundred thousand? *I* have *been known to like an older woman.*

I goggled at him, thunderstruck. Could it be? "Bennett, what's your last name?"

"Somerset."

He was the one who didn't show up, the one whose absence set off—

I stopped. That was and had always been an irrational chain of thoughts. Nothing would have been any different had he come to the ball. And he didn't have to account for a misstep from almost half his lifetime ago.

He did, however, have to answer for his more recent actions. "What were you doing e-mailing and having lunch with Zelda?"

"You were my only score since I came back to New York," he replied cheekily. "I figured it would be easier to get you to put out again than to convince someone else from scratch."

I was taken aback—I hadn't expected him to be up-front about it. "You should have told her that was all you wanted."

"Right. Next time I see her, I'll tell her that I have the biggest hard-on for you."

He said it with a smile, his tone perfectly casual. My reaction, however, was anything but casual. Now that the shock of his identity was beginning to wear off, all the sexual fantasies I'd woven about his raging hard-on for me flashed across my mind's eye, a highlight reel of ferocious kisses and frantic disrobing.

I inhaled, a shaky, shaky breath. "You could have just told *me*. Zelda heard wedding bells."

He was unchastened. "Come to think of it, I'll marry you any day of the week."

Even though it was abundantly clear that he couldn't be less serious, the playfulness of his tone, peppered with affection, somehow made my heart turn over, a sensation at once delightful and terrifying.

This man was more dangerous than I'd remembered.

"Your patents on electroceramics are going to be worth a mint," he added. "I'll make sure to refuse to sign any prenups."

"Huh," I said. "I don't date gold-digging groupies."

He laughed softly. "Running into you, Professor, is the best belated Christmas present I could have asked for. Are you busy? Can I buy you a drink?"

And then what? We go back to his Park Avenue apartment for sex?

Part of me wanted that, a lot. But already I wished that I hadn't run into him. Face-to-face it was impossible to discount the fact that he hadn't reached out since August. That as much as I loved to romanticize our encounter, I'd been just an opportunistic bang for him.

"Don't tell me you aren't the least bit curious about why I never showed up in Paris," he said, as if he heard my intended refusal. "You know there had to be a terrific scandal involved."

"Is that what you're going to divulge?"

"Only if you let me buy you that drink. This is a special one-time-only offer that expires in the next few minutes."

He was also a lot more predatory than I remembered. It occurred to me that last time he'd handled me very carefully, a thought that was a blare of alarm in my head.

"If it was a real scandal, I should be able to Google it."

"You can't—not yet, as far as I know." He studied me—this time not as a man looking at a woman he'd like to take to coffee—or to bed—but more like a physician inspecting a patient who presented puzzling symptoms. Or perhaps a DA considering a less-than-cooperative witness. "You know, it's at the top of my to-do list to call Zelda after she comes back from her trip and invite the two of you to dinner. Her flight lands day after tomorrow, right?"

I remembered that he'd been in touch with Zelda for a while. In hindsight it was clear that he had been laying the groundwork for something. But what?

A few beats passed before I tilted my chin toward the grand Beaux Arts facade of the Metropolitan Museum of Art, just steps away. "I was going to the Met. Would you like to come along?"

WE DIDN'T SPEAK AS WE walked up the steps to the museum, then across the great hall to check our coats and get our tokens. I was upset, and unsettled by the fact that I couldn't figure out why I was upset. Was it because he had been scheming behind my back? Was it because not texting him—or even turning down a drink with him—was no longer sufficient to keep him out of my life? Or was it because some part of me was breathlessly, extravagantly thrilled that the matter was out of my hands, that he was here to stay no matter what I did or didn't do?

"How was your Christmas?" he asked, as he secured his token to his charcoal jersey.

"I worked most of the time. Yours?"

"Taken up by a medical mission to Guatemala."

I almost stopped in the middle of the grand staircase. "Doctors Without Borders?"

"No. There's a Buddhist group that organizes missions to developing countries—and here in the States too. I've been going with them for years."

"What do you do? I don't imagine you can perform heart transplants."

"No, but I can do heart valve repair. And I can serve as translator."

"Now you are actually impressing me," I said, not without some reluctance.

"I know. All that *and* a nice ass—it's the pinnacle of modern manhood."

I laughed in spite of myself. "Watch it, God Complex."

He smiled back at me. The sight of those green eyes, their corners slightly crinkled, made my heart thud like a swooning Victorian debutante landing on the ballroom floor.

"Okay, enough small talk," I said sternly. "Let's hear about your scandal, and make sure you give me all the salacious details."

"*All* the salacious details? Suuure," he drawled, his voice full of mischief. "Let's see. It started when I was sixteen. I was in Spain for a semester as an exchange student. My host mom was a professor at the University of Salamanca, and one of her colleagues was a gentleman by the name of José Luis Dominguez Calderón."

"You say that name with a lot of relish," I told him. "A lot of villainous relish."

"You'll see why." He grinned. "One day my host parents invited Professor Dominguez and his girlfriend to dinner. The girlfriend was American. I missed speaking English, so I monopolized her that evening."

"How old was she?"

"Thirty-eight."

"So she was twenty-two, twenty-three at the time?"

"No, she was thirty-eight."

My jaw fell. "No."

"You're thirty-two. You think in six years you'll be of absolutely no interest to teenage boys?"

Come to think of it, some of the freshmen I taught were still teenagers. And from time to time one would develop a crush and visit my office hours with unwarranted frequency. But at least a nineteen-year-old was an adult. A sixteen-year-old was a minor.

"Besides," he continued, "she was hot, and she didn't look a day over twenty-six."

I screwed up my face. "Did she pounce on you, cougar-style?"

I could only hope that in a few years I wouldn't be going after tenth graders.

"No, not really. I hit on her."

"What?!"

Bennett laughed. "Come on, Professor. I told you she was hot. Which part of that didn't you understand?"

"But she was old enough to be your mother. And didn't you say she had a boyfriend?"

"I was an obnoxious kid who didn't see a fifty-year-old boyfriend as any kind of obstacle."

I blinked. "Just how obnoxious were you?"

"Let's see. When I was fourteen, I was pissed at my dad for something—I can't even remember what now—so I paid a hacker friend to engineer a fake takeover bid for one of the family holdings, making it look as if someone behind an anonymous entity in Grand Cayman was trying to get a controlling share. Gave Dad heartburn for weeks."

"That *was* obnoxious. But she was a grown woman. You could hit on her all you want—how did you get her to want to *be* with you?"

"Isn't that simple? I was hot too."

"Eww."

He glanced at me askance. "You don't think I'm hot?"

"That's different. It's not creepy for me to consider you hot."

"If it will make your puritanical soul feel better, she didn't think I was hot—at least not in the beginning. I called her a few days after the dinner and asked if she wouldn't mind showing a poor, homesick kid around Salamanca. She agreed—because she was nice, not because she wanted to molest me.

"We spent the whole day together in the old city, had lunch and dinner. José Luis was livid and they had a fight over me—he saw what I was up to but she didn't. Not at all. To get back at him, she asked me if I wanted to see some of the countryside too. So of course I exploited their rift for all it was worth."

A sixteen-year-old who knew how to exploit the rift between a thirty-eight-year-old and a fifty-year-old? "That's freaking scary."

"I told you I was obnoxious."

"So you just wormed your way into her heart?"

"More like I wormed my way into her bed at first."

We were walking through the European halls. The Virgin Mary we passed looked quite constipated. In fact, an entire row of Virgin Marys were stiff with disapproval. "Why do I feel that I might be led away in handcuffs if I listen to any more of your story?"

"Hey, you asked for salacious details."

"You were sixteen. That was illegal. She should have gone to jail for statutory rape."

"The thought crossed my parents' mind when they found out, but I was over the age of consent in Spain. They shipped me off to Eton instead, away from her reach."

"But she still got through to you somehow?"

"No. We didn't see each other for sixteen months. We met in online chat rooms. We wrote actual letters. I called her from phone booths with calling cards—remember those?—and waited for my eighteenth birthday."

"Just waited chastely?"

He shrugged. "I was in love."

My heart recoiled against an abrupt stab of pain. "What did your parents make of all this?"

"They were hoping the separation would do the trick. But the day I turned eighteen, I walked out of Eton and flew to California, where she was based."

"And your parents just let you go?"

"No, they chased me to Berkeley and it was ugly. But since I was already eighteen they couldn't do anything. Eventually they left." His voice turned somber. "I haven't seen them since—except once, at O'Hare. I don't think they saw me."

"Is that why you moved back here, so you could be part of the tribe again?"

He glanced at a painting we were passing, which happened to be a family portrait, three rosy children clambering over an elegant, serene mother. "If I said yes, it would be the first time I admitted it to anyone."

A strange thrill shot through me. "That's a yes, then."

He didn't answer immediately—I was reminded of the night we met, those few heartbeats during which he stood by his car, motionless, as if he'd acted without thinking the matter through, and must pause to reassess the situation.

"Yes," he finally said.

My breath caught—did it mean anything that I was the first one to hear it? "You do know that you can ring their doorbell anytime and say, 'Hey, Mom and Dad, I've missed you'?"

"I could. But that would require courage and maturity. Much easier to go on wallowing in indecision."

"The new pinnacle of modern manhood."

This made him laugh.

That great laughter, those green eyes…I simmered with a sharp emotion that I didn't recognize at first.

Possessiveness.

"Sir, ma'am," an attendant called to us, "the museum is closing in fifteen minutes and we need to clear the galleries."

"Would you like a drink at my place?" Bennett asked as we made our way out.

My stomach flipped. Was this an invitation to sex? "Where do you live?"

"At Seven Forty."

Manhattan's most prestigious apartment buildings were known by their street numbers, and few were as storied as 740 Park Avenue, where Jackie Kennedy had lived as a young girl. "You couldn't have bought something on Central Park West? It just had to be Seven Forty?"

"Of course. That was how I informed my parents I was moving back to the city."

When an apartment at 740 changed hands, it made news, at least among a certain subset of Manhattanites. Even if Bennett's parents didn't pay attention, they'd have friends who did.

Outside the museum I stopped. If he was determined to have dinner with Zelda and me, that was fine. But I shouldn't spend any more time alone with him.

In fantasy, he was perfect. In reality, he could only be trouble.

"I have something I'd like to discuss with you," he said as I mustered the will to decline his invitation. "Something that is unrelated, or only tangentially related, to my inability to save myself for marriage whenever you are around."

"What is it?"

"Let's just say I've been cultivating Zelda for the same reason."

I spent a moment pulling on my gloves, wondering whether I could at least postpone the inevitable for some time. Anything that concerned Zelda would eventually concern me, but did I have to deal with it tonight?

"I promise I'll behave myself in the kitchen," he cajoled. "There will be absolutely no copulatory acts against counters or cabinets."

A very, very narrow promise—outside his kitchen I would be fair game. I shook my head. "Lead the way, then."

He'd worn me down at last.

Chapter 4

740 PARK AVENUE WAS LESS than ten blocks from the Met. An unassuming entrance led into a foyer that had an Art Deco touch, to give it a glimmer of hipness back in 1929 without making the genteel folks of Park Avenue feel that they were being contaminated by too much of what was going on in Central Park West.

A private elevator ferried us directly to the penthouse. The elevator door opened and I stepped into an entry hall that could have been used as a movie set for *The Age of Innocence*. The walls were papered in a soft, faded gold, the furniture American antiques of the Federal style. Pots of pale narcissus bloomed everywhere, delicately fragrant and delicately beautiful.

The only splash of color came from a huge portrait that hung over the fireplace. The subject was a woman in a gown of bold carmine, with a king's ransom of rubies glittering over her throat and breast. The signature belonged to John Singer Sargent. A small plaque on the frame of the painting said, *Her Ladyship the Marchioness of Tremaine, 1894*.

"My great-great-grandmother," said Bennett, noticing the direction of my gaze.

"She was pretty hot," I said, unbuttoning my coat.

"She was also pretty scandalous back in the day. Almost divorced my great-great-grandfather."

"What stopped her?"

"I'm not sure. Rumor had it he was too good in bed."

I laughed—because it was funny, and because I was more than a little jittery.

"Hey, I must have inherited it from somewhere."

All I could think of was the sensation of him inside me, driving me to one brink after another. "Don't look at me. I've never been to bed with you. Now, where's my vermouth?"

He led me into the living room, which was less Gilded Age than the entry, and cooler in feel. The floor was bamboo. The curtains on the floor-to-ceiling windows were blue with a subtle undertone of grey. A pair of antique chairs upholstered in pale rose flanked a sizable blue-grey leather chaise.

Bennett poured vermouth for me and tonic water for himself. "Would you like something to eat?" he asked as he handed me my glass. "I have enough food on hand to feed two."

I supposed we might as well talk about whatever it was he wanted to talk about over dinner. "Sure."

He went to the kitchen and came back a minute later. "The soup needs to warm up in the oven for half an hour. Want to see the view?"

"It's just the skyline, right?" I said, setting down my drink.

"It is. But I've been away long enough that I still get excited about it."

He flicked a switch; the lights turned off. Another switch and the curtains rose on the Manhattan skyline. I gazed at the silhouette of my great city, a blaze of luminosity against a pitch-black night. Bennett's footsteps, soft and sure, came up behind me. His fingers were gentle as they brushed against my jaw. Then he lifted my hair and kissed me underneath my ear.

Our first encounter had been incredibly hot, but it had also been one of those things that happened largely because of a random intersection of circumstances. This time I was not a rain-soaked woman at her most vulnerable in years; this time I was put-together and poised; this time I would know how to handle myself.

The ferocity of the sensation that hurtled through me dwarfed anything I'd ever experienced, a pleasure so sharp and vivid…it was as if months of simmering, unspoken desires had become a magnifier that turned the slightest touch to chaos and upheaval.

I clenched my fingers so I wouldn't gasp out loud.

He kissed a different spot. I shivered.

This was coming to resemble my fantasy too closely. In real life I was supposed to slip out of reach, and maybe laugh a little while wagging a finger with playful reproach. In real life I wasn't supposed to be swept away by raging needs, like a canoe dragged over the edge of a powerful cataract.

"I thought…I thought you were going to discuss something that had nothing to do with this."

"We'll discuss it over dinner, which isn't for at least another twenty-five minutes." He punctuated his answer with a nip at my shoulder.

I swallowed a whimper. "I told you, I'm saving myself for marriage."

"Then why do you keep leading me astray?" He kissed me on my earlobe. "I think about you every time I masturbate."

Did my knees buckle? I wouldn't know, because he picked me up at that exact moment.

"You see this?" he asked as he laid me down on the chaise. "When I come back from thirty hours in the hospital, I don't even bother going up to the bedroom. I just sleep right here. But before I go to sleep I masturbate, and I think about you—under me, over me, and maybe bent over the armrest. Every time, without fail."

I was unbelievably turned on.

He yanked off my boots. Reaching under my skirt, he peeled away my tights and my underwear. Now he undressed, smoothed on a condom, and pushed my skirt up around my waist. Then, in one motion, he was all the way inside me.

How did this happen? How did I lose control so quickly? Was it because in my heart I had never wanted any result but this?

I shut my eyes tight and wrapped my legs around him. God, he was strong. When he drove into me, it felt as if I were making love to a race car. I had a death grip on the back of the chaise, so that he wouldn't propel me clear off it.

"Do you know why I think of you?" He spoke directly into my ear. "You make me come instantly. I put my hand on myself, picture you naked, and I come like a fourteen-year-old."

The pleasure of his body was volcanic. The pleasure of his words was a conflagration. I was already on the verge when he said, "I come so fast that sometimes I have to masturbate one more time. And when I do that, I imagine fucking you all night long."

My orgasm was a bullet to the head, a shocking starburst. His was similarly thorough and ferocious. But he didn't stop. He kept going, kissing my face, my throat, my breasts, until I was trembling again.

Until together we fell over the edge again.

MY BREATH WAS IN TATTERS. So was something far more important: my composure. Fortunately the dazzle of nighttime Manhattan was only a shimmer on the walls, the room dark enough that I didn't need to worry that he'd see my confusion—and the beginning of my distress.

Bennett kissed me on the shoulder and asked, as if it were an afterthought, "When was the last time you got lucky?"

Should I lie? It would be a good idea here. "You should know," I said. "You were an eyewitness."

He kissed my cheek. "I'm busy. What's your excuse?"

I have closed myself off—and I prefer it that way. Who are you and how did you manage to strip me naked? "I'm incredibly incompetent at getting laid. I could stand in the middle of Times Square on a Saturday night, waving a 'Free Pussy' sign, and get no takers."

"Liar. I'll bet I ruined you for other men."

I would have laughed if I could. "So says the man who can't put his hand on himself without thinking of me."

He chortled softly. "Put me in my place, why don't you?"

And with that, he pushed off to get dressed. By the time I slowly sat up, pulled down my skirt, and straightened my top, he was already presentable. He gave me my panty-and-tights tangle, and then my boots. And when I had everything in place, he turned the lights back on and brought me the vermouth I hadn't tasted yet.

"We'll have time to finish our drinks before dinner, like civilized people."

I wanted to ask him whether he really fantasized about me every time he masturbated. If it was true, then he was almost as sexually obsessed with me as I was with him—and that might be some consolation. But I had a feeling he would smirk at me and ask, *What do you think?*

And other than laughing it off, what response could I give? If I said I believed it, I would come across as hopelessly naive. If I said I didn't believe a word of it, then why did I bother to ask? Even laughing it off would at best be an awkward recovery from a full-blown faux pas.

So I said instead, "Do you really sleep on the chaise when you come back from the hospital?"

"When I'm on call."

"So you just sit here and…spank the monkey?"

"You know what happened one time? I had two days off and slept the night in my bed. The next morning I came down, grabbed some breakfast, and sat down to read the news, and ten minutes later I had an erection the size of the Empire State Building. I've turned myself into Pavlov's dog."

"Now you have to stay away from the masturbation couch the rest of the time?"

"I might have to move it somewhere else. Imagine if I had a party and accidentally sat down on it."

We were still laughing when the oven chimed to let us know that our soup was ready. But my laughter sounded a little brittle in my own ears.

Bennett set the table and served a salad for the first course. "By the way, Zelda showed me the picture with you in a tiara. Pretty breathtaking."

"Thanks. I usually deny that I'm the one in the picture, since in person I look like a halfhearted knockoff."

"Really? The first time I saw you, you looked almost exactly like that."

My brows shot up. "When I was out walking Biscuit in Cos Cob?"

"No, I first saw you in Central Park last summer, at a wedding."

I looked at him in surprise—I'd indeed attended a wedding in Central Park the past summer.

"I went for a run in the park and I was walking back when a wedding party came over the bridge. And when they all passed by, you were there at the other end of the bridge, looking down into the water."

"Oh," I said, more than a little unnerved. "I didn't notice anyone."

Weddings sometimes got to me. Despite the divorce rate, it was still even odds for the bride and groom to make it all the way, to become one of those white-haired, affectionate couples I envied and admired so much. And that day in Central Park was one of those occasions when I looked into my own future and saw nothing but loneliness.

"No, I don't expect you did," he said softly. "The water under the bridge was exceptionally interesting."

We were quiet for some time. I worked diligently on my salad, though I didn't taste much of anything. And then I asked, as much to fill the silence as out of curiosity, "And how's work for you?"

He took a sip of his water. "I feel like I can perform a lobectomy in my sleep these days."

"That's the removal of a lobe of a lung, right?"

"Uh-hmm. Between Thanksgiving and when I left for Guatemala, we had a string of patients who needed the procedure. There were a couple of cardiac procedures too, a valve replacement and a transmyocardial revascularization."

"I'm almost more impressed that you can say it than that you can do it."

"I told you, pinnacle of modern manhood."

This had me smiling again, despite myself.

We made more small talk as we polished off bowls of leek-and-potato soup. Then, during a lull in the conversation, he cleared the table and brought out poached pear halves. I sensed we were about to get down to business.

"So tell me why you've been stalking Zelda."

And why you've been Googling me so hard.

Bennett poured me half a glass of dessert wine before sitting down again. "When you first called me about Biscuit, you said something like, 'This is Evangeline Canterbury, Collette Woolworth's house sitter.' Your name rang a bell, but it was only when I was on the train Saturday morning, going back to the city, after we'd…"

"Done it against a wall," I offered.

"Yes, that." He looked at me with an expression that was almost a smile, but not quite.

An expression that caused a flash of intense heat low in my abdomen.

"Right," I said briskly. "So that was when you finally figured out why my name was familiar. I'm surprised you were able to. When Zelda first brought you up as 'the Somerset boy,' I drew a complete blank."

"I might have done the same if my mom hadn't kept repeating to herself, the last time we were all together in one place, 'I can't believe we left poor Evangeline Canterbury in the lurch.'"

He had a faraway gaze, as if reliving the chaos, acrimony, and heartache of that day. Then he shook his head. "Anyway, after I moved back east I realized I didn't have a strategy in place. When I left, I cut my ties pretty thoroughly. I don't have anyone here who can serve as a liaison, to ease me back into my parents' social circle. And I need someone like that before I can start the process."

I dipped a piece of pear in the pool of chocolate sauce at the center of the plate. "I hate to sound like a broken record. But if you are serious about reuniting with your family—and you must be to have moved three thousand miles—you can just pick up the phone."

For a long moment he said nothing. Then, "I can't."

Something about those two words, a certain rawness, perhaps, made my chest constrict.

But your mother is waiting for you to call, I almost answered. Then I remembered what Zelda had said: *The real rupture is between the boy and his father.* For all that Frances Somerset had been open about her own desire to hear from her prodigal son, she'd been resolutely silent on her husband's sentiments.

Now the purpose of the liaison was clear. "So you want a reconciliation, but you want it on your own terms—no apologies, no olive branches held out, no appearing at all as if you actually came to make amends."

He exhaled. "It's scary how accurately you're reading me, but yes, exactly. I want everything to seem organic."

"And that's where Zelda comes in?"

"No, that's where you come in."

I stared at him, a forkful of pear hovering before me.

"For me to cultivate friendships that have been dormant for fifteen years would be both too obvious and too cynical. A girlfriend is a much better idea: A brand-new girlfriend is still a legitimate girlfriend."

I set down my fork and took a swig of the dessert wine. "I'm not your girlfriend."

But did he want me to be?

He looked at me, his gaze clear yet…impersonal. It struck me just how much I'd deluded myself with my Munich fantasy. I didn't know him. I didn't know him at all.

Then his expression softened—and something came over me, a sense of sweetness and wonder. But only for a fraction of a second. When he spoke again, he was all business.

"We don't need to apply labels if that'll trip you up."

What did that even *mean*?

He leaned forward an inch. "Don't you see? There's something remarkably perfect about how everything has come together. Zelda is my mom's friend, so there's an overlap between your social circle and my parents'. As your plus-one, I'm bound to bump into them at various events. And since we were neighbors for a whole summer, which is God's truth, it wouldn't surprise anyone to learn that we've hooked up."

He wanted me to be his *pretend* girlfriend. My disappointment was so sharp it took a second before I could respond. "I can see your logic. But you have to understand—no matter how much I might look like a socialite in my 'princess' picture, I'm not one, and I hardly ever attend events on the social calendar."

"But that's part of what makes you such a good fit. My parents would be impressed by your accomplishments. It would also make our 'relationship' seem more genuine."

"That's crazy. I'm not an actress either. I can't keep pretending to be what I'm not."

"But together we don't have to. When I'm standing next to you, anybody with eyes can tell that I want to sleep with you—and that you won't mind. With that in place, how much more do we need to pretend? We're two busy people with no plans for the long-term future. We're just enjoying ourselves in the present tense."

I shook my head. "No. It's insane."

"Explain to me why it's insane."

"Because…"

Because it would be like throwing someone with an alcohol problem into a sea of hard liquor.

It was bad enough that I succumbed at his touch. Now, on top of our already ill-defined association, he wanted to add the complications of a fake relationship. Maybe he'd be able to keep track of what was real and what wasn't; I didn't trust myself that much.

But I couldn't tell him I was turning him down because I was too into him. "Okay, how long would it take you to reconcile with your parents? Three months? Six months? A year? What if I meet someone I want to be with? What if you do? Are we stuck with each other because we have this crazy agreement?

"Also, how often are we supposed to go to these social occasions? I spent my Christmas working. I don't have that kind of time.

"Not to mention, you may not know people in town, but I do. I've lived most of my life in Manhattan. What am I supposed to tell everyone? What am I supposed to tell Zelda? There are so many complications I can't even begin to list them all."

Bennett was silent, his face turned to the window. I was again reminded of the night of our meeting. After he'd introduced himself, I'd thanked him coolly, wanting him gone. He'd glanced toward his car then, as if he wished he'd never come out in the rain to talk to me. As if he was the one who might leave our encounter bruised and battered.

He looked back at me. "Except for the part about my parents, you can tell Zelda everything," he said, his voice calm and even. "That we hooked up in August and again just now. That I'd like for us to continue to see each other. That you aren't entirely sure yet. Same goes for your friends.

"I'm busy too, so we won't be out glad-handing every night—or even every weekend. As for time, three months is too short, but six will work. And if you meet someone you want to date while we're at it, you can take your out anytime."

He made it sound so easy. So casual.

I shook my head some more. "I'm sorry, but I can't."

Silence greeted my words. His face was shuttered. Realization burned in my chest: After my refusal, we wouldn't see each other again.

What was I thinking? Of course I would be his pretend girlfriend. Of course I would bask in his adoring gaze and giggle as he whispered snarky comments into my ear. And of course I would come back here with him afterward, still buzzing from the high of our public displays of affection, and let him take off my clothes and make love to me.

I clutched at the napkin on my lap. It was all I could do not to take back my refusal.

Bennett tented his fingers together. "At the end of our six months, I'll write a check for two hundred fifty thousand dollars to your favorite charity. Or to you directly, if that's what you prefer."

My jaw slackened. A quarter of a million dollars was a lot of money for doing little more than squiring him about town.

"Does that sound like something you can agree to?"

I took another swig of the dessert wine. I would regret my answer bitterly—I already did. "No."

Bennett didn't look displeased—he didn't even look surprised. "I don't know if anyone told you this, but I made a shit-ton of money when I was in California, and I'm willing to put it to use. If two hundred fifty thousand isn't enough, let's make it five hundred thousand."

My stomach flipped, as much from the extravagance of the offer as from...I couldn't be entirely sure, but something in the timbre of his voice had caught my attention, something that belied the impassiveness of his expression. "You could easily find someone else."

"Of course. But no one else on my horizon has received a MacArthur Genius Grant for her work. You'll make me look good."

I rubbed my temple. What did he actually want? And what did *I* actually want? "I never thought I'd see the day when I'm asked to become a Park Avenue trophy girlfriend."

"Look at it from my perspective—I never thought I'd see the day when a quarter of a million dollars wouldn't be enough to hire me a fake girlfriend."

I smiled weakly at that.

"As an added incentive, if we succeed in our endeavor, I'll write a check for an additional half a million dollars, a grant toward your research."

I should be flattered that he was so determined, but I was more than a little freaked out. "What's the catch?"

Other than that for six months we'd be working toward a common goal. When my friends talked about falling for their colleagues, this almost always came up—that they were teammates, obsessed with the same objective. I didn't want to be in the trenches with Bennett. I didn't want to be his partner and confidante.

"If I'm going to pay double, I'll be more stringent in my demands. At two hundred fifty I was willing to prorate. If you can only do four months, then I'll hand over a check for two-thirds of the agreed-upon sum. But at five hundred it's all or nothing. If you bail on me before six months is up, for any reason beyond acts of God, I keep the money."

It was my turn to look out the window—hope and doubt kept chasing each other in my head and I didn't want him to see that on my face.

I wasn't hurting for cash in my personal life and I'd secured sufficient funding for my research for the next several years. But Pater had been a businessman—an art expert too but a businessman first and foremost—and he had taught me that very few things in life were as eloquent as money.

Not that I'd describe Bennett's money as eloquent. It was more like a mysterious artifact, the writing on it in a language I'd never seen before. But its existence was significant enough that I couldn't dismiss it out of hand.

"Let me..." I grimaced. "Let me think about it."

Bennett exhaled audibly. "Take your time. But while you think about it, can you make me your plus-one at Charlotte Devonport's wedding?"

Charlotte Devonport was marrying my second cousin Sam in three weeks. "Are you related to her?"

"She's my mom's goddaughter. So my parents will be there, most likely."

"And I just ditch Zelda? She was going to be my date."

"You don't give my evil genius enough credit. She'll be receiving a ticket to a private concert Annie Lennox is giving in town that night as part of a fund-raiser."

Zelda was a huge Annie Lennox fan. She wouldn't turn down such an opportunity.

"In which case you can tell people that I'm a last-minute replacement for Zelda," Bennett went on, "somebody you asked on a whim."

I truly hadn't given his evil genius enough credit. "And you'll pretend, until you arrive at the wedding, that you had no idea who the bride was."

"Unless that claim seems too preposterous. In which case I'll say that I had some inkling who might be there, but since I didn't want to miss a chance to hang out with you…"

My heart pinched. *If only he meant it. If only it wasn't a Manhattan-size pretense.* "You should ask a woman who's more likely to take that six-month gig. Showing up at the wedding with me and then somewhere else two weeks later with another girlfriend might not give the impression you want."

"I'll decide who I want. You just say yes or no."

And he wanted me, even if it wasn't in the way I'd like to be wanted.

What's the harm? asked a part of me. *It's just a wedding.*

And this is just drinks at his place, retorted a different part of me. *Look at everything that's happened since you stepped into this apartment. Shut it down now. You can't leave the door open for this man. Next thing you know, he'll have taken over your entire life.*

"Please," he said, his voice so low I almost couldn't hear him, "I'm asking this as a favor."

Had he been looking at me, backed by the full force of his personality, I would have said no. But his gaze was somewhere in the middle of the table, that of a proud man who had run out of options.

"All right," I heard myself say, "we can go to the wedding together. Just the wedding."

Several seconds passed before his gaze lifted. I couldn't read his expression, except to know that he didn't seem glad, or even relieved.

"Thank you," he said softly. "You don't know what it means to me."

Chapter 5

IT WAS EARLY STILL WHEN we got up from dinner, but Bennett had to go to work—he was taking a night shift for a colleague who'd fractured an elbow skiing. After we put away the dishes, he grabbed the messenger bag I'd seen in his car, and we left together.

A cab was waiting for us downstairs. We got in and Bennett gave the exact address of my house. "The cab dropped Zelda off first the other day, after our lunch," he explained when I raised a brow.

There was no more vulnerability to be seen on his part, as if that despondent moment at the table had never happened.

"And how's Zelda, by the way?" he asked, all smooth amiability. "How's Turkey?"

"She loves Turkey, but she's already finished with the Turkish portion of the trip. Now she's in England, visiting her godmother."

"Ah, Mrs. Asquith. I miss her, the old battle-ax. Haven't seen her in a couple of years."

"That's right," I recalled with some surprise. "Zelda mentioned that the two of you are thick as thieves."

"She was—and is—a tremendous gossip, Mrs. Asquith. In fact, she used to tell me stories about Zelda, about how this man she really adored left her when he realized how serious her condition was."

This casual revelation flabbergasted me: Zelda had never mentioned such a man. "What else do you know about him?"

"He's a successful TV producer. Very low-key. Married forever to the same woman."

"Have you ever met him?"

"No, but I remember Mrs. Asquith telling me once that I'd just missed him. So they are on visiting terms—or they were, fifteen years ago." He glanced at me. "I guess this is news to you?"

I hesitated. "Yeah."

We were before the light at 5th and 79th, waiting to turn onto the transverse to cross Central Park. I stared at the grille that separated us from the cabdriver, trying to come to grips with this unknown side of Zelda.

She had long joked that my father married her only because of her bloodline, and she him because he was her ticket to America. I used to have this image of them sitting across from each other, Zelda smoking one cigarette after another—she quit only five years ago—while he jotted down the terms of their marriage with his Montblanc fountain pen.

Seemed like the sort of thing people did in the eighties.

But this man, this English TV producer, where did he fit in? And what had Zelda done with her heartbreak?

"Children are always the last to learn about their parents," said Bennett, breaking the silence as the light turned green. "A couple of years ago my sister mentioned that I was Mom and Dad's reconciliation baby. I can't tell you how shocked I was—I had no idea that they'd divorced and married again."

It was the first time he'd said anything about a sibling. "Is she your only sibling?"

"I have a brother too. He's four years older than me, and she two years younger."

I wouldn't have pegged him for a middle child. "They're not in the city, I suppose."

"Prescott lives in Singapore, and Imogene is out in Silicon Valley."

"Sounds like you get along just fine with them—your sister, at least."

"Before I moved back east, she and I used to see each other every week. My brother usually makes a West Coast stop when he visits the States."

I sighed. "One of them should serve as your liaison. I'm sure they'll do it for far less than a million dollars."

"What, and miss the fun of pretending to be a couple with you?"

That was the trouble, wasn't it? That it might actually be fun, until we hit the six-month drop-off date, and he thanked me and walked off into the sunset with his parents.

We were exiting the park when Bennett said, "I call Mrs. Asquith every few weeks. Would you like me to ask her about Zelda's old boyfriend when I speak to her next?"

I wavered for a moment. "Yes, I would. Thank you."

"Consider it done."

Consider it done. I remembered his text with that exact phrase. I could recite our entire exchange of texts from memory—and I sometimes did, silently, to myself.

The taxi came to a stop before my house. Bennett walked me to the front door and kissed me on the temple. "Sweet dreams."

THE NEXT EVENING, AN ALMOST freakishly beautiful flower arrangement came to the door, a profusion of tulips in a clear glass trough, the blossoms progressing from pure creamy white to pale blush to a deep purple, the whole thing at once delicate and dramatic.

A note came along. *Thanks for dinner.*

I reached for my phone. *Just for dinner?*

For sex you should send me flowers. Your orgasms were worth a dozen gladioluses, at least.

I shook my head, half smiling, and looked at that message for far too long.

The next afternoon I came home early to meet Zelda. I was turning the key in the front door when a big, black Town Car pulled up and disgorged her, sun-kissed from the walking holiday, a stylish new coat swishing around her knees.

"Nice!" I said as I hugged her. The coat was cobalt blue, a brilliant pop of color against the overcast winter day.

"A present from Mrs. Asquith."

"Did she get the car service for you too?"

"No, that's courtesy of the Somerset boy."

Whose evil genius I had once again underestimated. "I see."

I opened my wallet to tip the driver, who had lined up Zelda's luggage neatly inside our door. But he only smiled and said, "No worries, ma'am. The gratuity is all taken care of."

I still gave him something, on the off chance that Bennett was a terrible tipper.

Zelda and I hugged each other again. But no sooner had I put the kettle to boil than the doorbell rang. I thought perhaps she had forgotten something in the Town Car, but it was a deliveryman, holding a big brown bag.

Which turned out to contain a five-course dinner, along with a box of pastry.

"Bennett did say he'd send something around," said Zelda. "Doesn't do anything by half measures, does he?"

The man's manipulativeness was without bounds. "He called you?"

"Yes, during the ride. And apologized for being somewhat dishonest when we had lunch. He said that he already figured out you were his neighbor in Cos Cob, but chose not to mention it because he wasn't sure whether at that point you'd realized who he was."

"I hadn't."

"But you met again on Boxing Day and got it all sorted out. Isn't he a dish?"

"I suppose you could say that."

Zelda noticed the flowers. "Oh, my, did he send those also?"

"It's a take-no-prisoners charm offensive."

"Don't be so tough on the poor dear. It's about time some nice young man mounted a charm offensive for you. He did mention that you're a bit reluctant to go out with him, but that he's trying to change your mind."

I was both miffed that Bennett had preempted me in his practice of evil genius-ism—and relieved that I didn't have to explain anything. "All right, enough about him. Let's talk about you. Tell me everything."

She did. We polished off half a box of pastry as she showed me all the pictures, described her favorite places on the Turquoise Coast, and gave me the latest gossip about her cousins.

When she moved on to her visit to Mrs. Asquith, I was sorely tempted to ask her about the man from her past—whenever I wasn't thinking about my research or Bennett, my mind would come to dwell on this mystery boyfriend and the particular stretch of her past that was like dark matter, something that couldn't be observed except by its gravitational effects.

What forces did the heartbreak still exert on Zelda?

"Oh, that reminds me," said Zelda. "I spoke to Mrs. Asquith about the Somerset boy, and she showed me pictures they took when they visited Iceland."

"They go on trips together?"

"Isn't that lovely of him? I mean, granted, he's estranged from his own family and probably sees Mrs. Asquith as a surrogate, but still—not every man takes his actual grandmother to remote and beautiful places. You should give the boy a chance."

But every chance was a risk, and Bennett was a far bigger risk than most.

If I wasn't careful, he could become the kind of semisecret that people whispered about me. *Oh, you know there was a man, years ago. But no one else since. Wonder what happened. Poor Evangeline.*

"Are you trying to evict me, Zelda?" I asked, half jokingly. "Have you had enough of me as a housemate?"

"Oh, no, darling. All I want for you is a spectacular sex life, the kind that will shock people—and make them deeply envious."

I blinked. And then the two of us burst out laughing together.

"You had me for a moment," I told her, still giggling.

"Believe me, darling, I do want that for you. But more than anything else I want you to be madly adored." Zelda ran her hand through my hair. "It's what I've always wanted."

There was a lump in my throat. I cupped her face and kissed her on her forehead. "All right, I'll get on that—as soon as I achieve a sex life that will make people both gasp and choke."

THE WEEKEND BEFORE THE WEDDING, I had lunch with the Material Girls.

The Material Girls were my friends from college. We lived in the same dorm building, all majored in STEM fields—science, technology, engineering, and mathematics—and just kind of gravitated toward one another. I joked once that I always wanted to be referred to as a material girl, and thus was born our collective name.

After college, we were scattered for a while. But one by one we found our way to the Big Apple. I, the native Manhattanite, was actually the last to relocate six years ago, after I finished grad school.

Carolyn, our IT expert, was the one who'd given me the T-shirt that had caught Bennett's eye. Lara worked as a bioengineer. And Daff, who dropped chemistry for molecular gastronomy, picked the restaurant where we met—this time a new place in Williamsburg.

"So what's cooking in Hipster Central today?" asked Lara.

"Do not take the name of the hipsters in vain," admonished Daff, "for they shall spread the word of thy new establishment. When I have my own restaurant, I want all the hipsters to come and rave about it until the regular folks start giving me their money."

"At which point the hipsters can shove it," said Carolyn.

Daff laughed. "Exactly. Make my name and then they can go off to their next obscure, authentic discovery."

While we looked over the menu, we talked about everyone's holidays. Carolyn was still recovering from her visit home to Vancouver and a feast every day—her dad was a gourmet home cook who loved to entertain. Lara had been in Cabo, where her cousin got married over Christmas. Daff and I went nowhere—but for Daff that was a professional sacrifice; she'd be taking her vacation in a few days.

"You really have no life, E," said Carolyn.

"Thank you," I said. "And I worked hard for it too."

Lara nudged my shoulder with hers. "And is your vagina still on extended leave?"

My lack of a love life had long been a running joke among the Material Girls. But they, like Zelda, had bought into the explanation that as a tenure-track professor who must produce an explosion of papers to prove my worth, I simply didn't have the time. "Oh, come on, you don't believe that. You know my 'lab' is actually a sex dungeon."

No point bringing up Bennett yet.

"And how was the wedding, Lara?" I went on, turning the topic of the conversation away from me.

"Yeah," said Daff. "You never said whether What's-his-name was there."

What's-his-name was the guy who broke off an engagement to Lara to go out with her cousin—the sister of the one who got married.

Lara shrugged. "He popped in for like a second. I think he left before I even knew he was there."

Daff looked disappointed. "So you didn't shove your tongue down the throat of some other man right in front of him?"

"No, no hookups for me."

"There goes my hope one of us would do it with a random stranger and live to tell the tale," said Carolyn.

Someday, when I didn't feel anything anymore about my own random stranger, I might give them the story. But as movie Aragorn would say, *It is not this day.*

So I raised my glass. "Here's to a year of record-breaking sex. May all our vaginas be begging for an extended leave at the end of it."

"Hear, hear," said Carolyn.

The rest of lunch was the usual good time punctuated by laments that we didn't see one another more often, what with everyone being so busy. As we were settling the checks, Daff touched on the Annual Boyfriend Roundup, which took place every February after Valentine's Day. The event was started to give us a chance to introduce significant others to the group, but somehow nobody was ever in a relationship in February, so now it was just an excuse to dress up, go out, and enjoy ourselves.

"Who's bringing a boyfriend?" Daff asked.

As was our tradition, we all raised our hands.

"Good!" said Daff. "The liars' brigade is all here. Now go forth and wrangle some penises."

AFTER LUNCH I PAID A visit to Pater's grave.

He had died nine years ago this day, from a car accident that killed his third wife instantly. He'd lingered for a few hours at the hospital, long enough for me to sit by his bedside, his hand in mine, and live out our alternate history any number of times.

He'd remarried the year before, to a woman with whom he bickered constantly. And every other week they'd have a major fight. I couldn't be sure, since I hadn't been there, but I suspected that when the accident happened, they'd been in the middle of another one of their all-consuming quarrels.

When he'd opened his eyes in the hospital, he'd whispered my name. Then he'd asked, "How's Zelda?"

Pater was the kind of man whose negativity could drive a saint to Hulk out. Yet in his own way, he'd adored Zelda—had given her the house in the divorce because he'd worried about there being too many abrupt changes in her life. Losing her had been a heavy blow to him. And the new marriage hadn't been so much a rebound as a crutch—better to hate the one he was with than to be entirely alone.

"Zelda's fine," I told him, "in England visiting her cousins."

"Those damn cousins," he'd answered, wheezing. "They hated me—but at least they love her."

He'd fallen unconscious again after that. I stroked his fingers and imagined a very different January, starting with that long-ago night in Paris. In this alternate universe Zelda never got sick and she never left Pater. He would still be holding forth before dinner every night, a glass of vermouth in hand. And he would most certainly not be dying before me because the new wife with whom he couldn't get along had decided to drive after a few drinks too many.

His last words to me had been, "Make sure you don't settle for social-climbing district attorneys."

I kissed the bouquet in my hand and laid it on his grave, along with a note.

I miss you, Pater. And I haven't married a social-climbing district attorney—yet. Love, Eva.

CHARLOTTE AND SAM MARRIED AT City Hall, with only their parents in attendance. The evening reception was at the Mandarin Oriental on Columbus Circle. Bennett met me in the lobby of the hotel.

"The bride is going to kill you, Professor, for looking so pretty."

I looked decent. But Bennett…

Pater had been a clotheshorse with a closet full of Armani suits. He loved to expound on the intricacies of a good suit. In fact, just before his final admonition to me about not marrying social-climbing DAs, he'd said, *Never tolerate a man in an ill-fitting suit.*

He wouldn't have had to worry about that with Bennett. As a rule, men's clothes that weren't plaids or denim overalls did nothing for me. But the sight of Bennett's impeccable slim-cut blue suit, worn over a crisp white shirt, made my heart palpitate.

"Look at you, fashionista," I murmured.

"That means I-hate-you-because-you're-beautiful, right?"

"I don't know. In your mind, is there anything people say to you that doesn't mean that?"

He laughed and kissed me on my cheek. "Three weeks was far too long without you putting me in my place."

It didn't need to be three weeks. He had, true to his word, invited Zelda and me for dinner. But I'd declined for us. "I promise to put you in your place early and often tonight."

He whistled softly. "And Zelda, gone to her concert?"

"Like a little girl off to visit her first pony."

My dear, gullible Zelda had even repeatedly made the case that I should take Bennett to the wedding reception in her stead, not realizing that my demurrals were all for show. That I'd already committed to this evening with him.

"It's easy to make Zelda happy. You, on the other hand, are absolutely impossible, sweetheart."

No one had ever said anything of the sort to me. Yet the truth of it was like a kick to the chest. Was he being playful again, or did he really understand, deep down, that I wasn't the well-adjusted "sweetheart" I presented to the world?

"Watch it, Somerset. There are men who would pay a million dollars for this—sex not included."

"Ah, yes, you promised early and often. You are a woman of your word, Canterbury."

With that, he took my hand and started walking. I stared at our interlaced fingers.

He followed my line of sight. "It's okay. We don't have to be dating to hold hands."

We didn't. It was only the intimacy of the gesture that had jarred me.

The hotel staff directed us toward a flight of stairs that would lead us to the ballroom.

"Nervous?" I asked.

He exhaled. "Badly."

He had seemed perfectly at ease, like George Clooney about to work a crowd. But now I noticed the tension he carried in his shoulders.

"So if I come on to you inappropriately," he continued, "blame it on my nerves."

We were at the top of the stairs. I halted his progress. Everything about his outfit was perfectly in place, but I took a moment to smooth his collar.

Maybe he was all about exploiting me for his own purposes, but that didn't take away from the fact that he'd brought me out of the rain—and out of my misery—when I most needed it.

"Don't worry," I told him. "I got you."

He traced a finger across my cheek. "I know you do."

WHEN WE RESUMED WALKING HAND in hand toward the reception line, there were people looking at us—to be expected when a handsome and sharply dressed man showed up at a wedding. After a moment I realized that I knew some of those people, and they were surprised not so much by Bennett, but by me. It had been ages since I went anywhere with a man by my side.

I introduced Bennett to a couple of guests. Then it was our turn to congratulate the new couple. I hugged both bride and groom. Bennett shook hands with the groom and hugged the bride too. "Nice to see you again, Charlotte. I almost can't believe you're old enough to be married."

Charlotte looked nonplussed—she'd have been ten or eleven when he was disowned and probably didn't remember him at all. Her mother, farther down the line, gasped.

"My God, Bennett! It really is you. I didn't know you were coming today."

"I'm just here to keep an eye on Evangeline, but it's very nice to see you again, Mrs. Devonport."

"Yes, of course," said Mrs. Devonport, still dazed. "Evangeline Canterbury, is it? You were Zelda's stepdaughter."

"That's me. Bennett and I were neighbors for a while when I was housesitting for Collette Woolworth in Cos Cob. Now that I'm back in the city, we don't get to see each other as much. Since he's off tonight I thought I'd show him around a bit." I patted him on his sleeve. "The man works too much."

"I hope you have a great time," said Mrs. Devonport eagerly. "We have a fantastic deejay—or at least that's what Charlotte tells me."

We congratulated her and moved on. By the time we got to the ballroom, news of Bennett's presence had spread. Guests came and reintroduced themselves; those of the younger generation were his former schoolmates and neighbors, those of an older generation friends or acquaintances of his parents.

But no sign of the parents themselves.

"Are they not here?" I asked when we were finally able to sit down, after this bout of heavy-duty schmoozing.

"If they are, I can't see them."

We'd arrived a bit late on purpose, so that as we made our way across the ballroom, we'd be easily visible to the guests who were already seated. "You think they might be running behind too?"

Bennett shook his head, a grim look on his face. "For them, punctuality is next to godliness."

"But there isn't a set time for dinner."

The reception, despite its location, was a casual affair, with a small-plates buffet and no formal seating arrangements.

"If they were coming at all, they wouldn't miss the toasts."

As if on cue, the best man rose for his speech.

Speeches and toasts followed one another. I glanced at Bennett every so often. He laughed and applauded at all the right places, showing no signs of having been let down. When the bride and groom took the floor for their first dance, however, he laid his head on my shoulder and sighed.

My heart ached, as if his disappointment were my own. "There'll be other chances."

He sighed again. "I know. I'll be fine."

Without realizing what I was doing, I kissed him on his hair. He took my hand in his and played with my fingers. I felt…paralyzed. Part of me wanted to yank away immediately. And a different part of me would like for us to stay like this forever.

In the end Bennett was the one to straighten first, dipping a spoon into a demitasse of soup—he'd hardly touched any of his food. "I spoke to Mrs. Asquith a couple of days ago and asked about Zelda's ex."

I felt a flutter of a different kind of nerves. "What did she say?"

"He and his wife are in the middle of a divorce, which kind of took everyone by surprise."

"Is it because he found someone else?"

"Mrs. Asquith didn't think so. Seems like there was just nothing left."

"Did she tell Zelda?"

"I didn't ask." Bennett looked at me. "You think she'd still care, after all these years?"

"Yes."

"Why?"

"Because she has never mentioned him, not even by allusion: 'Oh, there was a man I once dated,' or, 'a TV producer I used to know.' It's like she erased him. You see what I'm saying?"

"Yeah, I do."

Hmm. Did he understand because he had done just that, expunging his ex from his existence?

No, what was I thinking? He'd never hesitated to bring her up, not from the very beginning, with that reference about having been known to like an older woman.

"Do you want to dance?" he asked.

I spied Mrs. Devonport approaching the buffet. "You go. I'll do some investigating."

"Seconds?" asked Mrs. Devonport as I drew up next to her.

"Absolutely. I love these little bowls of truffle risotto."

"I haven't had it yet, but I'm so glad you like it." She leaned in a little closer. "We've been wondering where Bennett has been hiding himself since he came back to town. I guess it's been with you."

"Not all the time. He's still doing his fellowship, and there's no end to the work." I also leaned in toward Mrs. Devonport. "I didn't know until Bennett told me just now that Charlotte is his mom's goddaughter—I said I had a reception to go to and would he mind coming with me, so he really had no idea who the wedding parties were. Are his parents going to be here, by any chance? I should probably prepare myself if things are going to be awkward."

"Oh, you don't ever need to worry about the Somersets being awkward in public," Mrs. Devonport hastened to reassure me. "Besides, Frances called me this afternoon and said she was still under the weather—the flu—and she didn't want to give it to anybody else."

"Phew," I said. "Crisis averted. Thanks for letting me know."

When I returned with my newly gathered intelligence, someone had taken my seat, a wavy-haired blonde in a cranberry spaghetti-strap dress.

Bennett rose and kissed me beneath my ear. "Sweetheart, I thought you were never coming back. I missed you."

"I was gone for five minutes, Doctor. You need to be a little less clingy."

He laughed. "Evangeline, this is Damaris. Damaris, Evangeline. Damaris and I took ballroom lessons together when we were kids."

"Bennett came with me to talent night at my school, and we brought down the house with our tango routine," bragged Damaris.

"Tango? Did you guys bring sexy back?"

"I thought so at the time. But then Bennett and I went dancing last June at a tango club and my God"—she trailed a finger up Bennett's lapel—"what a difference, dancing the tango with him all grown-up. How come we haven't gone back there since?"

"I told you," Bennett said coolly, "my work is too busy."

"Why? You can buy the hospital. Forget work."

"That's not going to happen," said Bennett. "But it's good to see you again, Damaris. Now, would you mind giving my date her chair back?"

Damaris stood up reluctantly. "We should tango here tonight and show everybody a thing or two."

"I don't think so. See you later."

Damaris made a sound through her nose. "I wouldn't feel so secure about your place if I were you," she said to me. "He went out with my friend a few times last summer and then dumped her like a bag of cement."

"Thanks for the heads-up," I answered with a smile. "I'll be sure to dump him first."

"You really are the best," Bennett whispered to me as we sat down in the wake of Damaris's hair-tossing departure.

"Next time, if you must reject a woman, try some subtle."

"I already tried subtle. The patient is forty-five percent inebriated and not responding to subtle."

Damaris looked back just then. Bennett wasted no time in pulling me toward him and kissing me on my cheek. "Now, why don't *you* get wasted and come on to me?"

I ignored that question. "Your mom has the flu. She called Mrs. Davenport earlier to say she wouldn't be coming."

This sobered him. "At least I don't have to wonder about that anymore."

We sat silently for a while; then I felt him touch the shell of my ear. The sensation of it all but skewered me. "What happened to waiting for me to get wasted first?"

"That's only one scenario."

"What's this scenario, then?"

"I'm just turned on by you."

His words were almost a greater peril than his touches. I nudged a pumpkin gnocchi around on my plate. "You're planning to use me to distract yourself from your disappointment. I don't do consolation sex."

I also didn't want to experience any more of his vulnerability. That sigh on my shoulder just about killed me.

"It's not consolation sex, just the straightforward, nasty sort," he whispered in my ear, sending sizzles of electricity along my nerve endings.

He was clearly angling for sex and sex alone, viewing me as a stressed-out society matron might eye her bottle of Xanax. Why, then, did I so desperately want to say yes?

I put on my sternest voice. "If you want to get laid, hook up with somebody on Tinder, or order an escort off craigslist."

"I'm morally opposed to paying for sex, and I don't want to deal with any more strangers tonight." He reached for a tomato tarte Tatin. "Guess I'll eat myself into a stupor then. Where's a gallon of cookie-dough ice cream when a man needs it?"

I got up and returned with an assortment of desserts. "Here, sex on a plate."

He bit into something triple-tiered, but his eyes were on me, his hunger unmistakable.

I pushed a slice of almond dacquoise along the edge of the plate, too flustered to eat. "Something doesn't compute about your situation," I said, so that I wouldn't stare back at him with the same intensity of lust. "Kids have screaming fights with their parents all the time and everybody says all kinds of mean things. And in the vast, vast, vast majority of the cases, by next Thanksgiving everybody is sitting down to dinner again. I don't get why your estrangement with your parents should have lasted so long. Did you and Ms. Cougar break up just now?"

"No, when I was twenty-three."

"Who holds a grudge for another decade?"

"I did mount a couple of real takeover attempts of the family holdings in my twenties."

I stopped pushing around the almond dacquoise. "So you were a raging asshole."

"That, I believe, is the technical term."

This changed things. "Are you sure your dad will forgive you?"

He dug a spoon into a thimble-size cup of chocolate crémeux. "No, I'm not sure at all. Which is why I need you. And you...you have no sympathy for a man trapped between his pride and his past asshole-ism."

He offered me the spoonful of crémeux, which was rich and bittersweet. "I have sympathy, just not enough to take off my clothes."

"You can keep your clothes on," he murmured.

The implication of his words...It was a wonder that the electricity sizzling along my nerves didn't short-circuit all the lights in the ballroom.

Applause erupted, startling me: The bride and groom were leaving. Bennett and I stood up and joined in the clapping.

"We should probably go too, if your purpose here is done," I said, once the newlyweds had exited.

"Are you going to jump into a taxi and head straight home?"

"Yes."

"And what do I do with my sad and lonely self?"

"Get drunk, eat ice cream, and don't operate on anyone."

He put an arm around me. "You are heartless. Why do I want you so much as my fake girlfriend?"

Why don't you want me as your real *girlfriend, you jackass?* "Because I seem—seem, mind you—to inhabit that sweet zone of obtainability: not so easy as to be worthless, and not so difficult that you'd give up all hope. Pretty basic evolutionary psychology."

He gazed at me. "You really know how to put a man in his Cro-Magnon place, Eva."

Pater had always insisted that nicknames were only for spouses and immediate family. He never referred to me in public except as Evangeline—and neither did Zelda, because he had been so adamant.

To hear Bennett call me Eva was a shock to the system, all the more so because I loved it.

Before I could reply, mournful, sensuous notes wafted across the ballroom.

A tango.

Damaris strode to the middle of the dance floor, struck a pose to a smattering of whistles and applause, and hooked her finger at Bennett.

He shook his head no.

"Come on," she wheedled.

He shook his head again.

"Pretty please," she pleaded.

Bennett hesitated. He turned to me, a gleam of calculation in his eyes. "Did you like *Dirty Dancing*? Did that movie turn you on?"

"Why do you want to know?" I asked cautiously.

"That's a yes then."

He shrugged out of his jacket and dropped it over the back of a chair. Then he pulled off his tie and extracted his cuff links. The music writhed and trembled. He approached Damaris slowly, almost casually, rolling up his sleeves as he did so. My heart stuttered at the sight of those beautiful forearms. The crowd was no less appreciative, the women cheering loudly.

All of a sudden he looped his arm about Damaris's waist and yanked her to him.

Catcalls erupted.

He drew a hand up her bare arm, over her shoulder, and cupped her cheek.

"*Mamma mia!*" said someone behind me.

Bennett flung Damaris away. She spun outward. He caught her by the fingertips. They stayed like that a moment, precariously balanced. She spun back into his arms. They were now pressed together from shoulder to groin, legs completely tangled.

He flicked one spaghetti strap off her shoulder. I heard myself gasp. He released her into a sweeping dip, then pulled her up so that their faces nearly touched.

The dance began in earnest. I'd seen tango, both as performance art onstage and in the clubs of Buenos Aires. But I'd never experienced another tango in which the man dominated the pairing quite so overwhelmingly.

The feral agility with which he moved had me slack-jawed. His turns and steps were as precise as an assassin's aim. His posture was gorgeous. And his understanding of the soul of the tango—the courtship in all its danger and complexity—mesmerized me.

Damaris was in thrall to his will, draped about him like a scarf. He was all cool provocation and heartless—or so I hoped—promises.

"This is better than porn," someone else said.

I was too flabbergasted to speak.

They sank into a deep lunge. While she remained in the lunge, he rose and walked away. She ran after him and lobbed her arms around his shoulders. He turned, lifted her, and dropped her into a reverse dip. Then he pushed her away, hard. They stared at each other. The music rose to a crescendo. She launched herself at him; he caught and held her, then slowly slid her down against his person, until she stood with one foot on the ground and the other hooked around his thigh.

The barest hint of a smile softened his mouth—power, control, and rampant masculinity in a bespoke package. The music stopped. He let go of Damaris, who immediately wrapped him in a hug. Something crooked and thorny poked into my heart—even more so when the guests burst into wild applause.

Then he was back at my side, reaching for his jacket. "Let's go."

Chapter 6

AS SOON AS THE ELEVATOR door closed, I yanked him to me. We kissed, devouring each other. The elevator could have crashed and I wouldn't have cared. Lust, need, and a crazy ache simmered inside me. I couldn't get close enough to him.

I couldn't get enough *of* him.

My fingers were in his hair. One of his hands was at the small of my back; the other cupped my bottom, molding our bodies together. Through his trousers his arousal pressed into me—a lot of arousal, that. I kissed him with even greater abandon.

Someone cleared her throat. We stilled: Without being aware of it, we'd reached the first floor and the door had opened on us.

Almost casually, Bennett kissed me at the corner of my lip, and then on the lobe of my ear, whispering, "I've never been caught in an elevator before, have you?"

I didn't make out in public, period. What in the world had come over me?

We pulled apart as if we'd engaged in nothing more erotic than a hug. Bennett took my hand. The next moment he turned stock-still, staring at the handsome middle-aged couple waiting to get in. They likewise gawked, in a way I wouldn't have expected of such a dignified pair.

The family resemblance struck me.

"Hi, Mom. Hi, Dad. You're late—the newlyweds have already left," said Bennett, with a nonchalance that gave no hint of how much he had schemed for this moment. He placed an arm around me. "Have you met Evangeline?"

Their gaze was more wary than curious.

"Hi, I'm Evangeline Canterbury. I believe you know my former stepmother, Zelda." I thrust my hand out. "It's great to meet you."

Mrs. Somerset visibly relaxed—so Bennett was right in wanting a known entity for a fake girlfriend. "Yes, of course," she said, shaking my hand. "Zelda never has enough good things to say about you. I'm delighted to meet you at last."

Mr. Somerset was less effusive but completely civil. "A pleasure."

Mrs. Somerset touched her son on his sleeve. "How's the fellowship, Bennett?"

"Inhumane, but I'm determined to persevere. How's work for you?"

"Good. Really good."

"I hear Custard is still alive. How is she?"

"Pretty well, actually. She had to find new places to nap once TVs became wall-mounted, but otherwise she hasn't changed much."

"Good to hear," said Bennett smoothly. "And please don't let us keep you. Enjoy the reception."

He tugged on my hand.

"It's really nice to meet you," I said brightly. "Have fun."

"Bye," said Mrs. Somerset, her gaze not leaving her son.

"Are the two of you going out?" asked Mr. Somerset, who hadn't said a word since our handshake.

Bennett looked at me.

I smiled at his parents. "We're playing it by ear."

"Just remember," said Bennett. "My biological clock is ticking, and I really need to settle down soon."

I laughed despite my nerves. We walked out of the hotel hand in hand.

I BROUGHT BENNETT TO A quiet café a few blocks away that served rib-sticking Russian fare. He sat down and dropped his forehead into his palm, his frustration palpable.

He had been so cool and unaffected in front of his parents—the contrast was stark. I'd known that this was important for him: He'd moved across the width of a continent to be in the same city as his parents. But now I understood in my gut just how much he wanted this.

How much he wanted to be home again.

"Thanks for not deserting me," he said after some time, two fingers pressed against the space between his brows.

I didn't need him to elaborate to know that he was thinking back on the exchange, trying to process the fact that his father didn't say a single word to him. Even when Mr. Somerset asked whether we were together, he'd been looking at me, and not his son.

I should probably comment on Mr. Somerset's aloofness. But I didn't know him; I only knew Bennett.

"You were too slick," I said. "There was no way for them to tell whether you still gave a shit about them. If I were the father you'd tried to bring down multiple times, I wouldn't have relaxed my guard."

He was silent.

"And don't forget, you've been in town for more than six months without making any attempts to contact them. As far as they know, you've written them off completely. I'd take it as an encouraging sign that they both came when they heard you were at the reception."

He nodded slowly.

I let him be, now that I'd said my piece. We both took out our phones. Multiple text messages were waiting for me, most of them from Zelda, whose concert had just ended.

People keep texting me about seeing you and Bennett together.

What's this saucy tango involving your date and Damaris Vandermeer?

Is it true? Did you run into Rowland and Frances Somerset?

I texted back.

You knew we were attending together.

Damaris and Bennett used to ballroom dance as partners. Revival performance tonight.

Yes, true. It was all very civil.

I didn't mention the part about Bennett and me accidentally making out before his parents. I figured they wouldn't either.

A new text came through from Zelda—*The boy can dance*—followed by a YouTube link. And when I clicked through, I saw the tango, captured by someone who kept whistling throughout the recording.

We put away our phones when the waiter came with our food.

"Did your mom text your sister, by any chance?" I asked.

"Good guess."

"Here's another good guess. Your sister texted you in return and you gave a completely noncommittal answer, along the lines of, 'Yep, saw them.'"

"Not as accurate. My sister was asking about *you*, so I waxed poetic about how good you are in bed."

I gave him a look.

"Fine," he said, smiling slightly. "How good you are out of bed."

I dug a spoon into my bowl of borscht. "Any plans for what to do next?"

"Somewhere in my head, I must have assumed that it would be like a movie: Put my parents and me in the same place at the same time, and magically all would be well. But we were all together just now and..." He exhaled. "And nothing has changed."

I sighed. "Welcome to Life Sucks 101, in which life doesn't work like movies."

Or Zelda would get well and never be afflicted again.

He cut into the blinis—buckwheat pancakes—he had ordered. Then his gaze turned to me. "My offer still stands, you know. If you say yes now, I'll date our agreement retroactively to the day after Christmas, so you get almost a month for free."

I stole a piece of blini from his plate. "Not that I don't think you're a generous man, but almost one-sixth of half a mil is a lot of generosity. What's the reason for the backdating?"

"My parents are going to the Amalfi Coast to mark their anniversary, which falls on the weekend after your symposium in Munich. If the dates don't conflict with anything else on your itinerary, will you come with me to Italy?"

This was why I hadn't wanted to agree to the wedding reception: It gave him another opening to reel me into his scheme. I stirred my soup. "Probably not. I have plans to explore the Bavarian countryside that weekend."

"I haven't gone down on you, have I?" he murmured. "Let it be said I'm willing to devote considerable hours to that particular pleasure."

I bit the inside of my cheek, trying not to betray how turned on I was. "If only your parents knew you were willing to prostitute yourself for them."

He snorted.

Neither of us said anything for a while. He steadily polished off his blinis. I finished my soup. The waiter came and replenished our tea.

When Bennett was done with his food, he wrapped his hands around a large tea mug and examined a picture on the wall, his profile to me. There was something to the set of his jaw, a resignation that was at once stoic and desolate.

He'd taken my silence as my final answer, a firm no.

I was not going to be mixed up in his schemes. I was not going to disrupt the quiet rhythm of my even-keeled life. I was not going to open myself up to false pleasures that came with an expiration date.

And yet…

Could I really abandon him? It was obvious that, left to his own devices, he would continue to play the part of the blithe, uncaring son. He knew this. That was why he had wanted my help in the first place.

Without a firm kick in the pants once in a while, he would flounder. His plans would go nowhere. And all the changes he'd made, uprooting his entire life, would be futile.

"I'll take that half mil for charity," I said before I could stop myself. "I'll come with you."

HE DIDN'T SAY ANYTHING, ONLY looked at me as if he couldn't quite believe what he'd heard.

Neither could I, exactly.

That silence lasted until we were in a cab, going uptown along Central Park West. We discussed logistics. On which day could I leave Munich? When was he setting out? And how long were we to remain in Italy?

Throughout it all, I was conscious of his gaze on me. His initial incredulity had worn off. Now his demeanor made me think of a mountain climber who had reached the Everest base camp, someone who knew that the easy part was over and the real trial was about to begin.

"I forgot to tell you," he said as we e-mailed each other our itineraries. "I'm paying a visit to Mrs. Asquith on the way back. Would you like to come with me?"

"I would. But I bought my tickets a long time ago, and my return flight doesn't pass through England."

"I can take care of that for you, if you want, along with your ticket from Munich to Naples."

"In that case, yes, thank you."

When the cab stopped before my house, he asked the driver to wait and walked me to the door. "I owe you, Professor."

"You're going to be out half a mil, at least. I'd say you don't owe me anything else."

"I did promise to go down on you, frequently and attentively."

Was it still January? Heat buffeted me from every direction. "That's not why I said yes, so there's no need."

In the coppery light from the street lamps, his gaze was steady, curious. "Then why did you say yes?"

Zelda and I used to build houses of cards together. A well-made house of cards actually stood pretty okay on its own. But because the construction material was so flimsy, and nothing held the structure together except prayer and careful placement, any kind of disturbance could bring it down—someone walking by too fast, a fridge door slamming shut, and once, a moving truck rumbling down the street.

Bennett's question was such a disturbance. Faced with its friendly directness, the lies that I'd told myself in the Russian café came crumbling down. I had not agreed to help him out of altruism. Or sympathy. Or even greed.

It had been fear, pure and simple.

He was consumed by his quest. If I turned him down, he would find someone else. Tonight, perhaps. Tomorrow at the latest. Maybe Damaris would get the call, maybe someone more restrained in her public demeanor. But no matter who, in two weeks' time, when he arrived in Italy, he would have a woman on his arm.

And the thought suffocated me. I would rather face far worse heartache later on than go home tonight with this huge weight on my chest, unable to breathe for the foreseeable future.

It was, without a question, the stupidest decision I'd made in a long,

long time.

"Because I finally remembered that a million has six zeroes to it."

His gaze remained unwavering. "You deal some dope bullshit, Professor. I admire that."

"A perk of being a materials scientist: My bullshit is well made on the molecular level."

He laughed softly. Then he leaned in and kissed me, a kiss of only our lips, gentle, unhurried, yet unbearably sexy.

Swoony.

He pulled away, looked at me another moment, and tucked a strand of my hair behind my ear. "Thank you," he murmured. "It's going to be one hell of an adventure."

I WOULDN'T GO SO FAR as to speculate that Zelda had been listening at the keyhole, but she did pop out of the living room with tremendous alacrity as I walked in. "How was your evening, darling? Tell me everything!"

I omitted any and all mentions of kisses, but otherwise gave a truthful enough account, up until our departure from the wedding reception.

"So it happened. They finally ran into one another. Yes, my brilliant scheme worked."

"*Your* brilliant scheme?"

"Why do you think I've been encouraging you to take the Somerset boy to the reception?"

I felt like an idiot for not realizing this sooner: Zelda knew Bennett's parents would be there. "And here I thought you just wanted me to date him."

"That I can only want. *This* I can do something about. Now, tell me what happened afterward. Did the boy say anything?"

"He was quiet for a long time. I mean, the encounter was really unexpected—we were already leaving."

That was a truthful enough answer.

"And then?"

Now the lying began. "And then he was mainly trying to convince me to let him join me in Munich."

"Really?" Zelda blinked. "For the whole conference?"

"No, the conference ends on Thursday. He wants to come sightseeing with me that weekend."

"And you said no?"

I grimaced, a genuine expression. "I should have but I didn't. It's not easy to keep saying no to the Somerset boy."

Zelda took a moment to digest this. "This calls for a pot of tea. Chamomile?"

"You go ahead," I told her. "I had enough tea tonight."

Zelda disappeared into the kitchen. I was almost one hundred percent sure that she'd gone to check her calendar. Sure enough, when she returned, she said, "Not that I don't love Bavaria, darling—beautiful place, had one of the best hikes of my life there—but the beginning of February is the wrong time of the year for Germany. Why don't you go to Italy instead? The Amalfi Coast isn't so crowded right now, and it's ever so lovely."

"Amalfi Coast?" I said the name doubtfully, as if I'd never heard of it.

"Yes. Hold on just a second." She reached for her iPad. "Here it is, La Figlia del Mare in Positano. It's a fantastic hotel in one of the most picturesque *comunes* on the Amalfi Coast."

"Have you been there?"

"No, but I have friends who rave about it."

And would one of those friends be Frances Somerset, who will be there shortly, and whose anniversary date you probably checked now to make sure that it fell on the same weekend?

Zelda moved closer to me and played the slide show from the hotel's website. "Isn't it gorgeous? Used to be a small private palazzo before it was turned into a boutique establishment. And you can get a pretty decent rate this time of year. They aren't officially open—February is when they train their staff for the season."

"You know a lot about a hotel you've never stayed at."

I'd met hotel aficionados who traveled with the express purpose of experiencing the best in hospitality, but Zelda had never been one of those: She was fine as long as a place was clean and convenient.

"Well, you hear things," Zelda answered rather vaguely. "Anyway, I've sent you the link. Think about it."

The kettle sang. Zelda set aside the iPad and went back to the kitchen. She returned a few minutes later with a teapot and a plate of dried apple rings. "You know, it's a bit ironic how things have turned out."

"You mean that the Somerset boy and I should have met after all."

"And that he should be completely smitten with you." Zelda sat down and poured. "I never told you this, but I suspected for years that the Somersets had something to do with your invitation to the Bal des Debutantes."

I reached for my cup, forgetting that I'd already had plenty of hot liquids for the evening. "Why?"

"You know your father wanted it desperately for you—well, for the prestige of the Canterburys, if we're being completely honest with ourselves. And I really wanted it for him, as a parting gift if nothing else. But it was always a long shot—the Canterburys aren't what they were, and I'm just a lot of people's third cousin.

"I remember telling all this to Frances—we were getting to know each other then. We talked about you and she came away impressed. Said she'd love for her son to meet you, except that he was all the way in England.

"No one knew anything then about the older woman—we thought he was at Eton because he wanted to be. So I told her that if you were selected for the Bal des Debutantes, he could hop over for a weekend and serve as your escort, and wouldn't that be a fun way for the two of you to meet.

"Frances agreed with me. The moment I told her of your selection, she asked if she could still volunteer her son as your escort. I said yes, absolutely. Of course, he didn't come, but it was only after a while that I put two and two together.

"Imagine that you are Frances and Rowland Somerset and you really, really want to remove your son from that awful older woman. But you know what young men in love are like—the more you bad-mouth their beloved, the more they dig in their heels. A much better fix would be to introduce him to someone else, someone who is essentially perfect—not to mention his own age—and hope that he'll come to see what he's been missing."

Zelda had an exaggerated concept of my perfection, and I'd long ago given up trying to correct her. "So the Somersets wanted to dangle me as a lure?"

"That's my theory, at least. It was too bad his eighteenth birthday fell on the day of the rehearsal and he bailed—could have saved himself and everybody else a lot of trouble."

"You think he'd have taken one look at me and dropped all his plans for California?"

"I thought it was—what do Americans call it?—a Hail Mary pass. But now I'm not sure everything wouldn't have worked exactly as they'd hoped. The boy is clearly wild about you."

I shrugged—and wished I didn't know better. It would have been a compelling narrative: the near miss, the long years apart, the accidental meeting, the fierce, instant attraction—the wedding announcement in the *Sunday Times* supplement all but wrote itself.

"By the way, he has plans to visit Mrs. Asquith on the way back, and he asked me to join him."

"That's wonderful," Zelda said immediately. "I'll ring her to let her know you're coming. She's been curious about you for ages."

We talked some more about Mrs. Asquith before we said good night to each other.

As I brushed my teeth, I picked apart Zelda's reaction. She was happy that I'd meet Mrs. Asquith at last. Mixed in, though, was a certain strain: Was she anxious that I'd learn too much of her past from her godmother?

But as I settled into bed, my mind drifted to Zelda's revelation about the Somersets and their possible string-pulling to get me to the ball. I couldn't narrow it down to anything specific she'd said; nor could I put a name to exactly what I was feeling.

I only knew that as I lay on my bed, staring at the ceiling, something chafed in my heart—and chafed badly.

Chapter 7

MUNICH, OTHER THAN THE ABSENCE of Bennett, went off almost exactly as I'd imagined. The paper I presented was well received. After a celebratory lunch with my collaborators that lasted three hours and left me a bit tipsy on Bavaria's famous beers, I went for a walk in the Englischer Garten—in the snow.

In fact, it snowed the entire time I was in Munich. By contrast, Naples, where I landed Friday afternoon, enjoyed a clear blue sky and bright, lovely sunshine.

My fake boyfriend waited for me at the luggage claim, in a gorgeously cut black trench coat worn open over a black suit that probably had Tom Ford's name on it. He was leaning against a row of seats, his eyes on his phone, and something about his posture was extraordinarily sexy—the relaxed shoulders, the slight slouch, the perfectly angled lines of his legs. I'd seen professional models on thirty-foot-high billboards who couldn't project half this much easy confidence.

Aspirational beauty, I suddenly thought. What he presented to the world was exactly the kind of magnetic stylishness luxury brands tried to associate with their products, the kind that made people anxious to wear the same clothes and sport the same watch, because they couldn't help wanting to emulate that powerful allure.

Because the assumption was that such a powerful allure could represent only the epitome of success and happiness.

Except he was a man who couldn't go home. Who couldn't even tell anyone, other than his fake girlfriend, that he wanted to go home.

After our first meeting, I'd been convinced he was made of rainbow and moon dust. At the end of our second meeting I'd come away feeling upended—he had been scheming, relentless, and possibly even unscrupulous in getting what he wanted from me.

But as he looked up and smiled, my heart quivered with a strange affinity: I understood what it was like to present an image to the world—and to be so good at it that no one ever questioned that image.

He came forward, took my carry-on bag, and kissed me on the lips. "I've missed you."

The desire that coursed through me was painful in its intensity. I dug through my tote for a pair of sunglasses, pretending to be unaffected. "Very convincing. Did you take acting lessons while you were out in California?"

"Sweetheart, I had a SAG card at one point."

I looked at him. "Seriously?"

The Screen Actors Guild did not give out those cards willy-nilly.

"My ex made films."

"What kind of films?"

He grinned. "You look suspicious, Professor. Are you worried I might have porn on my résumé?"

I pitched a brow. "Doesn't everybody in California have porn on their résumés?"

"In SoCal, maybe. But one of my ex's short films was nominated for an Oscar—so at least you know not everything she made was porn."

I was astonished. For a filmmaker to receive such a nod was a huge accomplishment, even if it wasn't for a feature film.

"Were you in that film?" If he was, then I'd easily find out her identity.

"That was after we split."

Still, I had to restrain my urge to start Googling right away.

Outside the airport, the temperature was a good bit cooler than the brilliant sunshine would have suggested. Bennett turned up the collar of his coat. Even though I understood now that his appearance was part of a facade, I still sucked in a breath—there was something innately stylish about my boyfriend.

It took me a moment to realize I'd forgotten to think of him as my *fake* boyfriend.

He told me he'd flown in the previous day and spent the night in

Naples. He'd also borrowed a car from a friend, which happened to be an adorkable little silver BMW i3.

"You do enjoy an electric vehicle," I said as he opened the door for me.

"I'm very fond of them, but I like my bicycles even more."

"I expected as much from a West Coast hippie."

He laughed. "It really is great to see you, Evangeline."

And just like that, more butterflies in my stomach than at a botanical garden in spring. I switched the topic to his work, and he in turn asked about the Munich conference.

The landscape was dominated by the great green cone of Mount Vesuvius. And just when I thought we had driven past it, the road turned west along the coast of the Sorrentine Peninsula, and the massive volcano came back into view again across the blue waters of the Gulf of Naples.

The foothills of Monti Lattari rose sharply to our south. The road was etched where the mountain met the sea, a narrow two-lane highway that drivers mistook for a stretch of the Formula One race. Then the hills dropped away briefly. The road turned south and cut across the peninsula toward the Amalfi Coast.

"Have you been here before?" I asked Bennett, as he seemed to take Italian roads—and drivers—completely in stride.

"Long ago. Somebody in the extended family has a house on Lake Como. We used to spend summers there—and come south once in a while for sightseeing."

"Were those summers idyllic or idyllically awful?"

"Lake Como is unbelievably gorgeous and I used to be unbelievably bored. I was sulky and ungrateful and in general drove my dad crazy."

He took the car up a steep incline, driving with a quiet competence that made me want to have his hands on me, touching me everywhere. I bit the inside of my cheek and looked out the window.

We'd gained elevation. The road clung to the side of hills, twisting and winding like lines on a topographic map. Vapors billowed across small valleys—the weather had turned foggy. Ocher roofs peeked out occasionally, and here and there the ruins of an ancient fortification high up the slopes.

"Speaking of driving my dad crazy," Bennett said after the i3 took its first hairpin turn, "I should let you know I'm expecting trouble on that front."

His tone, more than his words, made me glance at him. "What kind of trouble?"

"My ex passed away last October. There's going to be an exhibit of her work fairly soon, and chances are it'll include pictures she took of me—naked pictures."

I should have been more concerned by the probability of naked pictures of him coming to light, but it was the ex's death that caught my attention—October was so recent. "Did you attend her funeral?"

"I was on the West Coast for a few days."

I couldn't detect any particular inflection to his voice. All the same, my stomach dropped. Did he still love her? "You gave her eulogy?"

"No, I didn't have any special role. Her brother gave one eulogy, her longtime camerawoman the other."

"She never married?"

"She did at one point, after we broke up. But it lasted only a couple of years."

Which was too bad—a husband acting as the executor of her estate might be more reluctant to exhibit naked pictures she'd taken of another man.

The road veered around the edge of a hill and dropped down—we had crossed the peninsula and were now on the Amalfi Coast. The descent twisted and pivoted; a thick fog nuzzled the sheer cliffs.

"So when do you expect the other shoe to drop?" I asked.

"Weekend after next."

"What? Is there a nudity clause in our contract that says I can back out if and when naked pictures of you surface?"

He snorted. "Sorry, sweetheart. You're mine for the next four and a half months."

I swallowed—I'd rarely heard scarier words. But was I afraid those four and a half months would be too long—or too short?

"You know a lot about me," he said. "Is there anything I need to know about you, so I don't sound ignorant in front of my parents? Any significant past relationships?"

"No." And I didn't know a lot about him. Not enough, in any case.

"A straight-up no?"

I shrugged. "I've never dated anyone for longer than three months."

"Why not?"

I exhaled. One would think my allergy to anyone really getting to know me would be the reason that I couldn't stay in a relationship, but actually it had been mostly preempted by another, equally significant cause.

The Vermont farmer.

My parents divorced when I was two. My mother died seven years later. Her funeral marked the only time I ever remembered seeing her in person, a beautiful woman with too much makeup on her face, her hand literally ice-cold.

From what I could piece together, Mother and her second husband, whom she married the day after her divorce became final, had begun their relationship while she was still married to Pater. The affair was documented by private detectives Pater had hired, and because of that, he was able to get the judge to grant him sole custody of me.

That, however, didn't explain why she chose not to exercise her visitation rights. She sent letters and presents, but never herself. To make sense of things, I invented a fairy tale for her—and for me—as I pored over pictures of her with her husband, a Vermont farmer with a face as brown and craggy as a Sherpa's.

I imagined that this beautiful new marriage of hers so angered Pater that he exiled her forever from my life—and I accepted her banishment in the cause of true love. Her rugged, hirsute husband came to stand for all that was wildly manly and romantic in the world, the guarantor of happiness, the knight on a shining John Deere tractor.

Eventually I learned that when she'd died unexpectedly from bacterial meningitis, she had already separated from the Vermont farmer. But the damage was done. When I was sixteen I fell desperately in love with a boy named Jonathan—who had very little going for him except that at eighteen he'd managed to grow a full, luxuriant beard like the one my mother's husband had sported.

Every man I'd dated since had some trait that could be linked back to this fairy-tale man I'd never met. There was David in college, who fascinated me because he was an actual Vermont farm boy. There was Nick, also in college, whose collection of plaid shirts rivaled Mother's husband's. And there was Alex, who gave me palpitations because he knew carpentry—Mother had sent many photographs of rocking chairs, bookshelves, and once even a loom that her husband had made for her with his own hands.

But the Vermont-farmer fixation also had a flip side: Once I understood that my attraction to these men was but my psyche still acting up from the misplaced yearnings of my childhood, my crushes would peter out as quickly as they'd come to be, before a man had time to figure out I never told him anything about myself.

The older I got, the easier it became for me to see the Vermont-farmer connection. Sometimes I could spot it within a few minutes of that first stirring of interest. As a result, that interest would quietly die down, with a sigh and a shrug from me.

Bennett was a complete outlier: I kept dissecting his appearance and lifestyle, and there was *nothing* of the Vermont farmer to him. He might, in fact, be the anti-Vermont farmer.

And it scared me that I had no idea how to get over him.

"I like being single," I said.

"I know people who genuinely enjoy being unattached. They are not the ones who get melancholy at weddings."

My gut tightened. I wasn't used to anyone seeing me in my less guarded moments. "I wasn't melancholy, just contemplative."

The car rounded another sharp curve. "You, Professor, lie like a rug."

I could only be thankful that our road, hemmed in by cliffs on one side and overhanging a deep plunge into the fog-shrouded sea on the other, required all Bennett's attention. Or he might have seen me flinch.

I also wasn't used to being called out on my lies.

But I did have a few tactics for moving away from subjects that I didn't want to discuss. "My romantic history doesn't matter. What I want to know is why, with the threat of naked pictures hanging over your head, you took so long to get things moving? I mean, you were going out with Damaris Vandermeer's friend back in summer—that's a crowd of women who would have been perfect for your purpose. If one didn't work out, why didn't you try another?"

"First, there was no threat of naked pictures last summer. Even after my ex passed away, in the beginning it seemed like it'd take a while for the retrospective to get off the ground. It was only after the New Year that I heard differently.

"Second, I didn't go *out* with Damaris Vandermeer's friend. We met a few times for coffee. And I did check out the other women in that circle. But like I told you, they wouldn't have worked."

I studied him. His profile was as dramatic and chiseled as the cliffs to which the road clung—and about as revealing. "Am I really your only score since you moved to the East Coast?"

I couldn't have asked such a question back in December. But that was before he shoved a shit-ton of money my way.

The corners of his lips curved. "Are you feeling sorry for me? Please say you are."

My heart skipped a beat. "No, I only ever feel sorry for the masturbation couch. It probably had greater ambitions in life. I'll bet it gives you the side-eye every time you sit down, thinking, 'Motherfucker, how hard can it be to get laid these days?'"

He laughed. "True, not very. But I don't want my parents to get the idea that I'm a slut. They should believe that when I'm not saving lives, I'm making out with you in elevators."

I bit a corner of my lower lip, wishing I didn't react with such longing to what he described. "So…are you ready to run into your parents again?"

A beat passed before he answered. "I don't have to be ready when something is this important. I just have to be there."

Oddly enough, I was reminded of the first time Zelda suffered an episode after she came to Manhattan. I'd been five, too confused—and scared—to cry. So instead I held on to the guardsman teddy bear she'd given me and trailed Pater around the house.

Is she going to be okay? I'd asked, when I could bear the silence no longer.

Pater drained the Armagnac in his glass. *I don't know.*

So what do we do?

We don't have to do anything, he'd answered. *We just have to be here.*

"And hope for the best?" I murmured.

"And work for the best," answered Bennett.

THE EXTERIOR OF LA FIGLIA del Mare was a pure, deep vermilion, a color that seemed better suited to Versailles' drawing rooms, rather than the coast of the Mediterranean. Amid a cliff's worth of pastel houses, it could have stood out like a sore thumb. But instead it exuded a whimsical, old-world charm.

Bennett had booked a two-bedroom suite on the highest level of the hotel, with whitewashed walls, rustic furniture, and a large, private balcony overlooking the Bay of Positano. The setting sun was a distant glimmer of reddish-gold, barely visible through the fog. The steel-grey sea, two hundred feet below, felt less like the waters of the Mediterranean and more like those of the Atlantic.

All the same, it was beautiful.

And chilly.

Bennett draped his trench coat about my shoulders. "I love an opportunity to be gallant."

"You weren't wearing it."

He had taken off the trench coat to drive. Coming out of the car he had carried it over his arm.

"Even better. I love an opportunity to be gallant for which I don't have to suffer."

I smiled. He adjusted the collar of the trench coat, his fingertips brushing against the underside of my jaw. I had trouble sustaining my smile. Perhaps I also had trouble drawing in my next breath.

"Imagine people on the lower terraces looking up," he said softly.

"Are you an exhibitionist?" I tried to sound severe. "That's not part of our bargain."

His eyes were on my lips, gazing at me the way Caesar must have once gazed at Gaul—as something to be conquered and made his own. "Of course not. You want closed doors. All the closed doors in the world—and maybe some high walls too, just in case."

I swallowed. Was it a coincidence that his words were also an accurate description of my psyche? "Then why are you asking me to imagine people looking at us?"

"We should practice for when my parents might be among them." He drew me toward him by the lapels of the coat and kissed me below my ear, the graze of his stubble a hot singe I felt all the way to the soles of my feet. "I want them to think I have nothing on my mind except being inside you all night long."

There was no reason for me to feel jittery—I always understood that by becoming his fake girlfriend, I'd also said yes to more sex, possibly a lot of it. Yet my heart was slamming into my rib cage, and not only with arousal.

With every encounter I became less and less sure what he wanted from me. Not just sex, that much I knew. And I was under no delusion that he found me a fascinating puzzle. No, it was something else entirely.

Sometimes it seemed as if he already knew what I was hiding behind high walls and all the closed doors in the world. A few of his questions, in retrospect, felt like experiments—not looking for answers, but gauging how much and how instinctively I lied.

"You can't stay all night," I said. "I'm not a twenty-four-hour diner."

He smiled slightly. "But you are open dinner hours, at least? Six to nine?"

He smelled of fine wool and Provençal soap. Part of me wanted to bury my nose in his skin; the other part wanted to run far, far away. "That's still a long time."

"Not for what I have in mind." He guided me back into the sitting room, shutting the balcony door as he did so. "It's barely enough time to do you justice."

Inside it was quite warm. Or was it me, burning up at his words? He took the trench coat and tossed it onto the back of a chair. My leather jacket he unzipped and peeled off. Underneath I wore a form-hugging sweater—in a green that was an almost exact match for the color of his eyes.

Was that why it had caught my attention?

He pulled the sweater over my head and did the same for the camisole I wore underneath, exposing my bra. And then he pushed down my skirt and tights to reveal a pair of matching underpants. They were both basic black—I hadn't wanted to look as if I'd planned to be disrobed.

"Praise the Lord," he murmured, slipping off my undies, "for a woman who can bring me to my knees."

My heart thumped. "What use do I have for a man on his knees?"

He eased me down on a long sofa. "Begging for a demonstration, aren't you? Open your legs for me."

My hand gripped the back of the sofa. I might have trembled slightly. "What if I don't?"

He already destabilized me so; I was afraid to grant him any more access.

He traced a hand up my tightly clamped thighs. "Do you know you have the perfect face for a nun—as if you have only prayers on your mind? And then there are those times when it all changes, and you look pornographically turned on."

He pried open my legs and caressed the places I'd tried to conceal from him. Pleasure flooded me.

"Do I look like that now?" I heard myself ask, my voice raspy.

It was his turn to sound unsteady. "Yes."

He went down on me. And it felt so good, I had to bite down on my lower lip to not sound as aroused as I felt. But by the time he brought me to my third orgasm, I had given up any and all attempt to be quiet and contained.

Then he was inside me, huge and hard. And just like that, I was again pornographically turned on.

He watched me, his eyes a dark, dark green. I couldn't meet his gaze, so I wrapped my arms about him and buried my face in the crook of his shoulder, wanting only enough sensations to drown out any insidious feelings of need.

I was already high enough on the plateau that it wouldn't take much for me to tighten again, climbing toward the next tipping point. But just as I neared that point of no return, he slowed.

I moaned in protest.

"You want to come?" he murmured.

"Of course I want to come."

"Then tell me what you masturbate to—I've told you all about me."

How could I? Ever since last summer, every time I'd touched myself it had been to memories and fantasies of him. "Just fuck me. I don't want to talk."

He licked my nipple. "Answer or you won't get any more."

I was desperate to resume that upward spiral toward my next orgasm, desperate for one more pure, thoughtless release, a minute of blankness when I was wrapped warmly in his embrace and didn't have to remember why.

I squeezed my eyes shut, as if by doing so I would be speaking into a vacuum. "You. I masturbate to you."

At this he resumed that wonderful cadence that gave me so much pleasure. "Keep talking."

"I imagine..." I panted. "I imagine running into you unexpectedly, somewhere out of town."

"Somewhere like Munich?"

I quaked inside. "Maybe."

"And then?"

"And then you pull me into your hotel room, lock the door, and fuck me."

I was almost mindless from pleasure, but still I couldn't bring myself to admit the rest of it—the two of us lingering over dinner, then over drinks until we were the last ones left in the hotel's lounge, and then standing on the observation deck together, watching snowflakes big as feathers drift down from the dark sky above.

"Do I fuck you all night?" His voice was rough, demanding.

I closed my eyes even tighter. "Yes."

He rammed into me. "But you never called. And you never texted."

And I came like an asteroid striking ground.

THE WONDERFUL THING ABOUT HUGE, terrifyingly powerful orgasms was that one could pretend that they were memory bombs, wiping out everything leading up to them. I certainly did, floating in an erotic fog afterward. We lay intertwined on the couch, almost asleep but not quite.

Eventually he got up and draped his coat over me. There came the sound of water running. I was just about to make myself move when he came back, clad in one of the hotel's bathrobes, scooped me up in his arms, and carried me to the tub in my bathroom, which was already covered in a thick, inviting foam.

"Do you mind if I dump you here?" he asked playfully.

"Dump away." I loved baths, but rarely made time for them.

The water, when he lowered me inside, was the perfect temperature. But he didn't join me. "Dinner's in an hour."

The steam from the bath carried faint notes of basil and mountain thyme—the Mediterranean of late summer. Had we made the trip six months later, I would be sitting in this tub with my window open, breathing in the scent of orange trees. But now the window was closed, the fog wafting visibly outside.

My heart too felt…overcast. Bennett was certain to be attentive this evening, as we played the pair of lovers completely absorbed in each other. And the thought of it was oppressive. Painful.

When I came out of my room, in a long-sleeved, season-appropriate version of the little black dress, he was waiting for me. He had changed into a three-piece suit in grey with subtle windowpane patterns, the jacket slung over the back of the sofa.

He put away his phone and smiled at me. "I love punctuality in a woman."

No, not a trace of the Vermont farmer.

"I'm on the clock. Of course I'll be punctual." I needed to remind myself—and him—that I was here because we had a business agreement.

He tilted his head. "I didn't tell you that my parents don't arrive until tomorrow?"

"What? Are you sure?"

"They're still in Tuscany, spending time with friends. Tomorrow they fly into Naples."

I thought back to our exchanges regarding our trip and had to admit that at no point had he ever said that Friday was when his parents would check into the hotel. I'd simply assumed that to be the case.

A minute ago I'd dreaded the prospect of playing the smitten girlfriend in front of his parents; but now that I didn't have to do it, a different kind of anxiety stomped in.

The anxiety of not having a ready role for the evening.

"So…we'll just eat?"

He opened the door for me, his hand at the small of my back. "And relax, of course."

VINES OF BOUGAINVILLEA CLIMBED THE pillars and the vaulted ceiling of the hotel's restaurant. Potted lemon trees lurked in nooks and corners. Hundreds of votive candles flickered in chandeliers and tall, branched candelabras, the glow of firelight warm and golden.

The atmosphere was romance with a capital R—and all wrong for me. If I'd known ahead of time that Bennett's parents weren't here yet, I'd have asked for a sandwich in my room. And I'd have stayed there the rest of the evening with my door closed.

As if that could unspeak the words he had extracted from me under duress.

We were shown to a table near the arched windows. Almost immediately plates of *amuse-bouche* appeared on the table, along with glasses of mineral water. I accepted a menu with gratitude—reading it was a great excuse for not interacting with the person across the table from me.

"Bennett? Hi, Bennett!"

Did I sense a jolt of shock going through Bennett? But he smiled hugely as he rose to greet the two men in their late forties who had stopped by our table. "Hey, Rob. Hey, Darren."

They exchanged affectionate hugs. He then turned to me. "Evangeline, Rob and Darren, two of Berkeley's finest. We've known one another almost fifteen years. Gentlemen, this is Professor Canterbury, who is much too good for me but doesn't know it yet."

"Oh, I know it all right," I said as I shook hands with Rob and Darren, who laughed heartily. "It's great to meet you both. What brought you to Italy?"

"Rob and I have been talking about getting married for a while," said Darren. He had light brown skin and a hint of the Caribbean to his accent. "And we always thought that we'd have a huge ceremony and invite everyone we know."

"But when we started planning," said Rob, stroking the ginger beard on his face, "we realized that actually all we wanted was that piece of paper. So we went down to city hall with Darren's mom and my brother, and here we are on our honeymoon."

We congratulated the newlyweds. I lost no time in inviting them to sit down with us—to serve as the buffer between Bennett and me. Darren hesitated, but Rob accepted for both of them. Bennett asked for a bottle of champagne and we drank a toast to the bridegrooms' future happiness.

"Let me see," said Rob. "We saw you back in November, didn't we, Bennett?"

"October," Darren corrected him. "At Moira's funeral."

A woman's funeral in October, on the West Coast—could it be? And was that why Bennett had reacted as he had when he saw Rob and Darren? Because he knew her name was about to come up?

"Yeah, that's right. At that time we had a summer wedding in mind, but no concrete plans. And then a week ago we were just like, 'Screw it, we're making it legal right now.'" Rob turned to me. "Did you know Bennett was Moira McAllister's tenant for the longest time? We always joked that he was Moira's boy toy."

Moira McAllister? Moira McAllister the famous photographer? "Oh, wow," I heard myself say. "My college roommate had a poster of one of her pictures."

And unless I was very much mistaken, Zelda had a coffee-table book of Moira McAllister's work somewhere on the shelves at home.

"I'm always trying to convince people that I *was* her boy toy, but nobody would believe me," said Bennett, watching me.

Rob and Darren chortled. I managed to smile. Our waiter appeared to take our orders, and I used the reprieve to collect myself. Bennett had been *Moira McAllister*'s boy toy—I didn't know whether I was impressed or even more horrified.

"So." Rob turned to me once the waiter was gone. "Bennett left Berkeley all of a sudden last year. Was it for you?"

"I'm going to say it was, even though we didn't meet until several months after he moved to New York."

"But we could have met years ago if I hadn't gone out to the West Coast," said Bennett.

"So you're making up for lost time?" asked Rob, who was clearly the more talkative in the marriage.

Bennett glanced at me. "Absolutely."

I shook my head. "He's with me only for my patents. Look at him: The man was born for gold-digging."

After the laughter, Darren inquired into those patents. The conversation was briefly about my work before I asked them to tell me more about themselves. Rob was an architect and Darren an accountant—Moira McAllister's accountant, no less.

"And that's how we met Bennett," explained Rob. "One day she had a potluck party. We showed up, and there was Bennett—he'd just moved into her garage apartment. Where did you guys meet, in Spain?"

Bennett nodded. "Yeah, Spain. I was a high school exchange student and Moira knew my host parents. I looked her up when I got to Berkeley."

Talk about lying by omission.

He was watching me again. I forced myself to not fiddle with my champagne glass. "So what was it like, living with a famous artist?"

"Well, her house was old and stuff was constantly breaking, so I was usually fixing something or other."

"And he built her editing room, too," Rob told me with avuncular pride. "Darren and I were so impressed we had him come and build a deck for us."

I glanced at Bennett. "Are we talking about Mr. Fashionista here?"

"I worked construction for a couple of years to save money for college," said my fake boyfriend.

"I thought you worked as a stripper to put yourself through college. I thought you were a real American success story. You know, Magic Bennett."

Rob hooted. One corner of Bennett's lips quirked, his eyes full of a glossy mischief, all sex and glamour.

I poured the rest of the champagne in my glass down my throat, as if that could quench the unrest inside. Fortunately our appetizers arrived.

After we dug in, the conversation turned to other topics—old friends in California, Bennett's new life in the Big Apple, Rob and Darren's plan to bike the coastline from San Diego to Portland.

I was every bit the arch but secretly doting girlfriend. Rob and Darren were clearly pleased for Bennett. And from time to time Bennett looked at me with something akin to wonder, as if he couldn't quite believe how well he'd chosen.

Moira's name came up only one more time, when Darren mentioned that the Museum of Modern Art would be unveiling a retrospective of her body of work very soon.

Holy shit, Bennett's naked pictures were going to be in MoMA?

"You plan to go see it?" Rob asked Bennett.

"At some point," said Bennett. "Want to come with, Professor?"

I shot him a look. "I wouldn't miss it."

At the end of the evening we said our good nights with many hugs and smiles. But my smile dissipated the moment Bennett and I went our own way, the implications of everything I'd learned at dinner whirling about in my head like a storm of crows.

My silence failed to register on me until we were in the suite—I'd been standing before the mantel, turning a small box of complimentary chocolate around and around. And I couldn't be sure how long I'd been at it.

"Nobody knew even after you came of age?" I hoped my tone conveyed curiosity and not…anything else.

"My dad threatened a scandal that would end Moira's career if our relationship ever became public."

I fiddled with the lid of the chocolate box. "Could he have done that?"

Bennett braced a hand on the far end of the mantel. "Destroy her career? I'm not sure. Make things extremely unpleasant for her? Absolutely. And she was at a fragile point. The photographs that had made her name had been taken decades earlier. Her new works weren't resonating as well—or bringing in as much income. She was about to turn her hand to filmmaking, a much more expensive medium—and a scandal was the last thing she needed."

"Let me guess: This became a bone of contention between you two.

You wanted to shout your love from the rooftops, but she was afraid of the repercussions."

He looked up at the canvas above the mantel, a nostalgic photograph of the Amalfi Coast in the sixties. "It was the other way around: She didn't want to keep things quiet anymore, and I was hesitant to test my dad."

"This wasn't *the* reason you guys broke up, was it?" I thought of his multiple attempts to take over the family firm. Now his actions made more sense—he was angry at the restriction the old man had put on how he could live his life.

He shook his head. "That particular disagreement was at most the creaky stairs in a house slowly sliding off its foundation. But it got more notice because it was right underfoot."

I took a deep breath. "If you don't mind my asking, what *was* the reason the house was sliding off its foundation?"

He studied the couple in the image above us, standing on a balcony of the hotel, the man in a suit that wouldn't have looked out of place on a Beatle, the woman sleek and mod in her miniskirt. "Moira was a true rebel, but I was just a punk. And once I got the teenage rebellion out of my system, it turned out that I had a lot more in common with my parents than I could have guessed."

"Your parents are responsible, productive members of society. Hardly a demerit to be like them."

He shrugged. "Moira felt differently. And feelings are what they are."

I blinked. "Do you mean to tell me that *she* dumped *you*?"

"It was a mutual parting, but more mutual on her part than on mine."

I needed a moment to understand what he was saying. "You would have stayed and worked on the relationship?"

He was still looking up at the young couple from half a century ago. Was he remembering the heyday of his own romance? Was he seeing it through lenses tinted with just as much nostalgia? "Yes, I would."

The magnetic closure on the chocolate box snapped to with a click that reverberated in the stillness of the room. "And not just to prove your parents wrong?"

He looked at me, his gaze unwavering. "No."

Each sentence he spoke about Moira emerged as a straightforward, unequivocal declarative. Every word he had ever said about us, on the other hand, was like the fog that still lingered thickly outside: something that couldn't be pinned down.

Something without substance.

I opened the chocolate box again and took out a piece. "Okay, good night."

As I passed him, he caught my wrist. My heartbeat accelerated at once. But he only said, "Are you all right?"

I put on my most guileless expression. "Of course. Why shouldn't I be?"

His thumb slid down, drawing a line of warmth into the center of my palm. Then he let go of me. "Good night, then. And sweet dreams."

AS SOON AS I WAS alone in my room I Googled Moira McAllister, starting with her pages on IMDB and Wikipedia, then clicking through to the reference articles one by one. Some of the articles were from the archives of major outlets like the *New York Times*, *Vanity Fair*, and *Vogue*, others scans from magazines that had folded decades ago.

One thing was clear: Moira McAllister had indeed been hot. Not a classic beauty, but an unforgettable one, reminiscent of a young Anjelica Huston, all dark, brooding eyes and granitelike cheekbones.

And despite a sometimes uneven career, she had been an enormously accomplished woman, winning awards for her photography since she was a teenager, and racking up accolades for her short films even after her death.

Bennett's cradle-robbing ex had been a bit of a caricature in my mind, but now she was all too real, a woman who had lived and died, who had laughed in front of the camera and commanded a crew behind.

A woman who was in every way my antithesis. I had but to sit down at a table with his parents for them to understand that he had brought the un-Moira: No need to worry about Bohemian passions that flouted conventions, no worldview dramatically different from their own. I was safe and familiar; I was Bennett saying, without ever having to use those words, that he was ready to return to the fold.

I was, in fact, the very girl they had chosen for him almost a decade and a half ago, when they still hoped he wouldn't desert the fold in the first place.

All this I'd known the moment Zelda first told me about the Somersets' role in securing my invitation to the Bal des Debutantes. But now I understood in my marrow that I wasn't merely a facilitator in Bennett's quest; I was the very symbol of it.

I wished he were using me for my body instead. At least lust was visceral and sometimes specific. This, the reduction of all that I was into a quick shorthand for conventional respectability, lay upon me, a welt across my heart.

Chapter 8

I WOKE UP WHEN IT was still dark outside. As soon as I'd texted Zelda—she'd see my hello when she woke up—I Googled Moira McAllister again, this time searching for anything that included both her and Bennett. Google didn't autocomplete my search, but it did unearth an image of an outdoor meal on a picnic table, some dozen or so people on two benches, with Moira near one end of the table, Rob and Darren at the other end, Bennett standing next to them, everyone smiling at the camera.

It could have been the potluck get-together at which Rob and Darren first met Bennett—or it might have been a different party. But Bennett was young, eighteen or nineteen, a gorgeous, gorgeous boy in a white T-shirt, ripped jeans, and a pair of Vans.

I stared at him for a long time before I realized this must be around the time we almost met—if he had bothered to come to the Bal des Debutantes. Not that he'd have found anything in me to hold his attention then—he was clearly drawn to the sex and drama of a woman who had experienced the full spectrum of life, and I was but a young girl completely wrapped up in the state of her stepmother's mental health.

I hadn't changed much in the years since. I used to go to school and come back home right away. Now I went to work and came back home right away.

And my life had all the sex and drama of a filing session at a county registrar's office.

A WINTER STORM SHOULD SWEEP across the Amalfi Coast. Instead the sun rose in a bright, clear sky, and Bennett somehow managed to convince me that we should head out and see Capri.

We were on the ferry, not far from the island, when he set a hand on my shoulder. "You all right?"

"Yeah. Just enjoying the scenery," I said mechanically.

Although one *could* easily be rendered speechless by the sight of Capri: white sea cliffs rearing from cobalt blue waters, houses and roads clinging to dizzy slopes, and a lemon-bright light that had probably dazzled generations of artists.

"Let me know if you need anything," Bennett said softly.

Our ferry disgorged us at the Marina Grande. We rode the cable railcar up to the town of Capri and from there set out on foot toward the ruins of Villa Jovis, the retreat once beloved by Roman emperor Tiberius.

The street that led out from the center of the town was barely wider than a table runner. I stopped by a café and browsed the postcards for sale on a spinning rack. While I made my selections, Bennett ducked into a tiny shop across the lane and emerged with a bag of groceries. As I tucked my purchases into my purse, he offered me a handful of dried figs.

The way he peered at me, half-curious, half-concerned, made me realize that it had again been a while since I'd said anything other than, "Sure, we can go that way," or, "Do you mind if I have a look at the postcards?"

I took the figs and searched for something to say, something so banal it would be a waste of breath. *Nice weather. Beautiful place. Do you know what time is it?*

"What happened after you and Moira broke up?"

What was wrong with me? I used to be able to say all the right things.

Bennett shrugged. "I got smashed and then went out and got laid…or was it the other way around? You know, stuff everybody does—except you, I guess."

How did he do this? How did he turn the topic back to me—and always manage to catch me flat-footed? "Why do you presume I don't?"

"*Do* you?"

His voice held a hint of incredulity. And he was right; I never had. The ends of my affairs were always a relief, a return to equilibrium.

Or what passed for equilibrium for me.

I bit into a fig and wished I hadn't retorted. "Never mind me. So you do know how to get laid."

His eyes were on me again. Did he notice how ungainly my conversational pivot had been? How could he not?

"It's an acquired skill, like anything else," he said finally. "When Moira and I broke up for good, I was like a man in a midlife crisis: I'd been with one woman for so long, I had no idea how to work the room anymore. It took me months to rediscover my predatory instincts."

I'd have preferred a smirk in his voice, the usual masculine boastfulness. But he was matter-of-fact—dismissive, even.

"What did your predatory instincts tell you to do?"

I couldn't help my tawdry curiosity. I'd never bothered to glance at any celebrity sex tape. But I'd watch every second of his, aroused and angry at the same time, if there was one floating around.

"I learned that it worked pretty well if I went up to a woman and said, 'Hey, I just broke up with my girlfriend after seven years. Why are you here?'"

The first rule of communication: It's not what you say; it's how you say it. And the way Bennett said it, with sexual interest belied by aloofness—or was it the other way around?—did something to me. It made me, who already knew his story, want to know infinitely more about it. And it made me wish I were half so cool and nonchalant, that I too could take it or leave it.

"And what did you tell them about Moira when they asked?"

"Not many did—it's not that hard to keep people talking about themselves. And if anyone did ask, I told the truth: that she was my first and I wanted to spend my life with her, but it didn't work out."

I wanted to spend my life with her, but it didn't work out. A man perfectly capable of commitment, paying to pretend-date me, about as demonstrable an instance of noncommitment as possible...

"Lucky for me you never tried to pick me up."

But as soon as I said those words, I began to wonder. I'd always viewed our first time together as somewhat inevitable, from the moment I rather unsubtly invited myself to his house for tiramisu.

Had I been looking at a limited picture? What if everything he had done—tossing me the key to his car, walking away, promptly saying good-bye in front of his house—had all been calculated to put me at ease and gain my trust?

"You wouldn't have fallen for anything like that," he said.

"I wouldn't?" I murmured. "How *would* you have picked me up?"

He dropped the bag of groceries into his scuffed messenger bag and stuck his hands into the pockets of his trench coat. We walked for a minute in silence, me wondering whether my question had gone unheard, before he glanced at me.

Our gaze met. Electricity crackled along the surface of my skin. He looked away. Another minute passed before he looked at me again. This time I kept my eyes on my feet, not wanting to be so affected, but feeling the jolt all the same, the force of his attention.

"What's your name?" he asked.

There was no particular change to his voice, yet for some reason he came across as just perceptibly nervous.

"Evangeline." Did I sound similarly on edge?

"Do you come here often?"

I looked at the ornate wrought-iron gate we were passing, and the red-roofed villa inside—and imagined us instead at a crowded night-spot, with throbbing music, pulsing lights, and the odor of too many bodies pressed close together. "No, hardly ever."

"Why not?"

"Not my scene."

"Do you want to get out of here? Have a drink somewhere?"

"Why?" I countered. "Because a nice girl like me shouldn't be alone?"

"A nice girl like you should be alone as long and as often as you prefer," he said quietly. "But I want to be there for when you'd like someone next to you."

Pain pinched my heart, the pain of being understood when I didn't wish to be, by someone who was only playing a game.

"That's not bad." I put on my shades. "Look, we can see the sea again."

THE WALLS AND ARCHES OF Villa Jovis that still stood were massive. Despite two millennia of harsh maritime weathering, the mastery of their construction remained evident in the precision of the masonry and the levelness of the brickwork. And Tiberius sure knew how to pick a spot for his pleasure palace: The ruins, surrounded by a heart-stopping panorama of sea and sky, occupied the easternmost tip of the island, twelve hundred feet above a sheer drop to the waves below.

Bennett and I sat on a small outcrop overlooking a cluster of cliff-hugging pines and made a picnic from his bag of groceries—bread, cheese, olives, and a tiny bottle of white wine. I didn't eat much—and didn't take more than a sip from the bottle.

I should have driven by him that night.

I should have said no to everything that followed.

And I should have backed out the moment I understood what had made me say yes to his crazy scheme.

It still wasn't too late. People broke up all the time, didn't they, even in the middle of "romantic" trips to beautiful places?

"Tell me about the ball—the one in Paris," said Bennett, putting away the remnants of our lunch. "What did I miss?"

I frowned. What *had* he missed? I remembered very little of the ball itself—a flash of my stark red lips in a mirror, the iciness of Pater's fingers in mine as we danced the first dance together, the conspicuous absence of Zelda, kept back in our hotel suite with the kindly French psychiatric nurse who had agreed to come on short notice.

Ingrained by years of practice, my mind immediately turned away from those memories. This was where I'd find myself back on the night of the rehearsal, at the beginning of my alternate history. At the very last moment, when our hope was spent, my most generic Prince Charming would appear as if by magic, a little out of breath and full of apologetic smiles.

But I could conjure up nothing at all. Meeting the Somerset boy in person had destroyed my alternate history: He would never have come to us, not under any circumstances or in any parallel universes.

Yet now the one who had taken the road less traveled wanted to know where the other path would have led.

"You didn't miss much," I said, staring at a distant sailboat. "A bunch of girls in big dresses—by and large not having the time of their lives."

Bennett picked up a pinecone and ran his fingers along its scales. "I'm sorry I wasn't there. My parents asked again and again if I meant it—that I'd actually go to Paris as I promised. And again and again I said yes, even as I packed up all my belongings. I was afraid that if I answered truthfully, they would swoop in and do something drastic. And I needed the master of my residence house to give me my passport so I could take the flight to San Francisco that Moira had booked."

I shrugged. "The ball wasn't really my thing anyway. And your replacement was a count, so my father was satisfied on that front."

"I spoke to your father once, before my parents sent me to England."

I looked at him, astonished.

"My grandmother had left some paintings that would come to me on my twenty-first birthday—nobody knew which ones, but I'd hoped that it would include the Pissarro over her mantel that I'd always loved. Your father had come to our place to look at some pieces of art my uncle had bought. When he was leaving I met him outside and asked how much a Pissarro painting might be worth."

"But he didn't deal in Impressionist works."

"That's what he told me. But he also told me that if he were me, he'd hold on to the Pissarro for some time—he felt Pissarros were undervalued and would appreciate in a decade or two. And he was exactly right: Recently a Pissarro sold for almost twenty million pounds. He was exceptional at what he did, your father."

"Yes, he was." Pater had an encyclopedic memory and, even more important, an uncanny feel for the zeitgeist. He was almost always ahead of the trends, much to the delight of his clients, who had the pleasure of watching their investments quantum-leap in value. "Did you ever meet with him again?"

My father had not been the kind of man who inspired others to come up to me and talk about him. Perhaps for that reason, when it happened I was always struck by how much I missed him.

"No, but right after he gave me the advice about Pissarro paintings, my brother walked up and I introduced them. He was very taken with Prescott."

"Oh?"

"Most people my parents' age were very taken with Prescott. He was at Harvard then, a member of the debate club and the rowing club—all-around impressive. Still is today." Bennett tossed the pinecone in the air and caught it again, slanting a look at me. "Your father would have been surprised that you took up with the punk brother instead."

"Nah," I told him. "My father was used to being disappointed by my choices. All he ever wanted was for me to be a hostess with the most-est, and all I ever did was tinker in our basement with experiments that might blow up the house."

"Did you ever? At least cause enough smoke to have fire trucks come?"

"No, never. Still, he popped antacids at the sight of my science projects. He probably would have preferred it if I'd brought home a punk kid like you instead."

"Thanks for that backhanded compliment, sweetheart." He took a swig of the wine. "What about Zelda?"

"Zelda was always fascinated by what I was up to." I smiled at the memories. "We used to go through scientific equipment catalogs together and she'd help me order what I needed. She read books on her own to understand what I was doing. And since we were both in the basement all the time—her studio is there too—she'd come over from time to time and be my lab assistant."

"I've wondered about the unusual closeness between the two of you," he said.

Something about his tone made me nervous. Did he perceive that it wasn't just love that kept me in orbit around Zelda, her faithful satellite, but also fear?

He looked at me. "I've wondered about how it has made y—"

His expression changed.

"What is it?"

Wrapping an arm around my shoulder, he pulled me close and whispered, “My parents are coming this way.”

The tension in his voice vibrated in me. I took out my compact, opened it, and looked behind me with the mirror. There they were, his parents, picking their way down to where we sat.

“You ready?” he asked.

I suddenly remembered my need to distance myself from him—from this entire situation. His parents couldn’t have arrived at a worse time.

Bennett kissed me on my temple. “I’m so glad you agreed to come.”

We were on, then.

“You don’t know how much I looked forward to this trip,” he murmured. “How impatient I was to go away somewhere, just the two of us.”

His scent was that of winter, crisp, cool, with a bare hint of wood smoke. The sound of his voice, the caress of his words on the shell of my ear, the warmth of his palm on my nape…

“I think I have some idea how much you wanted this,” I managed.

“You can’t even begin to guess.” He pulled me to my feet. “Sometimes it scares me that we might have never met. That we could have spent years living a mile from each other and not once crossed paths.”

His thumb traced a line across my cheekbone. His gaze was intent, solemn. I couldn’t breathe. “You are the best thing to happen to me in a long, long time, princess,” he said softly. “I—Mom, Dad?”

I didn’t need to pretend to swivel around in surprise—caught up in Bennett’s “confession,” I’d forgotten about his parents completely. Could they see my disorientation? My embarrassment? Could they see the heat that scalded my face?

“Oh, hi,” I said, my voice half an octave above normal. “How are you? What brought you to Capri?”

“It’s our anniversary,” said Mrs. Somerset. “We’re taking a trip around Italy.”

I got off the outcrop and shook hands with them. “Happy anniversary. May you celebrate many more together.”

“And you two, are you on holiday?” asked Mrs. Somerset, sounding a little breathless.

It hurt, how much she wanted her family back together. I wanted to hug her, but I had no choice but to play my role. "I had a conference in Munich, and Bennett had a few days off. So we thought we'd meet up on the Amalfi Coast, even if it isn't the best time of the year. Quite a fog yesterday—we could hardly see our way to our hotel."

"We missed that," said Mrs. Somerset. "We got into Naples last night—and before that we were in Tuscany, where the weather was wonderful. For February, at least."

We women were definitely doing the heavy lifting here, while father and son…Mr. Somerset didn't exactly glower, but neither did he look pleased at this unexpected wrinkle to his anniversary trip.

This was a man who did not enjoy being thrust into situations for which he hadn't prepared.

I made the executive decision to give him the time to prepare himself.

"Are you staying here on Capri?" I asked.

"No, we're staying at La Figlia del Mare in Positano," answered Mrs. Somerset.

"What a coincidence. That's where we are too—Zelda raved about the place so much we had no choice but to try it."

"Maybe it's not so much a coincidence as an inevitability," said Mrs. Somerset. "I also picked the hotel because Zelda recommended it a while ago."

There was no time to ponder Zelda's inexplicable love of La Figlia del Mare.

I set my hand on my fake boyfriend's arm. "Bennett and I were about to head over to Anacapri and Mount Solaro. But why don't we have dinner together tonight, if you and Mr. Somerset don't have other plans?"

Mrs. Somerset must have come to a similar executive decision. She didn't consult her husband—or even look at him—before she answered. "We would love that. I hear the hotel's restaurant is excellent."

"It's exceptional. Should we say eight?"

"That would be wonderful."

"Well, see you tonight then. Enjoy Capri."

I tugged on Bennett's hand. It took a couple of tugs, but he muttered a "bye" and followed me up the path that would take us across the ruins and back to the road.

"What's the deal?" asked Bennett, once we were out of his parents' earshot.

I was afraid he might be miffed, but he only sounded puzzled.

"Your dad doesn't care to be thrown like this. I mean, how did you feel when the elevator door opened and they were standing right there?"

"Hmm," he said.

"I know you want to be the one prepared and in charge. And I can see why you opted for the guerrilla strategy. But you've caught them unawares twice now. You won't get much more than this stoic awkwardness out of him. So why not give him that even footing he prefers? You'll have just as much time to prepare. It's fair to everyone."

Bennett exhaled. "You haven't seen him prepared."

"That's fine. I'm a big girl—and you are a grown man."

"It remains to be seen whether he thinks so—about me, that is," Bennett said quietly. "I'm sure he'll be duly impressed with you."

"By and large you are not a teenage punk anymore," I told him.

He cast a glance at me. "You're sure?"

I almost said, "Of course," before I stopped to think about it: the fake girlfriend, the major-dollar carrot, and the whole elaborate scheme—just so he could have this reconciliation on his terms.

"The truth dawns, doesn't it?" Bennett murmured as he extended a hand to help me climb over a half wall.

The truth—and what he had told me at the airport in Naples: He had once been a card-carrying actor. The "confession" a few minutes ago that had mesmerized me had been but lines delivered by a skilled player.

I looked up at the sky, hoping for an approaching front that would have us scuttling back to the hotel. "They come to me as boys and leave as men," I said. "So will you."

But no clouds in the sky—and no way out for me.

We were walking on a narrow *via*, along a shoulder-height privacy wall. Without warning, Bennett had my back against the wall. Our gazes held—and I was nothing but agitation and need.

Tell me you meant it. Tell me you meant everything you said.

He only kissed me, a forceful, hungry kiss that left me light-headed—and even more downhearted.

"What was that about?" I asked, trying to sound casual.

"You don't come to one of the most scenic places in the world with a beautiful woman and not kiss her—that's all." He let go of me. "Now, do we need to take a bus to get to Anacapri?"

Chapter 9

FOR DINNER WITH HIS PARENTS, Bennett dressed down significantly. Instead of a three-piece suit like the one he had worn for our meal the night before, his outfit consisted of a blazer and a turtleneck over jeans.

I took off the belt and the statement necklace I'd used to punch up my basic grey sheath and swapped out heels for a pair of oxfords. "Should have told me earlier you were going casual."

"My dad has an instinctive mistrust of men who are too fashionable."

"Why did he ever work with my father then?" Pater had taken great pride in his fashion-forwardness.

"His prejudice can be overcome, provided the man knows what he's doing. But we aren't at that stage yet, so...I'll pretend to own only jeans and humble blazers."

As you pretend about so many other things.

"Are you sure you don't feel a little defenseless in only jeans and a humble blazer? Like you are the Death Star with its shield down?"

He snorted. "I do, unfortunately. And thanks for that simile, by the way, since we all know the Death Star is doomed."

I patted him on the arm. "It's okay. I'll totally blow up Luke Skywalker to save your evil behind."

Such a beautiful smile spread across his face that for a moment I lost my breath. He laced his fingers with mine. "Thank you for being willing to destroy my childhood idol. And thank you, by the way, for setting up this dinner."

It never failed to startle me when he held my hand. "You might have spoken too soon," I told him, tamping down the fluttering in my stomach. "Thank me afterward if you still want to."

"I'll be grateful even if it's a complete disaster."

"Why?"

"Because you cared enough to make it happen." He kissed the edge of my palm. "Ready?"

WE ARRIVED AT THE LOBBY a few minutes before eight, but Bennett's parents were already there—as were Rob and Darren, who immediately greeted us. My heart sank as I smiled and hugged them—would Moira McAllister's name come up?

The older Somersets came over. Bennett introduced everyone and we engaged in a round of small talk. Rob and Darren had spent their day visiting nearby vineyards and were now headed out to dinner at a little place they'd heard about.

"Let us know if you like the restaurant," said Bennett.

"Will do," Rob said cheerfully.

I exhaled: They would go to their dinner and we to ours.

Then Darren, with an affectionate grip of Bennett's shoulder, said to his parents, "You have a great kid here. I was Moira McAllister's accountant. After she had cancer for the first time, she was kicked off her insurance and couldn't get coverage again. So when her cancer came back five years ago, the hospital bills started stacking up—eye-popping sums.

"But Bennett here rode to his old landlady's rescue and took care of everything—more than once. Which was truly a gift of friendship and generosity. You should be very proud of him."

All three Somersets looked stunned by this revelation, with Bennett also more than a little discomfited.

I quickly wrapped an arm around his middle. "Oh, they are," I told Rob and Darren, my voice as full of hearts and kittens as I could make it. "We're all beyond proud of Bennett. He's the best."

"Stop," Bennett murmured, "you'll make me blush."

I went the extra mile and kissed him on his cheek. "Please. I live for it."

Rob and Darren laughed. They wished us a good evening and left for their dinner. I let go of Bennett to face his parents.

There would be no airing of grievances at this particular dinner—that was for later, between father and son. Tonight was about the truce, about showing that they could sit at a table without being at each other's throats, to lay the groundwork for when they *could* be at each other's throats without once again tearing apart the fabric of the family.

It would have been better accomplished without Moira McAllister's name being brought up—but it wasn't as if she wouldn't have been there anyway, the white elephant in the room.

I smiled at Mr. and Mrs. Somerset. "I admire a man who's willing to be the knight in shining armor to his ex, especially when they have both moved on. Now, should we head to the restaurant?"

BENNETT AND I HELD HANDS as we walked into the restaurant behind his parents—and let go only when we'd been shown to our table. The reluctance was not on his part alone: My stomach was knotted so tight I felt the strain all the way up in the vertebrae of my neck.

It was too late to run; I was in the trenches with him. If he didn't succeed, then I'd always carry this failure with me.

But we certainly *looked* like a family, at least attire-wise: Mr. Somerset too wore a blazer over jeans, and Mrs. Somerset's dress was a strong echo of mine, except hers was a cheerful coral in color.

As the waiter handed around the menus, Mrs. Somerset asked her son, "You're still a vegetarian, Bennett?"

"Uh-hmm," he answered, scanning the wine list.

What? I almost said aloud. In hindsight it was painfully obvious: I'd never seen him eat anything that used to walk, swim, or fly. But I was so distracted by the man I'd paid no attention to what he did or didn't put on his plate.

Beneath the apparent pleasantness at the table, tension rippled—until I placed my order. "I'll have the salad with scallops to start and the roasted duck breast."

"You're not a vegetarian, Evangeline?" asked Mr. Somerset, the first time he'd spoken since we exchanged greetings.

"No, I'm not."

"Bennett hasn't sung the virtues of a meatless diet to you yet?"

So he had been a militant vegetarian in his youth—probably as much to annoy his dad as anything else, I'd guess.

"Bennett would no more dream of changing my diet than I would of changing his," I said firmly.

My fake boyfriend sent me a grateful look. I gave his hand a squeeze under the table. He might be a man of many flaws, but his diet wasn't one of them—and he'd been completely unobtrusive about it.

I asked his parents about themselves. Mr. Somerset was semiretired—after having divested the shipbuilding portion of Rowland Industries, the family firm, he was using some of the proceeds to build a solar portfolio. Mrs. Somerset was a member of the managing committee at the Federal Bank of New York—and didn't see herself slowing down anytime soon.

"Rowland never really wanted to be a businessman, so he is more than happy to step away," she explained. "But I'm doing exactly what I want to do."

They in turn spent some time asking about my work, and I gave more detailed answers than I normally would, to satisfy their curiosity. After that the topic turned to Bennett's siblings: Prescott the economist in Singapore and Imogene the techie in Silicon Valley.

Apparently Imogene had a new boyfriend, but no one was particularly excited.

"My sister is a major player," Bennett said to me. "I had to tell her to stop bringing her current conquests to meet me, because I couldn't keep track."

"Imogene told me that she kept hauling her boyfriend du jour to lunch in the hope that you might bring a girlfriend," said his mother. "She claimed you never did."

He slanted me a glance. "I was waiting for the right one to come along."

My heart gave its usual pathetic throb. I smiled at his parents. "Please excuse Bennett. He does get a little carried away."

On second thought, that might not have been the best thing to say—they already knew how carried away he could get in a romantic situation. But Bennett only laughed softly.

"So you two are official now?" Mr. Somerset asked me.

I speared a piece of carrot that had been braised in duck *jus* onto my fork. "I'm a bit of a commitment-phobe, but...neither of us is seeing anyone else."

"Official enough for me," said Mrs. Somerset, leaning forward. "Do excuse a nosy old lady, but I'm dying to know how you finally met."

Bennett dug into his pasta. "Technically, it was on a dark and stormy night."

I gave an indulgent, didn't-I-tell-you-he-gets-carried-away eye roll. "That makes it sound like we met in the middle of a nor'easter. It was Cos Cob in August. I was taking a walk and Bennett stopped in his car because he was worried that I'd be flattened by a stampede of other concerned neighbors."

"It's that kind of neighborhood," he murmured.

"And that's how we met, more or less," I said.

"That was more or less it for Evangeline. But for me it was the culmination of weeks of internal debate over whether to approach her."

I turned toward him in surprise.

"Why the hesitation?" asked his mother.

"Because I thought it might turn out to be serious." He was smiling, the same kind of smile he had on when he'd said that he'd marry me any day of the week. "But once my lawyers and technical advisers evaluated her patents, it was a no-brainer: I had to get her before anybody else could."

If only I had a team of technical advisers to evaluate the bullshit content of everything he said.

"Aww," I said. "Dream on. You're not putting a ring on this until you sign on the dotted line of an ironclad prenup. I and my future billions will not be parted by a pretty face and a lot of sweet nothings."

"Hmm. Maybe I need to go back to gold-digging school. I'm obviously falling down on the job here."

At this, even Mr. Somerset smiled a little.

We had all sat down at the table rather stiff and cautious. But by the time appetizers appeared, Bennett already looked as relaxed as he had been at our dinner with Rob and Darren.

In stark contrast, his father became noticeably more taciturn and stern-looking. Against his severity, the lighthearted banter around the table took on a perceptibly artificial quality.

A silence fell after Bennett's remark. Mr. Somerset stared into the young red wine in his glass. To appear busy, I made myself cut and chew another piece of duck. Without any haste, Bennett worked on his pasta. This, actually, was the only sign of his nerves—usually he was a much faster eater and would have already finished the food on his plate.

Mrs. Somerset broke the silence. "Speaking of Cos Cob, your dad and I put in an offer for a house there about a year ago. But we were outbid. Your grandma Edith's old house—don't know if you still remember. She sold it when you were eight or nine."

Bennett looked up. "Oh. Guess I was the high bidder then. Didn't know you were also interested."

Mrs. Somerset glanced toward her husband, whose expression became even more foreboding. And going by Bennett's demeanor, I couldn't tell whether he was speaking the truth with regard to his ignorance—or spouting further bullshit. Couldn't tell *at all.*

I longed to drain my wineglass in a gesture of melodramatic frustration—but did nothing more than take a ladylike sip. "Aha, I did wonder why you had a house in Connecticut. Seemed a bit early, the town-and-country lifestyle, for someone who isn't done with his fellowship yet."

"Getting ready to become one of those golf-playing old doctors," he said.

Our waiter came then to clear the plates. When coffee and desserts arrived, Mrs. Somerset turned to her son and asked, "I'm curious, Bennett. I don't remember you ever being particularly interested in life sciences. Why did you go to medical school?"

It was a simple question asked earnestly. Bennett, however, hesitated for what seemed an unnecessary amount of time. I became aware that his father was frowning—either Mr. Somerset was concentrating really hard or it was an expression of open displeasure.

Eventually Bennett shrugged. "Just felt like it at the time—and haven't had any reason to regret that choice."

Mrs. Somerset delved further into his professional life—the kind of cases he saw, the schedule he kept, his opinion of his attending physician. Mr. Somerset listened attentively, but not happily. Bennett seemed not at all aware of the tension on his father's part; he was the blithe young man who had everything he wanted, and his parents were only incidental to his happiness in life.

When the check was presented Mr. Somerset took it. As soon it was settled, everyone rose from the table. I said good-bye to Bennett's parents with no small amount of relief: At least nothing untoward had happened—and we had better get out while that was still the case.

BACK IN OUR SUITE, WE didn't speak for some time. I perched on an ottoman before the fireplace; Bennett stretched out on the long sofa on which we'd made love the day of our arrival. The problem was, I couldn't judge whether the dinner had gone off as well as could be expected or whether it had, at some point, gone off the rails.

Beneath this uncertainty thrummed the chaotic refrain of Bennett's words. *Weeks of internal debate. Whether to approach her. It might turn out to be serious.*

My kingdom for an accurate bullshit meter.

Bennett rose, came behind me, and set his hands on my shoulders. Not until his fingers dug into my muscles did I realize how tense they were. He applied just the right amount of pressure and kneaded away the tight knots from the base of my neck, the tops of my arms, and the sides of my shoulder blades.

And then he walked away and lay back down on the sofa.

"Thanks," I said, my voice sounding unsure.

"You're welcome."

After a moment of not knowing what to do, I reached toward the paper bag on the coffee table, which contained the leftovers of the stuff he'd bought on Capri, and pulled out a handful of dried figs that still remained—I hadn't eaten much at dinner and now I was hungry.

I tossed a couple of the figs at my fake boyfriend.

He caught them and set them aside. "You okay, Professor?"

"I'm tight with my mother figure. So, yeah, I'm okay."

He covered his eyes with the heels of his hands and grunted. I guess I didn't need to ask him whether *he* was okay: He wasn't.

I had to resist an urge to go over and cradle his head in my lap. "When you were buying the house in Cos Cob, didn't you have any idea that you were bidding against your parents?"

"No, I didn't. None at all."

"Your sister didn't tell you anything?"

"We rarely talked about our parents. And this was January of last year. I didn't say anything to her about my move until April, after I'd bought the apartment." He set one hand on the back of the sofa and trailed the other on the rug. "But talk about being accidentally dickish on top of being intentionally dickish."

"Are you talking about those attempted takeovers?"

He stared up at the ceiling. "I went to medical school as a fuck-you to my dad."

A face-palm moment if ever there was one. I sighed and bit into a dried fig.

"He wanted to be a medical researcher," Bennett continued. "But when he was in his first semester in medical school, his older brother, the one who was always supposed to take over the family business, died. So he put aside medicine to become a businessman.

"I, on the other hand, made my fortune by being in the right place at the right time, with an inheritance from my grandmother that came at the exact right moment for me to invest in a passel of start-ups."

Zelda had told me something of Bennett's success. The inheritance from his grandmother had contained a lot more than a single Pissarro. His great-great-grandfather, the too-good-in-bed gentleman who had been married to the lady in the John Singer Sargent portrait, had been an important collector of Impressionist and post-Impressionist art—the contemporary art of his era. Over time the collection had splintered and diminished, but Bennett had still received a veritable treasure trove.

He sold some of the paintings at auction for twenty-five million dollars and invested in a number of start-ups. Within a few years the twenty-five mil had turned into more than six hundred mil: Half a dozen of the start-ups had been acquired by iconic companies, and a few more by less iconic companies whose money was just as good.

"My largely accidental good fortune as an investor came about at a low point. Moira and I had just broken up for good—and so much of what I'd planned for the rest of my life was with the two of us together. I was adrift and angry. Since it was easier to be angry at someone else than to be angry at myself, I decided that my dad was to blame, especially since he'd been eerily prescient about how it would all end.

"I hated that he was right. And I hated that I'd failed so spectacularly, that my great love had turned out to have been pretty ordinary after all. So after another unsuccessful attempt at taking over his company, I decided to make it even more personal. I would go to medical school and have what he never had."

I might have raised my brow a fraction of an inch.

"It's all right," he said. "You can be openly horrified. I was a very spoiled young man."

I didn't say anything.

His lips twisted in an expression of self-disdain. "And I might still be one."

Whereas his father, from just as privileged a background, had never been a spoiled young man. Had probably exemplified duty and sacrifice. And had kept *his* long-term relationship intact.

"It was a strange feeling," Bennett said slowly, "to realize that I admire him. That in a way I have always admired him, even when I thought he was both stodgy and despotic."

And he wanted his father to think well of him in return. But how was it possible when his wealth had come too easily—at least in his own view—and his profession was a giant middle finger to Mr. Somerset?

I dug into the paper bag again. There was, thank goodness, a chocolate bar at the bottom. I broke it in two, lobbed half at him, and gobbled up the remainder in two bites.

"You should have had 'asshole' tattooed on your forehead while you were at it—so your parents would never forget."

He sighed and broke off a piece of chocolate. "I'm surprised I didn't. When I made up my mind to go to medical school, I was high as fuck—having a shit-ton of money and no purpose in life never fails to lead straight to cranking out on a yacht in Saint-Tropez.

"Looking back, even though it was a decision made purely from spite, it saved me from myself. I had to sober up, for one thing—I was going to stick it to the old man even if it meant I had to actually study. And drugs and dissection"—he grimaced, as if remembering a particularly bad trip—"those two did not go well together."

I, who somehow managed to be on university campuses for fourteen years straight without ever smoking a joint, fished in the paper bag again. But it was empty of further calorie-laden solaces. Bennett gave the rest of his chocolate to me. "Don't worry. I haven't had any hard drugs in eight years. If anything, I miss smoking more."

That was only part of what bothered me. "Do you even like medicine?"

The thought that he might have devoted nearly a decade of his life to a field in which he hadn't the least personal interest, the only value of which was in how much it would rub his dad the wrong way…Something very close to a desperate unhappiness swamped me. "Because if you don't, you should get out right now—I don't care how close you are to the end of your fellowship."

He smiled a little, not the glossy, glamorous kind of smile, but one tinged with a trace of sadness. "You're a good friend, you know."

I wasn't. I was with him only because of a wretched covetousness that overrode my self-control.

"And to answer your question, I do enjoy medicine, far more than I ever expected to, paperwork aside. And I love going on medical missions—it's humbling to be able to actually make a difference."

Something in me fell back into place with a sigh of relief—perhaps I was a better friend than I thought. "Then you don't need to worry about why you started medical school. It will come through, that love—and your dad will see it."

He sat up slowly and pushed his fingers through his hair, the beautiful prodigal son who had come home, even though no father shouted in jubilation for a fattened calf to be slaughtered and a magnificent feast put on. "I hope you'll prove to be right."

"Give it time," I said softly.

He rolled up the now-empty paper bag. "Sometimes I wonder what it might feel like to be close to my parents. I wonder whether we'd ever be as close as you and Zelda."

"You mean having your menstrual cycles perfectly synced?"

He snorted. "Other than that."

You don't want to be as close as Zelda and me. You don't want every moment of joy counterpoised by a shadow of fear. You don't want to begin every New Year praying, Let this not be our last together.

"There is no substitute for how much care and affection you put into a relationship. So…baby steps."

He nodded, his expression contemplative as he studied me. I had the strange sensation that he wasn't thinking so much about what I'd told him, but what I'd kept to myself.

I stood up. "I'll go to sleep now. Good night."

He rose and barred the path to my door. I braced myself for a touch, or perhaps a murmur, but he only asked, "What do you do when you despair, and there isn't an August rain to drown your sorrow?"

I didn't think it was possible for him to ask me anything more penetrating than my personal sexual fantasies. I was wrong. Compared to despair, lust was nothing.

I made my tone light. "Then whatever weather would have to do, wouldn't it?"

He cupped my face. I swallowed—he would kiss me again. But he only pressed his lips to my forehead. "Thank you. I wouldn't have been able to handle dinner without you."

It's what you pay me for, I should answer.

Instead, I rested my hand briefly against his arm and told him, "I'm glad to help. Consider this my medical mission where I might actually make a difference."

Chapter 10

I DRIFTED IN AND OUT of sleep, dreaming of a rumple-haired, dirty-hot Bennett surrounded by beautiful girls, snorting lines of cocaine from a glass table.

I woke up disoriented and restless—and immediately Googled him. There were a couple of men with the same name who had fairly high-profile jobs—one a journalist, another an event promoter in LA—and pages that mentioned their names clogged the first dozen pages of search results. And when I Googled "Dr. Bennett Somerset," only a few meaningful results turned up, mostly from his medical school and the two hospitals where he had worked.

If he was on Facebook, the account was hidden. I found nothing on Instagram. A Twitter account, opened at the instigation of his sister, most likely—she was the only one with whom he'd exchanged tweets—had sat idle for several years.

I put aside my laptop, got dressed, and started to pack. But my progress was slow and haphazard. I couldn't stop thinking of the rudderless young man trying to distract himself with sex and drugs—and couldn't stop wishing I'd been there for him.

That was, of course, unrealistic thinking on a crazy scale. Had I been there, he'd have used and discarded me. But it was a powerfully alluring idea, that of saving a man from himself and winning his eternal devotion in return.

My phone vibrated—a text from Bennett. *Having breakfast with Mom at a nearby café. Be back soon.*

The hotel phone rang at that exact moment, startling me. I picked up, expecting the front desk. "*Pronto?*"

"*Buon giorno*. May I speak to Evangeline?"

Mr. Somerset.

"This is she. What can I do for you, sir?"

"I was hoping you'd have breakfast with me."

The thought of sitting down alone with Bennett's father chased away my appetite. "That sounds lovely."

"Excellent. How about the hotel's restaurant? And what's a convenient time for you?"

"I can be down in fifteen minutes."

"I look forward to it."

I reached the hotel restaurant in precisely fifteen minutes. Mr. Somerset and I shook hands, visited the continental breakfast buffet, and sat down together. We exchanged pleasantries. The weather had turned cold and foggy again. Bennett and I were headed out for the airport in an hour; the older Somersets would be staying another night on the Amalfi Coast.

A waiter came and poured coffee. Mr. Somerset took a sip from his cup; I took a deep breath.

"My wife and I are delighted to have met you."

I smiled like the paragon everyone believed me to be. "It's a pleasure to spend some time with you and Mrs. Somerset."

"We have met only one other of Bennett's girlfriends—you know something of the circumstances."

"Yes, I believe so."

Bennett's father studied me for a moment—as if my equanimity in the matter still surprised him. "There were quite a few things about that relationship that unsettled us. The age difference and that it had begun while Bennett was still a minor were the most obvious issues. But what mattered as much was the tremendous romantic delusion they had both been under. It wasn't so surprising that a teenage boy should be somewhat blind about his first great love. But for Ms. McAllister, a woman of sophistication and insight, it was beyond us how she looked at Bennett and saw only what she wanted to see."

I smoothed the napkin on my lap. "There's no age at which one becomes immune to the cognitive impairment love causes."

"You're absolutely correct. My wife and I used to sit in stunned silence after one of our encounters with Ms. McAllister and wonder whether she was right—whether we knew our son at all. When they eventually broke up, we weren't surprised, but a small part of me was disappointed: It would have been something remarkable had they managed to maintain their relationship. Even I, stick-in-the-mud extraordinaire, as Bennett liked to call me, couldn't be entirely indifferent to the force of such an all-conquering love."

I smoothed the napkin some more. "But it wasn't."

"No, it wasn't, in part because of that romantic delusion. Had they seen each other more realistically, the outcome might have been different."

I saw where this conversation was going. "And you'd like to know whether I'm also under some sort of delusion about who and what Bennett is."

"I hope you are not offended."

The irony of it. I shook my head. "No, I'm not offended."

"Then do you mind if I ask what you think of my son?"

He was a forthright man, Bennett's father, not given to pretenses. I wondered what he had made of Bennett's apparent ease and good cheer the night before. A stranger walking by would have seen a dazzling young man, one who already had everything he could possibly desire. That young man did not need his less wealthy, less glamorous parents; he was happy to humor them, but he had moved far beyond their sphere of influence.

I stirred my coffee. "What I think of his flaws, you mean?"

"Yes."

Weeks of internal debate. Whether to approach her. It might turn out to be serious.

Flaw 1: He spouts so much BS.

What do you do when you despair, and there isn't an August rain to drown your sorrow?

Flaw 2: I'm afraid he sees through me.

"There's an excess of pride to him," I said, breaking off a piece of a chocolate croissant. "A healthy amount of arrogance. Opportunism, too—he's not above being exploitive. I think I may safely call him a shark, your son."

"Yet you're with him," said Mr. Somerset.

"Yet I'm with him."

Should I be concerned at how convincing I sounded? Had I become that good an actress, or was it something else that gave force and gravitas to my words?

"Why?"

"You mean besides the obvious? I like that he's always been upfront with me, especially about his flaws. I like that he isn't pissing away his money on hookers and blow. And I like…I like that he challenges me."

Strangely enough, I might not be lying outright on the last part. As much as I hated it when Bennett called me out on my BS, in a way it was also something of a rush. Nobody else did.

The only thing I didn't like was that he was only my pretend boyfriend and I the set dressing for his newfound maturity and seriousness.

"Thank you," said Mr. Somerset. "I'm glad—and relieved—to hear it."

I wasn't as glad to have enumerated reasons Bennett's hold on me grew more tangible with each passing day. But this wasn't about me. "He's really quite remarkable, your son."

"Yes, he is," said Mr. Somerset. "And has always been."

A declaration of fact on his part, rather than one of pride, as if he were stating Bennett's age or height: This was a man who had a clear, unsentimental view of his son.

We fell back into small talk. Ten minutes later, coffee and pastry consumed, we were once again shaking hands, wishing each other safe and pleasant trips.

"Bennett is very lucky to have you," said Mr. Somerset.

"Who knows, maybe I'm the luckier one here," I answered. "I hope to see you again when we're all back in the city."

Mr. Somerset smiled. "Yes, I'd like that."

BENNETT AND I HAD AN uneventful flight to London. At Heathrow Airport we were met by Mrs. Asquith's man, Hobbs, who drove an old-fashioned sedan with a partition between the front and the back seats. Her house was forty minutes away, a small estate tucked into the Berkshire countryside—not far from Eton, according to Bennett.

"Did you like going to the school?"

"It was okay. I liked playing rugby—always thought American football too wimpy, all those helmets and paddings."

My lips curved very slightly at that. "Why did your parents put you there, rather than somewhere nearby to keep a closer eye on you?"

"Two years before we met, Moira was arrested in London for being rowdy and in possession of narcotics, so she couldn't enter Britain. My parents gave my passport to the master of my residence house, so I couldn't leave. It was a pretty clever plan on their part."

"So you visited another old lady instead."

"Huh," said Bennett.

He gave me a dirty look, but its effect was undercut by a smile. I found myself smiling back at him. And then we were looking at each other and not smiling.

I felt as if there were nothing solid underneath me, as if I might do something regrettable at any moment. Breaking off eye contact, I opened my purse and pretended to check inside. "Did Mrs. Asquith know about Moira?"

"She did after I told her."

"How'd she take it?"

"With cautious delight. She loves a scandal, that one. I think at one point she almost started the process to get the Home Office's ruling overturned, so Moira could visit. But in the end she became convinced I'd knock Moira up, and that would be a bigger scandal than even she could handle, especially if it came out that she had something to do with it."

My head snapped up. "Jesus."

"I know, as if we'd never heard of contraceptives."

He was observing me again in that way of his, and I felt like a mechanical watch with its covers taken off, all the wheels and gears inside clearly visible.

"I was talking about Mrs. Asquith almost taking leave of her senses."

"You *wouldn't* want a nice young man to see his girlfriend, whom he missed desperately?"

"I'd rather buy you a hooker for your birthday."

I almost winced at the hard edge to my answer: I was jealous of a dead woman, of the single-minded devotion she had once inspired in my lover.

He cast me a sidelong glance. "Interesting positions you take, Dr. Canterbury."

I stared at him. I wanted him to touch me. To ignite and then annihilate me. I wanted the opportunity, even if it was only for a few minutes, to pretend that the fire of lust was something far more substantial and all-encompassing.

His eyes darkened. They lingered on my lips. Then he gazed back into my eyes, and I forgot how to breathe. When he looked at me like this, it was easy to believe that no other woman existed but me, that I was indeed the one he had been waiting for all along.

He tilted his head slightly. My heart beat ridiculously fast. My fingers dug into the supple leather of the seat.

The car door opened. "Here we are," Hobbs said cheerfully. "Mind your step."

AT FIRST GLANCE, MRS. ASQUITH didn't seem like the kind of woman to help with a boy and his more-than-twice-his-age lover: the sharply tailored royal blue dress, the triple strand of pearls, the perfectly coiffed, snow-white hair—if she were to introduce herself as a dowager countess, nobody would blink an eye.

Then she smiled, a smile full of mischief and the-hell-with-it attitude, and suddenly I could see her as a coconspirator in all kinds of outrageous schemes. "Bennett, you scamp. And Evangeline, my dear, how wonderful to meet you at last."

The skin of her hand was papery, but her handshake was strong. "And may I introduce Mr. Lawrence de Villiers?"

I'd noticed the man to her side the moment we entered the room. He was in his late fifties, with the look of an older Mr. Darcy—he bore a striking resemblance to the actor Colin Firth.

"I rang up Mrs. Asquith a few days ago, and when she said you were going to be here, I asked if I could join you," Mr. de Villiers said to me. "Zelda and I knew each other from before she emigrated to America."

He was Zelda's old boyfriend, the one who left. I'd hoped to learn something more about him from Mrs. Asquith. But here he was in the flesh, a clear-eyed, handsome man to whom Zelda obviously still mattered, or he wouldn't have invited himself to meet her former stepdaughter.

"Very nice to meet you," I said.

We sat down to a late lunch of piping-hot soup and warm sandwiches—steak with caramelized onions on ciabatta for the meat eaters and a toasted Camembert sandwich for the vegetarian.

Bennett teased Mrs. Asquith, who had probably never turned on a stove in her life, on her much improved culinary skills.

She harrumphed. "As if I would have given you anything more than tea and plain toast, when you were always using my telephone to ring your girlfriend in America."

Bennett slanted her an I'm-disappointed-in-you look. "Aren't you going to tell the full story?"

"All right, so you did pay for a new central heating system and better plumbing. And a new roof. And solar cells. But that was years later. For the better part of a decade I had only my own kindness for consolation."

"Huh," said Bennett. "You used to listen in on my calls."

Mrs. Asquith grinned, entirely unrepentant. "They were my telephone and my telephone line." She turned to me. "He was a very naughty boy."

"I've reformed," Bennett protested. "I'm respectable now."

Mrs. Asquith scoffed. "You are still a scamp. All your respectability is in this young lady here."

Bennett glanced at me. "Are you really *that* respectable, Evangeline?"

I put down my sandwich. "Please. At Buckingham Palace they ask themselves, 'What would Dr. Canterbury do?'"

Mrs. Asquith cackled. "When Bennett said you two were seeing each other, I dug up old snaps Zelda had sent of you and said to myself, 'Lovely girl, but maybe too sweet and gentle for him.' I see now I needn't have worried."

"I keep him on a short leash," I said. "He's gone the moment he shows his true colors."

"Didn't I tell you I'm afraid of her?" said Bennett to Mrs. Asquith. "Always looking to kick me to the curb, this one."

"What can I say?" I dipped my fork into the minted pea puree on my plate. "Zelda raised no fool."

Mr. de Villiers, who had been quietly listening to our exchange, reached for his water glass. "When Zelda was younger, she was convinced she could never handle children."

I looked at him full on. "She did very well when the time came. She was the best part of my childhood."

He shook his head slightly. "I couldn't have imagined. Or perhaps I should say, I didn't quite trust my imagination."

"No one can predict the future," Mrs. Asquith told him. "You made rational choices, Larry. No need to second-guess them after almost thirty years."

"No, I suppose not," he said.

But he didn't sound convinced. We fell silent, and ate for a minute or so without talking. Mrs. Asquith restarted the conversation by making Mr. de Villiers tell us about his work in television: He had produced several iconic shows and been involved in a score more in one capacity or another.

"I was a junior second assistant producer, on my third show ever, when I was assigned to find a composer for the theme music. And that was when dear Maggie here"—he nodded toward Mrs. Asquith—"introduced me to Zelda, in the hope that her connections in the music industry might help me.

"She actually composed the music herself. But the show was never broadcast, so she put some lyrics to the song, gave it to Polygram, and they made a moderate hit out of it."

"I believe she paid for new insulation on our house a few years ago with royalties from that song," I said.

"Did she? That's lovely to hear."

There was a yearning in his voice, a hunger for such small, mundane news. Did Zelda feel likewise? When she thought of him, did she wonder whether he still liked his morning toast the way she remembered, and whether he had kept using the same soap and shampoo?

"Now, now, Larry," said Mrs. Asquith. "I agreed you could come on condition that you reveal all about the next season of *Bowyer Grange*. I'm old and I'm impatient, so you'd best start right now."

FOR THE REST OF LUNCH, Mr. de Villiers answered Mrs. Asquith's questions about upcoming plot twists of the hugely popular show. When we rose from the table, Mrs. Asquith asked if I'd like a tour of the grounds. I said yes, and Mr. de Villiers was volunteered to be my guide.

We bundled up and went outside. My companion dutifully pointed out features of interest. When he mentioned that the house was built in the 1880s, I expressed my surprise at its relatively recent origin.

"What's the term one uses for those big new houses in America?" asked Mr. de Villiers.

"McMansions, you mean?"

"Yes, that. This is an example of its Victorian counterpart—a prosperous man of business building a country retreat for himself and his family. Thousands of these were torn down in the postwar years—too costly to maintain and too new for the state to consider them of historical value. Fortunately for Maggie, hers is small enough that the upkeep falls within her means.

"Or almost, that is. Out of respect, we tend to look the other way when faced with signs of a house's dilapidation. But Dr. Somerset was just American enough to make the necessary arrangements for workers to show up, so Maggie could harangue them with her demands."

This unlikely yet enduring friendship between Bennett and Mrs. Asquith was making me like him all too much. I sighed inwardly.

We were inspecting a large, bare plane tree, planted in memory of a son of the house who had died in the Battle of the Somme, when Mr. de Villiers said, "I don't suppose Zelda has ever mentioned me."

At last. What we had come to talk about. I glanced at him, imagining the dashing young man he must have been thirty years ago. "No. It was Bennett who first told me about you—he'd heard a bit of the story from Mrs. Asquith."

Mr. de Villiers wrapped his muffler more tightly about his neck—the cold of the day was the kind that seeped in slowly. "We were seriously involved for a while, and it was the most marvelous time of my life. When I made up my mind to propose to her, I commissioned a specially designed ring. Are you familiar with Tolkien's works?"

I smiled to myself. "Very."

"Then you'll know what I mean when I say I wanted the ring to look like Nenya."

I nodded, a sharp pinch at my heart. There were three rings of power the Elves had kept for themselves. Nenya, the Ring of Adamant, was wielded by Lady Galadriel.

Zelda would have loved that engagement ring.

"Finally the ring came back from the jeweler. I booked a holiday for us." He looked up at the sky, heavy with the promise of snow. "But before we went, she had an episode."

I'd expected those exact words. Still my stomach lurched.

"I knew she had a therapist and a prescription for her condition. But since I had no experience with mental illness—not up close, in any case—at first I didn't understand what was going on. She had boundless energy, she couldn't get enough of me, and she became tremendously confident—which was very gratifying, as I'd been telling her for months that she was too modest in her self-belief.

"I began to grow alarmed when I realized she was hardly sleeping. When I woke up at night she'd be on the telephone, talking to friends in America, Australia, or anywhere people were awake. During the day she brought back groceries by the car bootful, morning and afternoon. And she washed all the curtains, sheets, and tablecloths—again and again.

"And then it swung the other way and…" He took a deep breath. "You probably don't need me to describe what it's like."

I shivered, my fingers ice-cold inside my gloves.

"I was a very capable young man who believed that everything was within my power to influence and change. I focused like a laser beam on her condition. We visited the best psychiatrists, the best nutritionists, the best everything. I was convinced that with proper medication, a well-calibrated diet, a rigorously adhered-to schedule, her illness could be controlled like type-one diabetes—still an annoying problem to have, but one that shouldn't interfere with living a normal life in this day and age."

My brows knitted. This kind of micromanaging was so different from Pater's we-just-have-to-be-here philosophy that I didn't know what to think of it.

"It didn't quite work out that way. In hindsight, that I'd put so much pressure on her to become well and remain well was probably one of the reasons she was ill again a few months later. And that was a terrible episode—she had to be hospitalized for several weeks."

Zelda's first episode in the States, when I was six, had led to a hospital stay. The one in the wake of the ball also required institutional care. But each time she was back home in days. To need several weeks of hospitalization—I didn't even dare to imagine the severity of that episode.

"She recovered eventually. But I felt I'd lost control over every aspect of my life. A complete failure of a man. So I told her I couldn't do it anymore, that it was time for us to stop being a couple." Mr. de Villiers sighed. Before me he seemed to grow smaller. "Six months later I was married. Two months after that she married your father and moved to America."

Pater had been on a business trip to London when he'd met Zelda. Theirs had been a whirlwind romance, at most six weeks from introduction to wedding. Ever since Bennett first brought up the topic of her old boyfriend, I'd suspected that she might have married Pater on the rebound. What Mr. de Villiers said pretty much confirmed that.

"Have you seen her since?"

"Once at a party in London—she'd divorced your father the year before. We sat together and talked for hours. But when the party ended, we went our separate ways." He glanced up at the sky again. Tiny snowflakes meandered down, disappearing the moment they touched ground. "My marriage was already an entity in name only, but I was still unwilling to face everything that a relationship with Zelda would entail. I couldn't handle it as a young man; it seemed impossible I'd do any better as a man of middle age."

We left our spot before the commemorative plane tree and resumed walking. At the far end of the garden I said, "But?"

"But I never stopped thinking about her. My ex-wife and I decided we simply didn't have enough stiff upper lip to preserve our marriage solely for the sake of not having a divorce on the CV. The divorce became final in July of last year. I was about to purchase a ticket to New York when I heard that Zelda was ill again.

"Then she recovered and came to see Maggie in December. Twice I drove out here. But I was…too ashamed, I suppose, to call on her when she was healthy, when I stayed away during her illness. So I stood in front of the house and looked up at the window of the room where she always stayed, like a character from *Bowyer Grange*. Each time I drove away without seeing her."

A snowflake fell on my face, the chill from the tiny chip of ice drilling deep beneath my skin. I should have known. I should have guessed from the moment I saw him that he wanted to be together with her again, this man who had "managed" her into the worst episode of her life.

"If you'd like to know whether Zelda would welcome you back into her life," I said stiffly, "I'm afraid I can't tell you one way or the other."

"Nobody can tell me that except Zelda, and that isn't why I invited myself here today. Today I only wanted to meet you. She spoke a great deal of you last time we met, and I've long wished to see the young woman who stuck by her through sickness and health."

People persisted in misreading my character. When the Somersets looked at me, they saw nothing but reassuring good sense—as if I could ever bear to appear anything but even-keeled and pulled-together. To be otherwise was to feel the seams of my world breaking apart, to sense the distant rumble that would make the whole house of cards come tumbling down.

To Mr. de Villiers, I stood for all that was selfless and courageous—when there was and had only ever been a stark fear of losing the one person who loved me unconditionally.

Usually I shrug off such mistaken praise—giving false impressions wasn't my intention, merely a by-product of protecting myself. But now, as we stopped walking again next to a stone sundial at the center of Mrs. Asquith's garden, I realized that Mr. de Villiers hadn't just wanted to meet me.

He was hoping for my blessing.

"May I ask you a question, Mr. de Villiers?"

"Of course. And please call me Larry."

"Does Zelda know about the holiday you'd booked?"

The seemingly inconsequential nature of my question surprised Larry. "I never mentioned it to her, but I believe Maggie did a few years ago. Zelda was visiting and they were looking through some travel magazines together, and according to Maggie, when she came across a picture of La Figlia del Mare, she said, 'Oh, look, that's the hotel where Larry meant to propose to you.'"

The wildly romantic La Figlia del Mare, which Zelda had been recommending to everyone since.

I placed my hand on the sundial, feeling nothing but a searing cold. "Obviously my opinion doesn't count. But since you sought me out, Larry, I'm going to assume that it does matter to some extent: I believe you'll make a wonderful companion for someone, somewhere, but that someone isn't Zelda."

He flinched.

"Our life in New York isn't perfect, but it's pretty good. She has great friends there and a solid support system. You don't sound as if you'll be retiring anytime soon. If the two of you get back together, Zelda will be the one expected to relocate, since her studio is much easier to move across the pond than a TV production.

"And then what? We don't live in fairy tales and true love cures nothing. It's more or less inevitable that someday she'll suffer another episode. You'll feel as if you lost control over your life again. You'll feel like a failure again. And where does that leave her? Stuck with a man who can only see her illness?"

Larry's lips moved, but he made no sound. My stomach twisted at how stricken he looked, but a fierce protectiveness burned in me. This man had his chance and he blew it. What made him think he could just waltz back into her life and pick up where they'd left off?

"I want to believe I have changed," he said at last, his voice cracking a little.

My fingers clenched together. "And you would bet her well-being on that?"

He had no answer for me. We started walking again. The insubstantial snow continued, leaving no evidence behind of having ever been there. I looked up once to see a curtain flutter in the house. Was that Mrs. Asquith, looking out? Or was it Bennett?

"I have a business trip to Manhattan in early May," Larry said, as we neared the house. "I was hoping to have dinner with Zelda, Bennett, and you. I suppose you'd prefer that I didn't contact her at all."

"I'd prefer that before you did anything, you ask yourself whether it would be good for her—or only good for you."

We climbed up the wide, shallow steps leading up to the front door. Under the portico I stopped and turned to Larry. "I'm sorry that nothing I said was anything you wanted to hear."

"The fault isn't yours," he said sincerely, if wanly. "I have only myself to blame."

"I'm sorry," I said again, suddenly exhausted. "Thank you for showing me the garden. It was very kind of you."

WHEN WE WALKED BACK INTO Mrs. Asquith's drawing room, it was already time for Bennett and me to say our good-byes. Mrs. Asquith presented my fake boyfriend with an elaborately wrapped gift.

"Happy belated Christmas, my dear young hooligan."

"Not again," said Bennett, shaking his head even before he undid the wrapping paper to reveal a hardcover notebook.

Mrs. Asquith chortled. "You ingrate. Something from the best stationer in London isn't good enough for you nowadays, is it?"

Bennett stuck the notebook into his messenger bag and hugged her. "You bought this on High Street for a quid fifty, you old liar."

"What was that about?" I asked when we were in the car, being driven to the airport.

"Long-running gag. She gives me one every time she sees me, for me to record my sexual shenanigans—then submit for her perusal, of course. When I was younger I used to cut out passages from vintage porn, paste them in, and send the notebook to her."

I smiled a little at Mrs. Asquith's gleeful perversity. "Did you tell her about how scarce your sexual shenanigans have been lately?"

"No, I told her about our encounter with my parents." He paused for a beat. "And I tried to persuade her to let me listen to her heart, but she wouldn't have it. Said she didn't trust a young man with a taste for old ladies."

Had I been there, I'd probably have laughed out loud at Mrs. Asquith's snark—it was still funny in the retelling. But a sober undercurrent to Bennett's words caught my attention. "Why were you trying to examine her? Is she okay?"

"Not as robust as she'd like us to believe. And asking for spoilers to a TV show?" He frowned. "That's not like her at all. She hates spoilers."

He pulled the notebook out of his bag and flipped through the empty pages. The scent of crisp, new paper perfumed the warm interior of the car. He traced a finger along the edge of the notebook, then turned his face to the window, lost in thought.

The sedan cut smoothly, almost soundlessly across the countryside, the fields and riverbanks of which were still green after a long winter. In the silence my conversation with Larry began to replay in my head, my own voice echoing, every syllable harsh and unforgiving.

In Mrs. Asquith's garden I'd felt as righteous as a mother lion protecting her cub. But now that moment of adrenaline had passed, I began to see that my instinctive growling and teeth-bearing had been but another manifestation of the fear in my heart, the one constant emotion that undergirded everything in my life.

Except this time the fear could no longer be shut in and locked away. This time the fear had been in control of me, throwing words like grenades toward Larry de Villiers.

Near the airport traffic turned knotty. We had to rush through the terminal to make our flight. It was only after we were airborne, with the fasten-your-seat-belt sign turned off, that Bennett asked me, "So, what do you think of Larry?"

I chose my words carefully. "He seems to care about Zelda still. And he seems to be a kind and considerate person."

Bennett raised a brow. "So you told him to stay away from Zelda?"

Flaw 2: I'm afraid he sees through me.

I didn't bother to issue a denial, but only shrugged.

"Ladies and gentlemen"—a flight attendant's voice came over the PA system—"we have a passenger in need of medical attention. If you are a physician, please press the call button nearest your seat."

Bennett pressed his call button. "On a plane this size, there's probably more than one doctor."

As if to contradict him, a flight attendant materialized almost immediately and asked him to come with her. I craned my neck to follow their progress, but she pulled the curtain behind her and blocked the view into coach class.

I fidgeted in my seat, half of my mind going around in circles with Larry and Zelda, the other half worrying about what was happening at the back of the plane.

After a very long twenty minutes, Bennett returned. "Is everything okay?" I asked.

"Uh-hmm. A little girl was traveling with a cast on her foot. The foot swelled from the low pressure in the cabin and cut off circulation to her toes. So we pried her cast open. I'll check on her again, but for now she's fine."

I exhaled. "That's good to know."

He switched on his in-seat entertainment system and brought up the movie menu. "I'm curious. What did Larry say that set you against him?" he asked, still looking at the screen.

"I don't know that he'd want me to repeat our conversation," I said, as much out of a desire to not face probing questions as out of concern for Larry and Zelda's privacy.

"Remember I'm Mrs. Asquith's favorite young hooligan. At this point I'd say I know a lot about Larry and Zelda's relationship, probably more than you do."

My lips twisted. Why did he have to be so well connected to *my* life? "I didn't like how he micromanaged her illness or how he just up and left."

He turned toward me. His eyes met mine in a green, level gaze. "Don't you think that despite your objections, the choice of whether Zelda and Larry de Villiers will get together should be left to *them*?"

I made no reply. Part of me wanted to explain my actions, but a different part said that it would be no use. He couldn't possibly understand.

"I won't presume to know how you feel," he said. "I can only tell you what I know: Moira suffered from fairly debilitating depressions—the can't-get-out-of-bed kind."

"She did?" His Lolita-esque love affair was turning out to be nothing like what I'd imagined.

"All her life—since she was a teenager. She never hid it from me. In fact, before I left Eton, she told me that she wasn't well. But, of course, I thought she was down because she missed me. I thought the moment I showed up she'd be fine. Better than fine.

"I showed up. But the stress of dealing with my parents only made things worse. Even after they left, she didn't get better. I was ignorant and impatient. I pushed her to go out, to invite people over—I didn't understand depression then, didn't know that it had a power of its own. I thought she just needed cheering up.

"Then, when I did understand, I panicked. I'd given up everything to be with her, and she was too lost in this bleakness to care that I was there."

But I saw a picture of you guys around that time, I almost said, *at a picnic table with Rob and Darren and a bunch of other people. You looked happy.*

I knew as well as anyone did that depression wasn't a uniform experience. Some days were more manageable; some days a woman in the grip of clinical depression laughed and enjoyed herself. But that didn't mean she'd seen the light at the end of the tunnel. The next day she could very well be in a pit of despair again, with no way out—and no way for someone who loved her to reach in.

"I almost left," said Bennett. "Almost threw in my towel and admitted I got in way over my head."

Shock slammed into me. "When was this?"

"About two months after I got to Berkeley."

Somehow I'd come to view their relationship as a gradual decline, the thrill and sexual fascination of the initial attraction slowly dissipating over time. I'd never thought of the rough patches they must have overcome along the way. "But you stayed."

"I didn't leave—there is a difference. And I didn't leave because, one, I didn't have any money; two, I didn't have anywhere else to go; and three, I was too proud to have my new life collapse so soon after I told my parents that they were too bourgeois to understand the depth and intensity of my great transcendent love.

"So I hung around, essentially. I found a job, made sure she ate, and cleaned up her house because I didn't know what else to do. And then she got better and our life got back on track. I mean…you've been there; you know the cycle."

I tried to imagine him in the role I knew all too well: that of the caretaker, the one who worried, prayed, and waited. "This shatters the mental image I had of you guys boinking like bunnies once you got to California."

He smiled slightly. "Don't worry. We more than made up for the initial lack of boinking."

That smile did possibly illegal things to me. My fingers tightened on the blanket on my knees. "Of course you did."

He looked at me for a second before he said, "Larry de Villiers is a man of action. My dad and my brother are both men of action. Men of action feel themselves responsible for everything under the sun and find it excruciatingly difficult not to take charge and attack all the issues head-on. My mom had to divorce my dad before he understood that she really meant it, that he had to back the fuck off and let her handle her own life. To Larry Zelda's problem *was* his problem. He'd have gone about it the way he'd gone about every other problem in his life, full-tilt and damn the torpedoes. And when he realized it wasn't a problem he could solve, no matter how much he threw himself at it, he still had to do *something*, even if that something was a permanent break he'd always regret.

"I, on the other hand, was a kid. Moira and I had a totally different dynamic—I was never the one expected to make everything all right. In the end, that was what made the difference—that I managed to stand not being in charge of our destiny long enough to have a say again."

He shrugged. "Of course, this would be a better story if Moira and I had actually stayed together until the end. But my point is, we don't know everything that happened back then. Maybe Larry quickly realized he'd made a mistake—but couldn't do anything because, ironically, he was a man of action and he'd already married someone else."

"You are very understanding," I murmured.

"Only because I've made every mistake in the book—and a few more besides." He was looking at me again, in the way he had that made me feel unbearably transparent. "Someday you should tell me what it's like to have never set a foot wrong in your life."

I snorted.

The next moment I gripped his arm. "Moira—I assumed earlier that she'd died from cancer. She—it wasn't anything related to her depression, was it?"

"No. And it wasn't cancer either. She died from double pneumonia."

I expelled a breath and let go of him. "I see."

He seemed as if he wanted to say something more, but after the space of a few heartbeats he glanced down at his watch. "I'd better go take another look at that girl before I start a movie."

I stared for some time at his empty seat before I put on my earphones and selected a movie for myself. But in my mind's eye I kept seeing the photograph Google had found, all those happy people at their cheerful potluck dinner.

The lives of others were like icebergs, largely hidden from view, even for someone standing only a short distance away.

"Is the girl okay?" I asked when Bennett came back.

"Fast asleep," he answered, pressing start on his movie.

"She's lucky you happened along."

He looked at me, surprised. "Thanks."

Just as I was lucky, too, that you happened along.

But I did not say that to him. I resumed my movie and put those words away, along with everything else I never said to anyone.

Chapter 11

THE NEXT AFTERNOON I WAS in the office when my phone trilled. Bennett. My pulse accelerated—he rarely called.

"Hey."

"Hey, Professor. When were you going to tell me you had breakfast with my dad back in Italy?"

Preferably after I'd fully processed everything that had happened over the weekend. In ten years or so.

"Fairly soon," I answered. "He's amenable to getting together in the city. Zelda's birthday is coming up. I haven't had a chance to talk to her yet, but when I do, I'll ask her to invite your parents to her party. That way you'll see each other again on neutral territory."

"Sounds good. So, what did he say? Did he give a reason why he wanted to meet with you?"

"He didn't come out and say it, but he wanted to make sure that I didn't have any grand romantic delusions about you."

"Of all the things he could worry about," Bennett murmured. "And if you did, was he going to set you straight?"

"That's not how I perceived his intentions. Your estrangement came about because of a woman. It makes sense that now that he and you are crossing paths again, he'd want to know what kind of impact he could expect from me.

"I'd take it as a good sign that he wanted to see me alone, to have a better sense of you via our 'relationship.' You do understand it was impossible for him to get a read on you, right?"

He didn't reply.

"Sorry," I said. "Is it too early in the day for putting you in your place?"

He laughed softly. "No, it's all right. Anytime is a good time for that."

Neither of us said anything for a second. I missed him, I realized. And I wasn't used to the sensation that part of me was now somewhere across town—or rather, I wasn't used to feeling like that for anyone who wasn't Zelda.

"Anyway, if you come to Zelda's birthday party as my significant other, that means we're taking our 'relationship' public."

"That's fine with me."

"Well, there's a small wrinkle. Zelda's party is two days after my friends' Annual Boyfriend Roundup. Everybody who has a boyfriend is supposed to bring him to the roundup—or risk getting expelled from the group."

That was me being melodramatic. If they found out, my friends would give me grief, but not kick me off the island—especially since in time they'd learn that he was a fake boyfriend. But I wanted a legitimate-sounding excuse to get together with him again—one that could be considered a natural tangent of our mission.

"So I'll be looked over like a prize hog at a county fair."

"Pretty much. You up for it, Porky?"

"Sure."

I had to give the man credit—even a real boyfriend might have shied away from the roundup. "It's on, then."

"What about Valentine's Day? Want to go for dinner somewhere?"

On a *date*? "Are your parents going to be there?"

"No. But wouldn't it look a bit odd to Zelda if we didn't?"

I struggled with it—the idea of the two of us alone for an entire evening was as formidable as it was pleasurable. "Don't worry about Zelda. I'll make up a plausible enough excuse."

"Well, I can't deny you are really, really good at that."

Was it an accusation? His tone was without a hard edge anywhere, but for some reason I felt an impulse to defend myself. I tamped down that irrational desire. "Make sure you're free for the Boyfriend Roundup and Zelda's birthday party."

"Text me the dates and the times and I'll finagle my schedule."

"I'll do that. Take care."

"You too," he said.

There, a friendly but businesslike good-bye. Exactly as it should be.

I was about to hang up when he asked, "And how are you, by the way? Feeling any better?"

I had never, as far as I remembered, admitted to feeling anything but normal in front of him. And really, was it a fake boyfriend's place to be concerned about my actual well-being?

I'm not better, if you must know. I want you with the kind of covetousness that might bring down plagues. And I'm afraid my fear is getting out of hand. It might be taking over the driver's seat—or maybe it took over a long time ago and I didn't even know. I'm fucked-up, Doctor. All fucked-up.

"A little tired," I replied. "I've been awake since half past three this morning. But other than that, I'm good."

"If you say so, Professor."

Was there a hint of disappointment in his voice? But he had already disconnected. I put the phone back in my purse, sighed, and took a sip from my thermos. Then I stared at the thermos. Zelda and I both had the same one in different colors. I'd bought them and had them engraved with, *Not all those who wander are lost*, a famous line from *The Lord of the Rings*.

The words had been meant as encouragement for Zelda, to let her know that even if her life must take many more twists and turns than she wanted it to, she was still on the right path.

Now, however, I saw the quote in an entirely different light.

Not all those who wander are lost.

But those who never set a foot wrong often were—that was the reason they did and said all the right things, so nobody would realize that they'd lost their bearings long ago.

I WAS YAWNING AS I came out of the train station on 79th—it was past midnight in Italy and I had to stay awake for a few more hours yet. But as I approached my house, some of my sleepiness turned into tension.

Bennett and I had landed late, well past Zelda's bedtime. Because of the time difference, before she got up I was already out of the house, leaving behind a note and a necklace made from squares of cobalt-blue glass that I'd bought for her on Capri. We'd texted each other throughout the day but hadn't talked yet—one might make the argument that I was trying to put off a certain conversation.

Zelda already had coffee waiting when I walked in the door. I hugged her. "What would I do without you?"

The question of my life.

"And to have with your coffee…" Zelda handed me a box of miniature pastries. "From the Somerset boy."

Who had also sent an extravagant arrangement of mango-colored calla lilies. I pulled out the accompanying card. *Thank you for a lovely interlude. I hope for many more.*

So did I, with an intensity that scared me. The Somerset boy was an agent of chaos—like Gandalf, appearing out of nowhere to shove innocent, unsuspecting folks who just wanted to live safe and secure in their nice hobbit holes into messy, dangerous adventures.

"Still not sure about the boy?" asked Zelda.

I realized I was scowling at the card. "It's early days. Anyway, we had an interesting time. Had dinner with his parents. Did Mrs. Somerset tell you about it?"

"Yes. Bennett too."

"You already talked to him?"

"About half an hour ago. To thank him for all the lovely food—he sent dinner also, by the way. Guess what he asked me? Whether I knew where his parents would be staying on the Amalfi Coast when I strenuously recommended La Figlia del Mare to you. Catches on pretty fast, doesn't he?"

"Doesn't he indeed."

"Made me feel like quite a mastermind. Anyway, I invited him to my birthday party and he said he'll try to get that weekend off."

"You'll also invite his parents?"

"Of course. It's for a good cause."

There was a mastermind at work, all right, but it wasn't Zelda. "Looks like you've got their reconciliation well in hand."

"I certainly hope so. But of course there's only so much use to these civilized encounters. Nothing changes when everyone is polite. They have to shout, hurl accusations, and then break down in tears and sob about how empty their lives have been without one another."

She was being melodramatic, but she was right. If Bennett wanted to be part of the family again, at some point he must openly admit that not only did he care, but he cared a hell of a lot.

Somehow I couldn't see him doing that.

I bit into a custard tart that was hardly bigger than a quarter and wondered what to say next. I could tell Zelda more about my trip to Europe, but I'd only be postponing the inevitable.

"By the way, Larry de Villiers called yesterday. He said he invited himself to Mrs. Asquith's place when he heard you'd be there."

The custard tart was stuck in my throat. What had he told Zelda? "I was about to tell you that."

Zelda's tone was tentative. "So I guess you know about us now."

"He gave the CliffsNotes version."

Zelda smoothed the fabric of her long plaid skirt. "You must be wondering why I never told you anything."

"I—I assumed it was because it hurt too much."

"Well, he isn't the easiest subject for me, but it isn't as if I never talk about him. Sometimes Mrs. Asquith will have news about him for me, sometimes one of my cousins, or an old friend who knows both of us."

I carefully folded my hands in my lap. "So it was only me you never told?"

"Only because I didn't want you to think I didn't give my all to my marriage with your father."

"Oh," I said. That had never occurred to me.

"I know I sometimes joke that it was an old-fashioned marriage of convenience—and in a way it was true: He wanted a good mother for you, and I wanted someone who didn't try to fix me. But I did love him. And sometimes, knowing how badly the divorce affected him, I wish we hadn't gone through with it. I thought there was no point sticking it out any longer, since we couldn't make each other happy. Only later did I realize that it wasn't in Hoyt's nature to be happy—he just wanted to not be alone."

My father, the misanthrope who desperately needed companionship.

Or simply the presence of another.

"You shouldn't think like that," I said. "You shouldn't need to be miserable for him to not be alone."

"I know." Zelda tucked a strand of her beautiful grey hair behind her ear. "But he took such good care of me while we were together—I've never met anyone else who was completely unfazed by my problems."

That was Pater. He'd been the worst kind of pessimist—yet at times that pessimism turned into a stoic strength. Since he expected everything to end in tears, Zelda's condition never bothered him.

We were silent for some time, me slowly sipping my coffee, Zelda drinking from her cup of green tea.

"So, Larry de Villiers called," I said in the end, bringing the conversation back to the present.

"He was glad to have met you and Bennett. And we chatted a bit about everything—his children, Mrs. Asquith, my work, his work—just catching up."

Part of me almost wished he'd spilled the beans about my interfering ways. I was used to concealing things from Zelda, but I'd never before kept my mouth shut about something that had a direct impact on her.

I set aside my coffee cup. "If he wanted to get back together with you, would you give him a chance?"

Zelda was nearly twice the age she'd been when she first came into my life. And—I realized with a jolt—it had been a very long time since she'd been in a significant relationship.

Not since her divorce from Pater. A longer drought than mine. Had she not met anyone, or was it also intentional?

"I don't know," answered Zelda, looking sincerely indecisive. "I really don't know."

AROUND EIGHT THIRTY THAT EVENING I was nearly comatose. But after I lay down in bed, the coffee kicked in. I turned one way, then the other, adjusted my pillow several times, peeled off a layer of blanket—but it was no use. I'd become thoroughly awake, the kind accompanied by throbbing temples and a faint ache behind the eyes.

Against the unruliness of Zelda's illness, I'd fought long and hard for stability. But now that stability was under attack from all sides. There was Larry, still carrying a big, bright torch for Zelda after almost three decades. There was Bennett, who asked too many questions and perceived too many answers. Together they threatened to disrupt our quiet, orderly existence.

Together they were the barbarians at the gate.

I pushed my fingers along the ridges of my brows, trying to relieve the tension there. Several soft dings came from the direction of my nightstand. I grabbed my phone, hoping it was Bennett texting me.

It was the Material Girls.

The first text came from Lara, who was this year's hostess for the roundup. *OK, ladies, time to put our cards on the table. I'm bringing a hot, single congressman. He's conservative in his politics, but a freak otherwise. What have you got?*

Pfft, replied Carolyn. *I've got a Pulitzer Prize–winning investigative journalist who just escaped from a Yemeni prison. The stories the man has.*

Daff, of course, was not to be outdone. *I will have you know that my man is a famous Olympic figure skater. A famous gay skater, but I've turned him bisexual.*

Trust my friends to always bring a smile to my face.

I feel really lame, I tapped, *for having bagged only a surgeon. But he's actually a hotshot Silicon Valley investor with a net worth measured in shit-tons of dollars.*

It's going to be great, replied Carolyn. *Filthy-rich doctor can pay for everything, and the skater can make out with the congressfreak while the journalist records it for posterity.*

I chortled. Then I noticed that I had an unread e-mail. It was from Larry de Villiers.

Dear Evangeline,

I reached out to Bennett for your e-mail address—I hope that is all right with you.

As you can probably imagine, our conversation still echoes in my head. I hear bits and pieces of it as I go through the day, and in more complete sections in the silence of the night.

The more I weigh my character and my choices, the more I realize that you are right. By the time Zelda and I parted ways, I had become a man who could see her only in the context of her illness. And in that regard, I have not changed very much in the intervening years, or I would not have put off visiting her the moment I heard that she was unwell.

Thank you for saying those difficult words that needed to be heard.

Yours,
Larry

I set aside the phone and covered my face with my hands. From the moment I'd realized that "those difficult words" had been propelled not by protectiveness but fear and fear alone, I'd been trying to avoid coming to this realization.

But I couldn't deny it anymore.

I too had let Zelda's condition become the defining factor in our relationship. I too thought of it first and foremost. The only difference was that instead of running away, I hovered ever closer to her. Instead of cutting my losses, I doubled down and went all in.

I fell asleep dreaming of myself standing alone in Mrs. Asquith's garden, my hand on the sundial, the cold seeping in endlessly.

Chapter 12

THE MORNING OF THE ROUNDUP I remembered that when the Material Girls first inaugurated the event, we'd declared it a black-tie affair—because why the hell not.

If you have a tux, wear it tonight, I texted Bennett. *It's black-tie.*

Hours later—he usually replied to my texts right away, except when he was in surgery—his response came. *OK.*

Late in the afternoon a flurry of texts landed on my phone. Daff, in charge of the restaurant at a venerable Upper East Side hotel, rarely had Friday nights off—practically the only time she allowed herself such an indulgence was for the Boyfriend Roundup. But two of her chefs were out sick and she had to work the dinner shift.

Instead of rescheduling the whole thing, we decided to move the roundup from Brooklyn to the lounge of a hotel around the corner from Daff's, and push back the time to ten thirty in the evening.

I arrived at the hotel in a gown of ivory crepe. Bennett, in a three-piece tux, was already waiting in the lobby. Both the man and the woman behind the registration counter had their eyes fastened to him.

"You've been waiting to bust that outfit out, haven't you?" I said as greeting.

He put away his phone. "This old thing? It's what I wear to fix stuff around the apartment."

In lieu of a bow tie, he'd worn his shirt open at the collar, over a silver-grey ascot scarf. I touched the cool silk of the scarf. "Nice."

He didn't say anything, but only looked at me. I flushed, wondering whether my face had betrayed me again by appearing pornographically turned on. "Come on. We're meeting in the bar."

He took my hand and leaned close. "You look beautiful, as always."

I did my best to ignore the heat that propagated through me. "Have I told you that you might be the only man present?"

"No."

"Have I told you that nobody is expecting you?"

He laughed softly. "This is beginning to sound fun."

The lounge was an old-fashioned space, with golden-hued murals and curved armchairs clustered near small round tables. I spotted Carolyn and Lara at a table against the back wall, chatting animatedly, Lara in a backless lavender number and Carolyn, the most fashion-forward of us all, in a stunning gown in midnight blue, sprinkled with golden stars.

As Bennett and I approached, my friends looked up, only to blink in confusion and then outright incredulity.

"Wait a minute, what's a man doing here?" asked Carolyn.

"I said I was bringing one," I answered.

"You always say you're bringing one," said Lara indignantly. "Last year you said you were bringing a vineyard owner from upstate, and a world-famous whistle-blower the year before."

"No, that was me," said Carolyn. "The year before E was going to bring a superstar furniture restorer."

"Well, anyway, you can't sit down," Lara told Bennett. "This whole thing is just a cover for us soon-to-be hags to bemoan how hard it is to find a man in New York—and to indulge in some hot girl-on-girl action while we're at it. You're going to spoil our game plan."

Bennett smiled and pulled out a seat for me. "You must be Lara. And you, Carolyn. Nice to meet you both."

Carolyn's parents were Chinese, and Lara was half-Ethiopian, half-Russian—they weren't difficult to tell apart.

"I managed to find a man with functioning eyes," I said. "Aren't you guys proud of me?"

Bennett sat down between Lara and me. "*I* am proud of you, sweetheart. But how come you've never told me you were such an earthy type? I didn't know you were into vintners and artisans."

Until he'd mentioned it I hadn't realized the influence of the Vermont farmer on my selection of fantasy boyfriends. I looked him over—no, still no trace.

Daff, our resident redhead, rushed up in a slinky green sequined dress, still putting on her dangle earrings. "Lara, you sneak. You did get lucky at the wedding, and you didn't even say anything about it."

"I didn't bring him," said Lara.

Daff turned to Carolyn. "Did your parents finally get off their asses and fix you up?"

"No, they're still very much on their asses and ignoring my sell-by date like it's the Mayan apocalypse."

Daff scanned the scrumptious man who had taken the trouble to come in black-tie, even if he'd done away with the literal black tie. "Did you wander in off the street and sit down at a table full of beautiful women?"

"No," said Bennett, glancing at me with a cheeky smile. "I was bribed with hours and hours of sex."

Daff's eyes bulged. "Seriously, E. *You* brought this one?"

I shrugged. "I went out to the wilds of Manhattan and bagged him all by myself."

My fake boyfriend extended his hand. "I'm Bennett. Nice to meet you, Davina."

Daff shook his hand, still goggle-eyed. She pulled up a chair and squeezed in next to Carolyn. Carolyn draped an arm over her. "I know what you're thinking, Daff. He's an escort E hired for the evening."

"Right?" said Lara. "Evangeline, we thought you donated your vagina to science ages ago."

"That's how I first saw her vagina," said Bennett. "I was still in medical school, on the West Coast. And her vagina was so unforgettable that I tracked her down across the country—and here I am."

I decided I might as well go along for the ride. "It's true. And if a man shows up at your door, saying, 'Hi, Dr. Canterbury, I've brought your vagina back,' it's only polite to invite him in and have him help you test out whether said vagina still works after all these years."

Lara all but spit her drink into her napkin. Daff and Carolyn leaned on each other, cracking up.

A server came by and took orders from the latecomers; then Carolyn was all business. "Lara, did you bring the questionnaire? We have to put him through the questionnaire."

"Oh, yes," seconded Daff. "Release the questionnaire."

"What is this Kraken of a questionnaire?" asked Bennett.

Carolyn cackled. "Ask your girlfriend. It was her brainchild."

Last year, at our usual all-female Boyfriend Roundup, I'd not only suggested that we come up with a list of questions with which to torment our eventual victim, but contributed a large share. It seemed a foregone conclusion that somebody would reel in a sucker someday; I'd just never imagined I'd be that someone.

In fact, I'd forgotten about the questionnaire altogether.

As had everyone else, apparently. Nobody could even remember what we'd done with the questions we'd come up with. I breathed a sigh of relief—from what I could vaguely recall, some of those questions had been highly personal.

"Yes!" cried Carolyn triumphantly. "I knew I had it. I typed it into this list-making app on my phone and it's still there."

I pulled a face.

"Now I see what I'm in for," murmured Bennett.

Carolyn literally rubbed her hands together before she picked up her phone again. "Okay, here goes. What's your full name?"

"Bennett Oliver Stuart Somerset."

"What do you do for a living?"

"I'm a cardiothoracic surgeon."

"Where were you born?"

"Ten blocks from here."

Phew. Maybe I'd misremembered. The questions were all right.

"How old were you when you lost your virginity?"

Nope, not mistaken after all.

"Sixteen."

"What's the most number of times you've had sex in a twenty-four-hour period?"

Oh, God. That was one of my questions.

"Seven."

"Jesus," said Daff.

"There might have been some kind of drug cocktail involved," Bennett told her gleefully. "And multiple women."

And a yacht in Saint-Tropez, no doubt.

For some reason, all the women around the table stared at me as if I were responsible for Bennett's excessive fucking.

"Come on," I said. "Did you really think the ultimate good girl would hook up with someone who wasn't a freak?"

Daff accepted her drink from the server. "I guess there's that."

"Okay, back to the questionnaire," ordered Carolyn. "What do you think of anal sex?"

Daff promptly choked on the first sip of her drink: The question had been one of her contributions.

"Depends on the anus," said Bennett.

"Good answer," said Carolyn. "Have you ever been married?"

"No."

"Incarcerated?"

"No."

"Are you paying for all our drinks tonight?"

"Yes."

"Are you rich?"

"Yes."

"How rich?" asked Daff. "When Evangeline's done with you, can I use you for a sugar daddy?"

"Sorry, Daff, that's not on the questionnaire," decreed Carolyn. "Now, Bennett, have you performed oral sex on our Evangeline?"

"Yes."

"Has she returned the favor?"

"No."

"Make the boy work, E," said Lara. "Good for you."

I could probably fry an egg on my face. "That's right, grasshopper. Watch and learn."

Carolyn continued. "What is Evangeline's favorite position?"

Hoist on the petard of another one of my questions.

"She likes them all."

This had Daff whistling. "Oh, E. We never knew ya."

"Sorry for being undiscriminating," I said.

Bennett touched a strand of my hair. "It's okay, sweetheart. I like you horny."

Carolyn and Lara hooted. Daff shook her head. "Wow, so you really are having sex again, E. Blows my mind."

"Okay." Carolyn resumed her most brisk tone. "We're almost done with the questionnaire. Bennett, where did you first meet Evangeline?"

"At a sex party in Greenwich Village."

What the hell? "That is not true!" I protested.

He had a dirty gleam in his eyes. "Prove it. Next question."

"When did you fall in love with her?"

"It was love at first sight."

"Wait," said Lara. "First sight of her vagina at medical school, or first sight of her in person?"

"In person."

"At the sex party?"

"Central Park. Last June. We wouldn't meet at the sex party for another seven weeks."

It was just like him to mix together enough likely-seeming tidbits with complete nonsense, so that I couldn't tell how much was truth and how much bullshit.

"The penultimate question: Do you have your engagement ring all picked out?"

Another one of my inane contributions.

"Yes."

"Last one: When's the wedding?"

"August."

"Why August?" asked Lara.

"'Cause she'll have passed tenure review and I'll have finished with my fellowship. And we can have a nice long honeymoon before her schedule goes crazy again in September."

I eyed him up and down. "Talk about perfect timing."

He rubbed my arm through my sleeve. "Didn't I say I'll take care of everything, sweetheart?"

"Okay, lovebirds, flirt on your own time," said Carolyn. "Now we have to tally up the score."

There were scores?

"What kind of scores can a man get around here?" asked Bennett, vastly amused.

I had to give it to him: He was game and unflappable. A pretty high bar had been set for future victims of the Annual Boyfriend Roundup.

"Well, it starts at 'He's just using you.' And then there's 'Okay, but not great.' After that, it's 'I'd bang him too.' Above that, 'A real keeper.' And if you score any higher than that—"

"It's been a while. I can't remember everything," said Daff. "You can score higher than 'A real keeper'?"

"Uh-hmm." Carolyn looked straight at my fake boyfriend. "You scored higher than a hundred percent. According to our scoring table, that means you're an actor from an off-Broadway show, and this is a gig for you."

BENNETT WAS WASTED IN MEDICINE: No actor from a show, off-Broadway or on, could have played a better boyfriend. My friends clearly found him something of a unicorn, but he was a fun unicorn, and two hours passed in no time at all as we chatted and laughed.

"So what color bridesmaid dresses for your wedding, E?" asked a tipsy Carolyn from the back of the cab. "I have—I shit you not—thirteen of them, and they cover the entire visible light spectrum."

"We're doing a hipster ugly-bridesmaid-dress wedding," said Bennett. "Come in the one you hate the most."

"Oh, God. I hate all of mine," muttered Daff, who was drunker.

"Another delivery run for you," I said to Lara, always the still-sober one at the end of the night.

She blew me a kiss. "I'll get them home."

As their cab drove away, I turned to Bennett. "A Greenwich Village sex party? Really?"

He was unrepentant. "Better than 'I found her wandering the back lanes of Cos Cob and promptly took advantage of her.'"

Our cab pulled up. We got in. Bennett told the driver, "Park and Seventy-third."

A frisson of excitement shot through me. "Why are we going to your place?"

"Ten minutes ago you said you were hungry. I have ravioli."

The garish blue-green light from the TV screen installed between the two front seats shouldn't have been flattering on anyone, yet the contours of his face were as beautifully lit as if a photographer's assistant had been holding a reflector a few feet away. "I can have a snack at home."

"But I don't want you to go home yet."

It was warm in the cab. He pulled off his ascot and my eyes were immediately riveted to that small vee of skin exposed by the opening of his shirt. "Then why didn't you say so?"

"What kind of straight shooter do you take me for? Someone as skittish as you needs to be manipulated into my apartment."

I looked back up at him, half smiling and all predatory. *I think I may safely call him a shark, your son.* Now the shark was circling me. By habit I clung to my raft—but a part of me, maybe most of me, longed to be devoured. "How are you going to do that? I could easily have this cab let you out and then drive me to my house."

He leaned a little closer. "Would you like to see the engagement ring I picked out?"

Had I been dropped on my head, I couldn't have been more stunned. "Wh-what? *Why?*"

"I'll tell you if you come up."

It's a trap, shouted Admiral Ackbar from *Star Wars.*

It's bullshit, said my common sense.

Who gives a fuck? countered the woman who couldn't wait for the shark to drag her into the waves.

When I didn't answer, Bennett took my hand in his and traced a fingertip along the edge of my palm. I bit a corner of my lip, embarrassed by the heat that speared into the crook of my elbow. He grazed the pad of his thumb across the back of my hand. Inside my high heels, my toes curled.

The urban canyon that was Park Avenue became quieter and emptier as we drove north. Our reflections were visible in the window of the cab, a man and a woman ostensibly behaving themselves: He looked down with the concentration of someone staring at his phone; my eyes appeared glazed, as if I already felt the lateness of the hour.

Except I was anything but weary. My heart drummed. My nerves sizzled. I had to count so my breaths wouldn't come in too quick, too shallow. Bennett's touch roamed along the lines of my palm, slowly climbing toward the tip of my index finger.

The next thing I knew, his palm had cut into the vee between my index and middle fingers. I almost gasped at the suddenness and, well, invasiveness of the gesture.

Did he hear my sharp, indrawn breath? Could he feel the tremors beneath my skin?

As soon as we were in his private elevator, before the doors had even closed, we were already kissing. At the top we stumbled out. Somehow he managed to get us up a flight of stairs to his bedroom.

He stripped off my coat. My clutch fell with a thump. Still kissing me, he pushed me down onto his bed. The impact of our bodies pressed together, shoulders to knees, made us both emit beastly sounds.

He pulled my dress over my head and made quick work of my bra. His teeth sank into my shoulder, the flood of sensation swift and fierce. I gasped.

"You are so fucking hot, Eva," he whispered in my ear. "Last time I got home from work I had to get myself off twice before I could go to sleep—I kept imagining you in my bed and kept getting these raging erections."

The words were as great a turn-on as his touches. Greater—when we were apart again it would be the words echoing in my head, an audible arousal.

I pushed his tuxedo jacket off his shoulders and kissed him below his jawline, an openmouthed nibble that had his hand tighten on my arm.

"You know what I want?" His voice turned raspy. "I want to fuck you before I go to work. And I want to fuck you right after I come back home."

I might have ripped apart his vest. I definitely heard shirt studs pinging into the headboard. *Keep talking. Keep telling me how much you want me.*

And don't ever stop.

"I want to see you naked against a wall again. I want to see the way you look at me. You have such hungry eyes."

I quaked—I didn't want to hear about my all-too-visible yearnings. I kissed him, every inch of skin I could reach, as my hand slipped into his waistband and wrapped around him.

He discarded the rest of his clothes and peeled off my panties. We were now skin-to-skin everywhere. He kissed me, deeply, thoroughly. I whimpered in the back of my throat—the kiss was as erotic as anything he had ever done to me.

"When I have to take care of myself I imagine all the things I'd do to you," he murmured against my lips. "And I think of all the sounds you'd make, from that first catch of your breath, to your screams when you come."

I didn't know how much more I could take. This was getting too intimate, and I was again feeling all too transparent. I closed my eyes and plunged my fingers into his hair. "Why don't you make me scream again? Do it. Fuck me balls-deep."

It was his turn to breathe harshly.

I nipped his shoulder, as he had done with mine. "You know I like it—every position, everything you do to me."

His response was a low growl of such arousal that my own already tattered breath grew even more agitated. He pushed off me. I thought he was getting the condom, but he only repositioned himself to go down on me.

I didn't want it. I didn't want to be the only one undone, the only one moaning and thrashing with pleasure. I begged him to fuck me. But he didn't, not until I'd come several times. Only then did he bury himself in me, making me whimper and tremble.

He bit my earlobe. "Do you know what I *really* want?"

"What?" I gasped.

"I want to fuck you bareback. Every inch of me, feeling every inch of you."

Damn him. Those words made me peak again—violently. At least he joined me this time, his orgasm equally untrammeled.

SO THIS WAS WHAT IT was like to be in bed with him, I thought when I could think again. This was what it was like when the shark had had his way with me.

He stroked my hair. We were on our sides, facing each other, and I had the unsettling sensation that though his face was nearly invisible—the windows were behind him—perhaps he was seeing mine all too clearly.

"Where's my engagement ring?" My voice held a hint of disapproval, like that of a teacher speaking to a student who couldn't produce his homework at the beginning of class.

"Give me a sec," he said, his words drowsy. "You melted my spine and I can't get out of bed right now."

"There is no ring, is there? You tricked me into coming here."

"Would I lie to you?" he mumbled. "Two minutes."

Half a minute later he was already asleep.

BENNETT'S APARTMENT, LIKE HIS COUNTRY house, was spare and elegant. Uncluttered. Zelda and I weren't hoarders, exactly, but we had bulging shelves in every room and walls full of framed photographs.

His homes, on the other hand, offered little glimpse into his personal life. The black-and-white botanical prints I passed as I came down the stairs had probably been selected by an interior designer, as well as the candelabra on top of the fireplace, its curves chrome and minimalist.

The opacity of the apartment echoed the opacity of its owner, of whom I knew so much and yet so little.

I sat down on the arm of a padded chair in the living room, feeling alone. The fault was my own: I'd always been anxious to distance myself from him after fantastic sex, for fear that if I didn't, I'd become too involved for my own good.

But I'd crossed that line long ago, hadn't I? Still, I'd slipped out like a thief in the night, instead of staying where I was. Where I wanted to be, warmly ensconced in that illusion of intimacy.

The stair light came on. Bennett descended in a white T-shirt and a pair of blue-and-grey-plaid lounge pants. "There you are. For a moment I thought you'd absconded. Are you still hungry?"

The way he filled out the T-shirt. The way the loose lounge pants hung from his narrow hips. The way he stood, his hand on the newel post at the bottom of the steps, his head cocked slightly, the expression on his face halfway between contemplation and inquisitiveness.

Yes, I'm still hungry. For you.

I rubbed the sole of my bare foot against the rug beneath the chair. "Does anyone become less hungry with time?"

He switched on the lights of the living room, then crossed over to the kitchen. I heard him turn on the tap and fill a pot. "What were you doing, sitting there in the dark?"

Thinking about you. And about what's the matter with me. "I thought you fell asleep."

There came the soft but unmistakable whoosh of a gas stove being lit. "Please. Give a doctor on his one hundred and fiftieth year of training some credit for being able to wake up in two minutes when he's promised to do so."

He came back into the living room and kissed me on my hair. "It's very, very nice to make love to you, but exhausting it isn't."

"Clearly I'm doing something wrong."

"You're not doing me enough—that's what you're doing wrong. You should keep at it until you break me."

I exhaled slowly. He really, really knew how to turn me on with words. "So, how long will it take for the ravioli to be ready?"

"After the water boils, a few minutes," he answered, sitting down on the other arm of the chair.

"That'll work."

He leaned in toward me. I was instantly nervous, afraid that he might kiss me. So I reached out and set my fingertip against his pendant, which happened to be outside the T-shirt. "I'm curious. Is there a story behind this?"

He glanced down for a moment. "Imogene bought it for me when our parents took us to Maui. I used to wear it all the time, including during my time in Spain."

The thought had never crossed my mind before, but suddenly I had the urge to see old photos of him, albums upon albums, both analog and digital.

"My parents found out about Moira toward the end of that semester.

They brought me back home. It was a bad summer, and it got even worse when they discovered that Moira had also come to the city and we were seeing each other behind their backs.

"I stopped talking to my parents. When they sent Imogene in their stead, I basically told her that she had to choose sides, and that if she wasn't on my side then I had nothing else to say to her either. Ever. She sat on the edge of my bed for a long time and then got up and walked out."

He stopped for a few seconds. "When I was shipped off to England, I left the pendant behind. But four years ago it came in the mail, along with a phone number—Imogene had moved to Silicon Valley. We met for lunch that weekend. After that, it was like I told you—we saw each other every week. And once that happened I met my brother too, the next time he stopped on the West Coast."

"And you started wearing the pendant again?"

"No, not yet. At the time it was just a sentimental relic—I put it in my nightstand drawer and went on with my residency. When we got together I never asked Imogene about our parents, and she didn't really bring them up. But inevitably they were mentioned in passing. That way I learned bits and pieces of what they'd been doing.

"Fourteen months ago I attended a medical conference in Chicago."

I remembered he'd told me that in all the years of their estrangement, he'd seen his parents only once, at O'Hare airport.

Something beeped in the kitchen. He stood up. "That's the timer for the water."

Without thinking I followed him into the kitchen. "And?"

"I was about to board when I saw them walking down the concourse. It had been thirteen years since our last meeting…." He gently swept the ravioli into the pot and set the timer again. "You know how you get used to living one way and you keep going? Because you're used to it. Because that's the way things have been for a long, long time."

Oh, did I ever know it.

"It was like that for me," he went on. "I'd been an orphan, essentially, and I'd become okay with it. Even when the topic of my parents came up with my siblings, even when they headed home for the holidays and I didn't, that was just how it was.

"But then, fifteen feet from me, my parents stopped to look at flight information. My mom said something to my dad, he smiled at her, reached over, and tapped three times on the face of her watch. That's their code for 'I love you.' They did that a lot in cars. When we were little, Imogene and I used to tease them mercilessly for it. Sometimes we'd belch together as soon as one of them did the watch tapping. Sometimes we'd shout, 'Who farted?' Prescott would try to stop himself from laughing, but he never really could. So my parents' romantic moment always devolved into this fiasco of stupid kids giggling and elbowing one another in the back of the car.

"The thing was, they never minded. I mean, sometimes my dad would mutter darkly. But then he'd glance at us in the rearview mirror, and he always looked…grateful."

Bennett took out a couple of pasta bowls and set them on the counter. Slowly, he traced a finger along the brim of a bowl. There was nothing particularly revealing in his expression, but something about the motion of his hand, the seemingly casual movement contrasted with the tension in his wrist…

I'd seen him frustrated at our lack of progress with regard to his father. Now I knew that I'd only seen the bare minimum of his reaction.

Now I knew that he'd kept a gnawing doubt—and any and all despair—to himself. Even I, his partner, wasn't to know.

Or perhaps I, his partner, particularly.

"It felt as if I stood forever that day looking at them," he went on, "when it was probably no more than a minute or so before they walked off. But everything changed. I wasn't an orphan. I had parents. And I wanted to go home—badly. As soon as I landed that day, I began looking into how I could transfer to a hospital here. It took some time to arrange, but by last May I was packing up my belongings.

"And when I did that, I came across the pendant and remembered that vacation. It was our last good vacation as a family—we were pretty happy with one another and glad to be somewhere fun and beautiful together. I put it on as a good-luck charm and haven't taken it off since."

He looked at me and smiled. "Sorry for the rambling answer."

Something in the wistfulness of his expression broke me. All at once I felt a fierce need to hold him in my arms—so much it hurt. So much I was dizzy on my feet.

"You all right?" he asked, concern in his voice.

I was not all right. I was desperately in love. More than I had thought I would be. More than I even understood to be possible.

I reached out and turned off the burner.

"The ravioli might need a few more—"

I silenced him with a kiss, a wild one. He took my face in his hands and kissed me back just as ferociously. We somehow crossed over to the living room, shedding clothes as we went.

I pushed him down onto the chaise and climbed on top of him. "It's two days before my period. If you tell me you're clean, then you don't need a condom."

His grunt of pure arousal made me shiver. "I'm clean."

I kissed him again and took him inside me, every inch of me feeling every inch of him. Such sensations—such hot, reckless pleasure.

He gripped the back of the chaise, his teeth gritted. "God, Eva."

I braced my hands on his shoulders. "This is what you want, isn't it? To fuck me bareback?"

For a minute only the sounds of our heavy, ungovernable breaths filled the air as my hips lifted and lowered, merging with him again and again.

Then he wrapped his arms around me and brought me close to him. "Yes, this is what I've always wanted, to make love to you with nothing between us."

And I was lost.

We were both lost.

Chapter 13

BENNETT WRAPPED ME IN A bathrobe and carried me upstairs to his tub, which was huge and deep, perfect for two. He didn't join me inside, but used the shower instead. And that was fine, because I needed a moment to myself.

I needed days, perhaps weeks, to recover from the shock of not only finding myself in love, but to such a disastrous degree. And why must it be with a complicated man, one whose heart was as tightly guarded as Fort Knox?

When Bennett came out of the shower, I closed my eyes, pretending to be half-asleep. He kissed me on the tip of my nose. "I brought a few things here that you can wear."

Then his footsteps descended the stairs—and my heart felt as if it were dragged behind him, bruising against every single step on the way down.

It was another quarter of an hour before I could leave the relative safety of the tub and put on a set of his flannel pajamas.

At the top of the stairs, I met him coming back up. "Late-night snack is ready, if you still want one," he said cheerfully.

Offer me your undying love; then maybe I'll think about dinner. "Smells nice, but it doesn't smell like ravioli."

"Ravioli got too soggy and bloated. I made grilled cheese sandwiches."

"Yum," I said mechanically.

But the sandwiches turned out to be scrumptious, the cheese inside hot and gooey, the bread gloriously butter-soaked.

I sighed as I finished my last bite. "So how long have you been a vegetarian?"

"Since I was nine. I read *Charlotte's Web* and that was it for me."

"Hmm, when I was nine, I watched *Babe* and stayed away from pork for all of one week before I scarfed down a slice of pepperoni pizza."

He smiled, a gorgeous man in a great mood. I didn't quite return his smile—hard to do that when I could scarcely breathe from falling hard and fast into that eventual abyss.

His expression turned more solemn. He touched the back of his hand to my cheek. "I bolted upright in bed earlier when I thought you'd escaped my evil clutches."

"You should have more confidence in them."

"Usually I do." He took our plates to the sink. "By the way, speaking of evil clutches, I already told Zelda you're staying the night."

A horde of thoughts stampeded across my mind, from, *Can I handle having sex seven times in twenty-four hours?* to, *Does this mean anything other than that we'll be having sex again in the morning?* "Don't tell me Zelda immediately sent over a change of underpants and my toothbrush."

"She offered to. But I already have spare brush heads for my toothbrush and a change of underpants for you."

"What?"

He turned around, braced a hand on the countertop, and grinned. "Hey, I'm a regular, hot-blooded male. I bought my fake girlfriend lingerie for Valentine's Day. Except she refused to go out with me, so the lingerie is still in a gift bag somewhere."

Was it wrong that I really wanted to see the lingerie he'd chosen? "I can't go home in the morning in an evening gown. Everybody will know I'm doing the walk of shame."

"As long as you aren't leaving at the crack of dawn, I can have some clothes delivered for you. So go ahead and sleep in."

With him? Lying side by side…all night? "I don't know if I can sleep in a strange place."

"We don't have to sleep right away. We can stream a movie. But the only TV that's set up for streaming is in my bedroom, so you'll have to come there for now."

"Okay," I said, still feeling uncertain, but resigning myself to the fact that I didn't have enough willpower to actually leave. "I guess we can watch a movie."

Even though it was getting ridiculously late.

I brushed my teeth. We pulled the curtains shut, tossed a few more pillows onto his bed, and started an action flick that promised to be entertaining and not terribly demanding. But less than ten minutes into the movie, I'd already stopped paying attention to what was happening on the screen.

Bennett nuzzled my neck, raining little drop kisses that turned into dangerous bursts of heat deep in my abdomen.

"You'll miss the next set piece," I told him.

"What a tragedy."

"Is this really the only TV that streams?"

"Of course not," he murmured.

And turned my face to kiss me, a leisurely kiss that led to another. And then another. He kissed my throat and opened the buttons on my pajama shirt. "I love how you look in these pajamas."

"Is that why you don't want to see me in them anymore?"

"Exactly. Everything you look great in must be stripped off."

Unhurriedly he kissed me everywhere. Without any haste he entered me. We kissed, our bodies joined, and went on kissing, until slow-simmering pleasures again more turned needy and frantic.

"I love the taste of your lips," he whispered in my ear. "I love the texture of your skin. I love the sound of your breaths. "

And then: "I love everything about…about this moment."

The orgasm that ensued was the most intense one yet.

AFTERWARD BENNETT CLICKED OFF THE TV and wrapped an arm around me. I snuggled closer to him, warm in his embrace.

Was this the illusion of intimacy I'd wanted?

"In *Henry V*, King Henry says to Kate, 'You have witchcraft in your lips,'" Bennett murmured sleepily. "Do you know where you have witchcraft, Eva?"

"Do tell," I answered archly, expecting him to heap praise on my private parts.

He pressed a kiss into my shoulder. "In your eyes."

What a dirty, rotten thing to say to your fake girlfriend, who'd have to carry around the memory for the rest of her life, wishing she could hear it again.

Everything he said about us always had that glossy patina of plausible deniability—compliments and declarations that were extravagant but ultimately insubstantial.

And I loved and hated them as Gollum loved and hated his precious.

Bennett's breath slowed to the deep, quiet rhythm of sleep, while I stared into the darkness, beset with an angst I'd come to know all too well, exactly the kind of turmoil I'd hoped to avoid by refusing him again and again.

Why couldn't he stick to business? I could handle business. I could even handle an occasional bout of frenetic coupling. But I was powerless before anything that lent itself to interpretations of deeper feelings on his part. *It was love at first sight. You are the best thing to happen to me in a long, long time. Yes, this is what I've always wanted, to make love to you with nothing between us.*

When he spoke like that, hope pierced me like arrows—and hurt almost as much. Because I wanted so much to believe every word, every sentiment, plausible deniability be damned. I wanted to forget that we were essentially onstage and focus only on his eyes, his voice, and those words of deeply felt avowal.

Don't fantasize, Eva, came my sensible-grown-woman voice. *You must look at the facts. You must—*

Forget lightbulbs turning on. No, this was every massive star in the sky going supernova at once: a blinding blaze of insight.

I was a scientist, a pretty damn good one too. A core principle of science was that the hypothesis must fit the facts: One didn't bend, ignore, or dismiss facts to suit one's hypothesis.

All along, I'd postulated that Bennett was using me for other goals. At the beginning my hypothesis made sense—he'd stated as much. But now I had many more facts at my fingertips, and...and...

I was almost afraid to think it. But if I looked at the entire picture objectively, it was much more likely that I wasn't simply a means to an end. I was an end in and of myself.

Take the time line. What had Damaris Vandermeer told me at Charlotte's wedding? *He went out with my friend a few times last summer and then dumped her like a bag of cement.* I'd put money on it that the friend was, on paper at least, perfect girlfriend material, with a strong connection to the Somerset family. Bennett hadn't gone out with her merely for fun, but to investigate her potential as a partner in his quest for reconciliation.

But then that had gone no further. Why? Because I came into the picture at the end of summer. Because our one-night stand—hell, our one-hour stand—had been as memorable for him as it was for me.

He reconsidered his strategy and started laying the groundwork for the professor. Had we not run into each other the day after Christmas, he'd still have made sure we met again via the new ties he'd cultivated with Zelda.

From that point on, it had been quite the pursuit. The million-dollar carrot aside, his parents aside, what had he been trying to do? To get me to spend as much time with him as possible. He didn't need to get to Amalfi Coast a day ahead of his parents. He didn't need to ask me out for Valentine's Day. He didn't need to scheme for me to spend the night.

He wanted to.

Only minutes ago, when he'd said, *I love everything about…about this moment,* that was him barely restraining himself from saying *I love everything about you.*

As for why he never told the truth except with a varnish of plausible deniability…It wasn't to play games with me, but to protect himself. I was a begrudging lover. I turned him down constantly. And I was almost always trying to put greater distance between us. If I were a man who had been badly burned in love, I'd approach me with the same kind of cautiousness.

In fact, I'd swerve wide to avoid me altogether. But that was neither here nor there.

My elegant new hypothesis thrilled and scared me in equal measure. If it was true—and I had a tremendous intuition that it was—then it changed everything. The man I loved didn't just return my feelings; he was crazy in love with me.

I took his hand and laid it over my heart. Could he feel it beating with astonished glee? Lacing our fingers together, I luxuriated in his closeness and smiled hugely.

It was a whole new world.

I WOKE UP TO THE aroma of fresh coffee brewing. A greyish light filtered in from the edges of the curtains—an overcast day outside. My dress and my underthings, last seen on the floor of the living room, had been neatly gathered in a chair, next to the lingerie Bennett had bought me for Valentine's Day.

No crotchless panties in the bag. He did get completely impractical items—I might have whistled softly at a set of transparent bras and panties—but there were also pieces that were both pretty and wearable.

As I put his pajamas back on over the see-through set—why not?—I studied the room. Above the fireplace hung a Pissarro, possibly the one he had mentioned to my father years ago. But otherwise it was empty of personal touches. The rumpled bedspread and his vintage Patek Philippe watch on the nightstand were the only signs that he'd slept here.

But whereas earlier I'd have felt an unhappy weight that I'd fallen in love with a man who didn't betray himself even in his own home, now I was…reassured. After all, my house, despite its coziness, was just as opaque in its own way: There was nothing of my mother. The stacks of photographs that she had sent me, the ones I used to pore over, had all been banished to the attic, denied a place among the pictures and memorabilia that constituted a visual record of my life.

A real relationship was beyond me. But in a fake one with a completely enamored Bennett, I had a chance. And the more opaque he remained, the more protective he was of himself, the more likely that we would continue exactly as we were: fun dates with my friends, sleepovers, and everything else that was desirable in a relationship without requiring either of us to open up.

I bounced down the stairs. Bennett was in the kitchen, hair still mussed from sleep, flipping pancakes in a San Francisco Marathon T-shirt that had a hole on the right shoulder. My heart tugged—he was unbearably appealing in his domesticity.

"I thought your culinary repertoire was limited to grilled cheese sandwiches," I said, leaning a hip against the kitchen counter and mentally adding "yummy breakfast" to the list of pluses that characterized our current arrangement.

"And you thought wrong. Until I turned twenty-one and came into those paintings I could auction off, Moira and I were pretty much broke. So the boy toy cooked."

Spatula in hand, he kissed me on the lips. We were practically a Norman Rockwell couple on this lazy Saturday morning, weren't we?

He returned to the stove and cracked eggs into a different pan. The sizzle of protein joined the aroma of buttery carbs. I tried to recall whether my real boyfriends had ever made me breakfast—only to realize that I'd never spent the night with anyone. That I'd always been the girl who went home by herself, no matter how late the hour.

"Speaking of Moira, isn't that MoMA retrospective of hers starting this weekend?" Instead of sour grapes, I was feeling a lot of goodwill toward Moira—without her, there wouldn't be this perfect fake relationship. "Have you been worrying about your naked pictures?"

"I've made my peace with the fact that there are going to be some. I'll just say I occasionally modeled for her when I was her tenant."

He plated the eggs and the pancakes and carried them out to the breakfast nook, with its big bay window facing the balcony. That was when I realized it was snowing outside—and had been for hours. A good four inches of powder blanketed the parapet. The potted evergreens along the balustrade too were covered in snow. The windows across the streets were lit from within by a soft, golden light—the whole scene looking like something out of an old-fashioned Christmas card.

"So much for a walk in the park for us," said Bennett, following my line of sight. "Do you have any plans today?"

Was he about to offer further proof to buttress my new hypothesis? "My grad students are out of town this weekend, so I have to go into the lab this evening."

Bennett returned to the kitchen to pour coffee into two cups. "That means you're free during the day. What do you say we actually watch that movie from last night and then go to Chinatown for lunch?"

Ding! Breakfast made from scratch, movie, and lunch in Chinatown—if this wasn't love, then I didn't know diamonds from graphite.

I pretended to think, cutting my stack of pancake into neat pieces. "Well, you've found my weakness—I can't say no to Chinatown."

"Me neither, as it happens," he said cheerfully, passing me the butter dish and a small cruet of maple syrup.

I looked at him a moment too long before putting a forkful of pancakes into my mouth. "These are good."

The banana-and-pecan pancakes were more than good: warm, moist, fluffy, the sweetness of mashed banana perfectly balanced by the subtle tang of buttermilk. With the addition of butter and maple syrup they were practically breakfast heaven.

"Before I went into construction, I was a short-order cook at a twenty-four-hour diner for a few months."

"Tough work."

"It was. But I was thrilled to find out that I could handle it. Up to that point in my life, someone else had always footed the bill. Bringing home a check made me feel like a man."

"Did you feel like a hundred times the man when the millions started rolling in?"

"You'd think, but I treasured my grease-smudged checks more. That was an honest exchange of labor for remuneration; the investment income felt like Monopoly money. Especially since I wasn't even that good an investor."

"You made a twenty-fold return on your original investment. No need to be modest."

"I'm not modest. I put half the money I cleared from the auction into start-ups my financial advisers recommended. The other half I put in random ones—like, pulling-names-out-of-a-hat kind of random—because I wanted to see whether my advisers would get me better returns than a dart-throwing monkey.

"And guess what? Seven of the nine companies that later sold for big bucks were out of the control group. So when I say I'm no Warren Buffett, I'm not being self-effacing; I was literally the dart-throwing monkey. Not exactly the sort of accomplishment to make me feel like

I'm swinging a twelve-inch dick."

"You aren't?" I said, my eyes very wide.

He laughed—and maybe blushed a little. Then he leaned forward. "You know what does make me feel like ten times the man?"

I rubbed the pad of my thumb against his stubble. "What?"

"When I can get you to say yes to anything."

My heart skidded. Twenty-four hours ago I wouldn't have understood. Twenty-four hours ago I'd have pointed out that I caved in to his demands every step of the way. But then again, twenty-four hours ago my grasp of the situation had been as backward as when people believed that the sun revolved around the Earth.

But now I was following proper scientific procedures. Now I saw how much effort he had put in where I was concerned. Now I knew I'd been given yet another piece of proof that my new hypothesis was not only sound, but ironclad.

"Well," I murmured, "you've found Chinatown. I always say yes to Chinatown."

AFTER BREAKFAST WE RESTARTED THE movie. But the poor flick didn't stand a chance once I showed Bennett what I was wearing under the pajamas he'd loaned me. In nothing but those fuck-me bits of transparent fabric, I went down on him with an almost trembling greed.

I'll never forget the reaction I wrought from him—his head thrown back, his pelvis coming off the bed, his hands knotted tightly in my hair. And the sounds he made, so much raw lust, a cascade of filthy imprecations that turned me on unbearably even as I drove him out of his mind.

He returned the favor and ate me until I was limp from my orgasms. And then we made love playfully, rolling around the bed, kissing, nibbling, and exploring at will.

The lunch crowd had half dispersed by the time we arrived in Chinatown, which meant we didn't need to eat with the speed of a house on fire. So we lingered over our lunch and talked, with Bennett asking me lots of questions.

I told him how the Material Girls came to be, and how we all ended up in the five boroughs. He laughed at our antics surrounding the Annual Boyfriend Roundup.

"STEM girls know how to have fun," he said.

"Absolutely. When nerds let loose, they really let loose."

For a moment he looked as if he might lean in and whisper something naughty in my ear. But he only said, "I remember you telling me that your father didn't care for your interest in the sciences. Was it ever a matter of contention between the two of you?"

I thought back. "Not really. I mean, he couldn't help letting you know how he felt, so I always understood it wasn't what he would have wanted. But there wasn't a sexist element in his desire for me to be a Manhattan hostess—he'd have loved to be its male equivalent, if he'd managed to marry a woman of sufficient means and status.

"And in a way, it was how we connected with each other. Nobody ever did anything to his standards, which meant that he was the one who stood over me as I practiced my handwriting. He was the one who gave me an education in art. And he was the one who taught me about fabrics and construction of garments, among other things."

"Did you enjoy your lessons?" asked Bennett.

Hmm, my inquisitive lover was feeling his way around me, but it was all right. Pater was not where my weakness lay.

"Not always," I answered. "He could be moody, and I never quite knew from day to day whether he'd be cheerful or glum or outright bad-tempered. But looking back I'm really glad we spent all those hours together, especially since he passed away so unexpectedly."

In my mind I saw my bouquet shivering before his gravestone. He was the parent I'd counted on to stay around the longest, and yet he was gone in the blink of an eye. For weeks following his funeral I'd remained in a state of shock. Every time a car screeched to a stop somewhere I'd start violently, my head flooding with imagined details of the crash that took his life.

My fingers tightened around my chopsticks. Perhaps I wasn't as immune as I'd thought.

"He was very proud of you, you know," Bennett said softly.

"It's what Zelda tells me." Though I wasn't sure whether I believed

Zelda one hundred percent.

"I told you I introduced my brother to him, right?"

"Yeah, when you asked him about your grandmother's Pissarro. You said he was taken with Prescott."

"Taken enough to tell him, 'Keep it up, young man, and maybe someday you'll be good enough to meet my daughter.'"

"Really?" I was astounded. Pater never had such compliments for me. *That's not too bad* was about as extravagant as his praises went.

"Really."

I half shook my head, then laughed, still incredulous. Bennett peered at me, his curiosity evident not so much in his expression as in the tilt of his head and the forward angle of his shoulders.

Instinctively I turned away from him. I was wrong. My lover had an intuitive sense of where all my weaknesses lay. *I know people who genuinely delight in being unattached. They are not the ones who get melancholy at weddings. What do you do when you despair, and there isn't an August rain to drown your sorrow? So you told him to stay away from Zelda?*

To cover for my abrupt motion, I dug into my purse, pulled out my phone, and looked at the time. Four o'clock exact. "It's getting late," I said. "We should go."

BY THE TIME WE STARTED in the direction of the Canal Street train station, the snow, which had stopped when we left Bennett's apartment, was coming down again. The day was bitterly cold, but I was warm in the clothes he'd selected for me: stylish, well-made pieces in camel and grey, plus a spectacularly comfortable pair of shearling boots.

We were at an intersection, waiting for the light to change, when Bennett took my hand in his and looked up at the darkening sky. I thought of my Munich scenario, the bit with us standing on the hotel's observation deck as snow fell all about us.

I was already living in my fantasy. So what if Bennett saw through me from time to time? I could cope with a little imperfection on the part of my fantasy lover.

"Is that your phone ringing?" asked said lover.

It was, the Rohan theme that signaled Zelda. "Excuse me," I said to Bennett. And then, to Zelda, "Hello, my love."

"Darling, I've been trying to get hold of you for the past hour. Where are you?"

I saw then that I'd missed a number of calls and texts. "Chinatown. Are you okay?"

"Oh, *I'm* fine. But you won't believe the news coming out of MoMA."

Shit. The Moira McAllister retrospective.

"At least two of my friends have called me," Zelda went on, "to ask whether I knew that there are pictures of Bennett at the retrospective, very artistic pictures but still, very naked pictures."

"It's no big deal," I said. "He was her tenant for a while when he was on the West Coast and he modeled for her."

"Well, my friends said there are thousands and thousands of pictures of him—their words, not mine."

Fuck. "Ah, in that case we'd better go take a look. I'll call you later."

"MoMA?" asked Bennett, not particularly perturbed. "The cat out of the bag?"

"Sounds like it." I took a deep breath. "Unfortunately, this cat might be the size of King Kong."

THERE WAS A LINE TO enter the Moira McAllister special exhibit. First-day crowd or onlookers drawn by the news of nudity where none had been expected?

Bennett had been quiet on the train ride uptown. He was equally quiet as we stood in line. But as we entered the first exhibit room, with no images of his naked body leaping out at us, he exhaled audibly.

We passed several more rooms without seeing body parts that belonged to him. I too began to relax. What thousands and thousands? At this rate I wouldn't be surprised if it were only a few snapshots tucked away in a corner.

We entered the next room and my jaw dropped. The other rooms were done up fairly typically for an exhibit, with one or two rows of framed prints on each wall, more or less at eye level. But this room, a sizable one, had its walls—and ceiling—papered over with images.

Literally thousands and thousands of black-and-white photos, fitted together like a huge mosaic, with some images as big as Oriental rugs, others barely larger than a thumbprint. And they were all Bennett, every single one.

Not all of them were nude pictures—even a quick sweep revealed that he was perfectly decent in many. But the biggest ones had him in various state of undress: Bennett standing before a window, a joint in hand, his back to the camera, his gluteal muscles astonishing in their perfection; Bennett sprawled facedown on a mussed bed, sleeping, all long arms and legs; a very much awake Bennett gazing into the camera, eyes heavy-lidded with lust and anticipation, his hand reaching south of the edge of the photograph, which ended a bare millimeter short of showing everything.

I turned around—everyone else in the room too seemed to be slowly spinning about, while whispering to one another, *What is this?* Who *is this?*

Bennett in the shower, water sluicing down his lanky form. Bennett lying on the carpet, wearing nothing except a strategically placed copy of *L'Étranger*. Bennett in the arms of a woman, equally naked, her face turned away from the camera.

Moira.

Seven years was a lot of time for her camera to be pointed squarely at Bennett. Bennett cooking, Bennett eating, Bennett brushing his teeth. Bennett driving, Bennett looking at a map, Bennett checking under the hood of a classic Thunderbird. Bennett washing dishes, Bennett vacuuming the carpet, Bennett putting together a bookshelf, a hammer in hand, several nails clenched between his teeth.

And it went on and on, the camera's—and the photographer's—profound interest in this beautiful young man.

The tide of visitors gradually pushed us out of the room into the next. And the next. There were no more images of Bennett. His years with Moira had been confined to one room and did not overlap with her other creative output—an accurate portrayal of the isolation of their affair, an intense experience she'd been forced to keep a complete secret.

The museum was closing when we left. Without speaking to each other, we walked into a nearby espresso bar and sat down.

Was Bennett shocked to see so much of his old life put up for public consumption? Did he feel betrayed, or did he understand that it was inevitable, that an artist who strove for expressions of truth would never consent to keep so much of her own life forever a lie by omission?

And how had he felt, inundated by so many moments from the past?

"Was that too much for you?" he asked, breaking the silence.

It *had* been too much for me. Not because he was naked for all the world to see, but because now I truly understood how much he had invested in that life. Beyond the first visual blast of nudity, everything was overwhelmingly domestic. And in every image he had looked...settled. For someone that young, there had been no restlessness in his eyes, no itch to be somewhere else, someone else.

I shrugged. "It isn't my ass up there. How are you?"

He set his palms against his temples. "On the one hand, Moira and I didn't part very well. After everything we'd been through together—her first bout of cancer, the embezzlement by her agent, the ups and downs of her career—I was resentful for a long time afterward that she just let go of me. So the exhibit is actually kind of nice seen from that angle, a public tribute to my place in her life.

"On the other hand, whether she meant it that way or not, it's also a giant middle finger to my dad. And the timing...shit."

The timing really was shit. Eighteen months ago Bennett probably wouldn't have cared. And if he and his father had successfully reconciled, it also wouldn't have mattered as much. But now, at this critical juncture, having his naked pictures splashed all over MoMA—and all over the Internet soon, if not already...

In this day and age, a few naked pictures—or even an exhibit room plastered with them—didn't constitute a deal breaker, especially not for a man with a shit-ton of money. But Mr. Somerset was old-fashioned. Such a display might tilt his opinion of his son irrevocably in the wrong direction. And if he were to come to the belief that Bennett had something to do with it...

"I wonder if he'll feel like a laughingstock," said Bennett, his thoughts proceeding in the same direction as mine. He exhaled slowly.

"It's going to be awkward tomorrow at Zelda's party."

It was probably going to be awkward for a long time to come—the elephant in the room now the size of a blue whale.

I added another packet of sugar to my coffee. "Your strategy was all wrong. Instead of a fake girlfriend, you should have knocked up someone for real. Nothing brings a family together like a baby."

Bennett looked into my eyes. "Can I knock *you* up for real?"

My heart thudded. It shocked me how much I wanted to say yes. If I were pregnant, of course we'd have to get married. And who wouldn't want to get married if marriage consisted mainly of hot sex, pancake breakfasts, and lunches in Chinatown?

"That's the nuclear option. That's for when the world finds out that Moira was actually your father's mistress *and* your mother's half sister."

Bennett shook his head, a reluctant smile curving his lips. "Is there a slightly-short-of-nuclear option?"

I bit the inside of my cheek. Would I sound too crazy? Like, batshit insane?

"You have an idea," he said. "Let's hear it."

"I'm already having second thoughts."

"Let's hear it anyway."

I threw caution to the wind. "Next to a baby, the second-most-effective diversionary tactic is a wedding."

Bennett sat up straighter, his expression that of a lost traveler in the desert, unsure whether he was seeing a real oasis or a mirage. "Keep talking."

Something in his eyes made me almost reluctant to say, "But we're not going to do that, because it's too unhinged even for us."

"Then what are we going to do?"

His shoulders slumped: He was disappointed that we wouldn't be staging a wedding. My heart melted into a puddle—could there ever be a better feeling in the world?

"We can do a fake engagement. You say you already have a ring picked out. If that's the case, we can announce it at Zelda's party—and that should preempt any other topic."

He might not have shown me any ring. But at this point, I was willing to bet a month's salary that such a thing existed. That he had again been telling the truth under the guise of plausible deniability.

He looked a little stunned. "You're willing to go that far?"

Doubt wedged into my happiness. He wasn't saying that the idea was demented, was he? "It's a lot less drastic than having your baby," I said, hanging on to my own plausible deniability.

He was silent for moment. Then he reached across the table and took my hands. "That's a wonderful idea. Thank you."

Did I blush? And could he tell, from his grip on my wrists, how fast my heart was racing? "That's a plan then."

We looked at each other and laughed at the same time. "God, it's nuts," I said.

"Hey, crazy situations demand crazy solutions," he replied. "Thanks for rising to the occasion."

He *was* glad. I could feel the contentment wrapped around us like a force field as we walked hand in hand to Broadway and 50th. Before I headed down into the station to catch the 1 train uptown, I laid my hand on the lapel of his coat. "Look after yourself."

He kissed me on my cheek. "I'll be just fine, now that we're engaged."

It was very possible that I floated all the way to the university, my feet a few inches off the ground.

Chapter 14

I DIDN'T STAY IN THE lab long: After an hour of bumbling inattention, I decided I'd better leave before I botched an experiment or lost valuable data.

On the train home my head swam with visions of Bennett and me as a companionable older couple: cycling along the winding country lanes of Vermont during peak foliage; strolling down a decked-out Madison Avenue at Christmas; doing the Sunday crossword puzzle together before a roaring fire while a blizzard plowed through the city.

Truly, a montage worthy of an AARP commercial.

I waltzed into the house. Zelda rushed up from her studio to meet me. But as she saw me, the anxiety on her face turned into puzzlement. "You don't seem particularly upset, darling."

Belatedly I realized that I'd been *whistling*. Rearranging my features into what I hoped was a more serious expression, I answered, "Well, you know, what's there to do but wait for the whole thing to blow over?"

"True, true. But I don't know…you don't even seem shocked about him and Moira McAllister."

I took off my coat and hung it up. "Oh, that I've known for a while. It floored me in the beginning, but it wasn't as if we had no inkling of the 'unsuitable older woman' in his past."

"I thought that meant a ten-year age difference. Moira McAllister was close to *my* age."

I sighed. On the one hand, Moira taking up with a sixteen-year-old would always be problematic for me. On the other hand, it had been a significant long-term relationship for both of them, with all the joys and difficulties of any romantic partnership that lasts beyond the initial infatuation—and that shouldn't be reduced to a one-dimensional portrayal of a cougar and her boy toy. "Well, if the situation had been less shocking, his father probably wouldn't have disowned him."

"There's that, I suppose," said Zelda. "So…will he still come for the party tomorrow?"

"As far as I know."

It was dinnertime. Zelda had already made a salad and pastrami sandwiches. We sat down at the table, busied ourselves with our food, and didn't speak for a couple of minutes.

In the silence, my conscience twinged. Larry de Villiers's e-mail still sat in my inbox, its humble sincerity a reproach every time I came across it. I didn't know how to answer him—or how to bring up the subject with Zelda.

It was a relief when she said, "You're taking everything in stride, darling. I guess MoMA doesn't change anything for you and Bennett?"

"Not really." But yes, really. How did a fake engagement proceed? Would we throw a party? Send an announcement to the *Times*? Would I actually wear an engagement ring everywhere? "It's not as if he'd been caught clubbing baby seals. He was just mostly naked in some of the pictures."

"I hope his parents will feel the same way you do."

That poured cold water on my frothy hopes. "Have you talked to his mom?"

"I thought of telephoning her. But what would I say?"

I set down my sandwich. I'd been so cocooned in that distant, beautiful future spun of my own dreams and wishes that I hadn't given any real thought to the here-and-now of the situation. And it wasn't only his parents Bennett had to worry about. "Oh, God. It's going to be messy, isn't it? I hope people at his hospital aren't going to be dicks."

"I hope people in your department aren't going be dicks," said Zelda, reaching for a pickle spear.

I hadn't even thought of it from that perspective—academia did not like to grant permanent membership to candidates with any personal notoriety. "Screw the tenure committee. They can—"

The doorbell rang.

"Delivery for the party?" I asked Zelda.

"No, everything is scheduled for tomorrow."

I went to the door and looked out the peephole. Bennett! I yanked the door open. "Come in! You look cold." He had on the same grey overcoat and blue scarf that he'd worn earlier, but now his nose and ears were all red and his boots looked as if they'd been left in the snow for hours. "Have you been out walking all this time?"

"Wasn't exactly in the mood to do anything else." He kissed me on my cheek. "Hi, Zelda. How are you?"

Zelda, who had peeked out from the dining room, glanced at me. I looked back at Bennett. "We're both doing better than you at the moment."

He smiled a little. "Well, thanks for that."

"Would you like to join us for dinner?" asked Zelda. "We have salad and some nice ciabatta rolls."

"I'm fine. I just came for a word with Evangeline."

"In that case," said Zelda, "you children have a lovely chin-wag and I'll see you later, Bennett."

When we were alone again he kissed me, the kind of kiss better suited for lovers reunited after long and hopeless separations, like Aragorn and Arwen at the end of the trilogy. Needless to say, I, who last saw him only hours ago, relished the hell out of it.

"You okay?" I asked, breathless.

"I was going to say it could be better. But then I remembered that I had sex with you four times in the last twenty-four hours, so maybe it doesn't get any better than that."

I might have preened a little. "I know. It's all downhill from there."

He smiled again and I was weightlessly happy—he had walked all over Manhattan and had come here, to my door.

I rubbed his cold hands with my palms. "Have you talked to your sister? Do your parents know yet?"

He nodded.

"What does Imogene make of all this?"

"Her current boyfriend is a lawyer, so she was going on about ways we can try to get the pictures taken down."

"Can you?" I felt a quick jolt of hope.

"I doubt it. I've signed any number of model releases for Moira, and the pictures I saw were all from when I was in California, after I turned eighteen."

Of course MoMA's lawyers would have done their due diligence.

"Besides, it's already all over the Internet—no use trying to latch that barn door."

"We'll tough it out," I told him, and pressed a kiss to the center of his palm.

He looked at me oddly. Was that too intimate an act? Or was it my use of the collective pronoun that had caught his attention? But of course it was "we" now, we who were on the verge of announcing our "engagement."

He reached into his pocket. "Anyway, I came to give you this."

"This" was a simple, antique ring with filigree work on the band and a modest, round-cut sapphire. "The one you picked out?" I said, trying not to squeal like a girl half my age.

"Yes. But I've reconsidered the engagement idea."

My hand tightened around the velvet box. *What?*

"It was a tremendous offer and I'm very grateful," he said quietly. "But my parents would rightly see the timing as suspect—as would Zelda. And I don't want anyone, especially not Zelda, to worry."

I should be proud of him—it was a very mature, very responsible decision on his part. But all I could think of was that mirage-beautiful, TV commercial–worthy future of ours. "So…no engagement announcement tomorrow?"

He reciprocated my gesture from earlier and kissed me in the center of my palm. "I can handle a scandal without hiding behind you—as appealing as that idea is."

Belatedly I remembered the ring in my hand. I glanced down. "Then what's *this*?"

"A present."

"What kind of a present?"

"A no-reason present." He leaned in and kissed me on my lips. "Don't look so concerned—nothing has changed."

Except I thought everything had.

BENNETT'S NAKED PICTURES MADE THE eleven-o'clock news that night—on two different channels, no less. The footage consisted of quick cuts of his face and his body accompanied by breathless copy-reading. *Who is this young man? And what made him so special to Moira McAllister, the great photographer?*

"Oh, I can tell you exactly what made him so special," said one female anchor, as her colleague chuckled.

It was far worse the next day. Not only had Bennett's name been dug up, but his address and his place of work too. The facade of 740 Park Avenue was splashed everywhere, along with a professional head shot of his, probably taken from the hospital's website.

"But this young man is no ordinary surgeon," said a midday news anchor. "In fact, we can safely label him one of the most eligible bachelors in Manhattan. There is that family pedigree, of course, but there is also the fact that he has been a very, very savvy Silicon Valley investor and made a huge fortune during his time on the West Coast."

"Money, art, sex, and a May–December romance. Phew," said his co-anchor, "no wonder people can't stop talking about it."

I monitored the coverage in every medium—it was important to know what Bennett was up against. But I did so as if from a tremendous distance—as if I were dealing with strange sequences of alien signals picked up by SETI dishes.

He'd broken our engagement. Why? What did it mean? Was my new hypothesis a mountain of appalling fallacies? I swung between a mute horror at being completely off base and a scalding embarrassment that he had rejected my grand overture after all.

I knew perfectly well that there had never been any engagement, other than the air-quote variety. I also knew perfectly well that he'd made the right call in not proceeding any further with a move that screamed diversionary tactics. All the same, in the end, this was what it boiled down to: I'd wanted to take our relationship to that proverbial next level and he'd said no.

Yet another ding from the Google alert I'd set up. I clicked through and winced at the masthead of a big gossip site. They'd found the YouTube video of the tango from Sam and Charlotte's wedding—and they'd tracked down Damaris Vandermeer and asked her a few questions on camera.

After Damaris went over the details of her association with Bennett—fortunately not exaggerating their level of acquaintance, as far as I could tell—she had this to add: "But I don't care how hot he is. He's a jerk. He went out a few times with a friend of mine and then just up and disappeared. I'll bet she's having the last laugh now. Her dad would have a heart attack if her boyfriend's butt was all over the Internet—so that was a lucky escape for her."

I closed my laptop and dropped my head into my hands. What a mess.

The media storm would move on: News cycles were ever shorter, and attention spans ever more reduced. The coverage would be intense and blizzardlike, blanketing every venue—but it would peter out just as quickly, all the outlets pouncing en masse toward the next scandal du jour.

The real consequences would take place on a more private, more personal level. How long would it take Mr. Somerset to get over this circus? Would he *ever* get over it?

Texts piled in from the Material Girls. Fortunately my friends had my back. None of them high-fived me for bagging myself such a nice ass or pointed me to any video coverage. They only asked me to let them know if there was anything they could do.

I texted back, assuring them that everything was okay and nobody was freaking out. And then, because I *was* freaking out, I texted Bennett.

You okay?

He replied immediately. *Holding up.*

Are there people outside your building?

I believe so.

The party was starting in an hour. *How will you get out?*

I'm at the Mandarin. Nobody's waiting here.

Smart choice. *If you want to sit out the party, I'll understand.*

So would I. But I never miss a chance to see you.

I stared at those last few words. In fact, I took a screen shot. And e-mailed it to myself. I'd probably have printed out a few hard copies too, if the idea weren't so over-the-top.

But why don't you want to be engaged to me?

I mentally slapped myself and walked downstairs to make sure everything was ready.

ZELDA HAD INVITED A MIX of our neighbors, her social friends, and her friends from the music industry. The Somersets arrived exactly fifteen minutes after the time specified on the invitation. Zelda introduced them to a couple of longtime neighbors, while I went and fetched glasses of wine.

Bennett's parents looked strained—and I probably appeared no more at ease. But we made a good show of comity and politesse. I asked after their well-being. They admired our living room decor—a hodgepodge, really, pieces of pop art Pater had left me, posters on atomic structure, and our collection of Middle-earth miscellany.

Bennett rang the bell half an hour into the party. I met him in the hall and took his coat. "They're here."

He was in a glen-plaid three-piece suit worn without the jacket, and a dark blue silk tie patterned with tiny skulls. I remembered what he'd said once about dressing down for his father. This time he'd dressed up, to shield and buttress himself.

I gave his hand a squeeze. "You can leave anytime you want."

"I'm your boyfriend," he said softly. "I'm staying till the end."

My heart turned over. "Look forward to a very long ninety minutes, then. Let's get started."

I led him to Zelda, for him to wish her a very happy birthday. She happened to be talking to Mrs. Vanderwoude, who lived three doors down from us, and introduced him as my date.

Mrs. Vanderwoude gasped. "I just came back from the Moira McAllister exhibit at MoMA. That's you, isn't it, all over that room?"

And so it begins.

Mrs. Vanderwoude was old and deaf and spoke at the top of her lungs. Half the guests glanced our way. But not the Somersets, who stood with their backs to the room, seemingly absorbed in a bright yellow-and-blue pop-art painting.

"I did some modeling when I was younger," Bennett answered. "It took a lot of odd jobs to get me through college."

Mrs. Vanderwoude turned her face rather coquettishly. "Must have been *something*, working with a great artist like that."

"Yes, it was. A memorable experience."

It was a you-are-getting-this-much-and-not-a-bit-more answer. Perfect civility, delivered with a smile, no less. But the underlying severity was not lost on Mrs. Vanderwoude. She put away her coy expression and ate a Brie puff from her plate before she asked, "So, how long have you and Evangeline been going out?"

Bennett glanced at me. "Not long enough. I hate to think of all the years I wasted without her."

"Cool it, lover boy," I murmured, even as I prayed for his words to be true. "There's a reason my friends think you're in an off-Broadway show."

"But Bennett is actually a surgeon," Zelda hastened to add.

"Beauty *and* brains—just what Evangeline has been waiting for all these years," said Bennett.

I shook my head and took his hand in mine. "Come on. Let me introduce this pinnacle of modern manhood to some more people."

The general public often had a mistaken idea of the lonesome scientist toiling away in a lab. Modern science not only required a great deal of teamwork, but also a lot of glad-handing in the never-ending search for funding. So I was no stranger to negotiating a crowd.

Still, this party was real work.

Within a short time, thanks to Mrs. Vanderwoude, news of Bennett's notoriety had spread. Some of the guests moved around surreptitiously to get a good look at him. Others were first shown his pictures by a phone passed around, and then they too craned their necks in his direction.

We the happy couple shouldered on against this high tide of curiosity. Nobody was openly rude. Nobody, after Mrs. Vanderwoude, even brought up MoMA. Which somehow made the atmosphere more oppressive, and the interactions more tiring.

I could only imagine how trying it must be for Bennett to know that not only had everyone in the room seen the pictures, but that they were likely speculating on his relationship with Moira and making all the shallower assumptions.

Not to mention being keenly aware, at the same time, that his parents were in the room and undoubtedly hating every second of it.

At last, our paths crossed before the appetizers.

"Hi, Mom. Hi, Dad," said Bennett, his voice even, friendly.

They nodded, Mr. Somerset coolly, Mrs. Somerset with undeniable anxiety.

"Sorry about MoMA, by the way."

"That's all right," his mother said immediately.

"We got a call from *Vanity Fair* this morning," said Mr. Somerset. "They want to do a feature story about you and Ms. McAllister."

I might have grimaced openly.

Bennett was unmoved. "This is right in their wheelhouse, so *Vanity Fair* will do what *Vanity Fair* will do. I just hope it won't bring negative attention on you, Professor," he said to me.

I was surprised and touched by his concern. "I'm okay. I'm more worried about what happens tonight when *you* go to work."

He smiled slightly. "At least most of my patients will be under anesthesia."

Mrs. Somerset turned a caprese salad skewer round and round on her plate. "Too bad the same can't be said of your colleagues."

"They can have some fun at my expense if they want to."

"And I'm sure they will," I said. "But in a week or two they'll get bored with catcalling you. Which reminds me"—I turned to Bennett's parents—"why don't we plan a get-together for once this blows over? There are tons of places in town that Bennett hasn't tried yet."

"Yes, that sounds wonderful," gushed Mrs. Somerset.

"Bennett, mind coming over here a second?" called Zelda. "I have someone I want you to meet. He's your attending physician's brother."

"Excuse me," said Bennett.

After he departed in Zelda's direction, Mrs. Somerset and I exchanged contact information. Mr. Somerset, who'd been silent since the statement about *Vanity Fair*, spoke again at last. "Have you seen the exhibit, Evangeline?"

"Bennett and I were there yesterday."

"Is it as sensational as the media has made it out to be?"

"Oh, it was sensational, all right. But…" I hesitated only a moment. "But I think you should go see the exhibit. There are thousands of images, and the vast majority of them aren't the least bit objectionable. They're more like a photojournal. If you've ever wondered about those years of your son's life, you won't find a better record anywhere."

"You're right," said Frances Somerset. "I'll go tomorrow."

Rowland Somerset wasn't so easily swayed. "But it isn't just a record of his life in pictures—it's also a record of a relationship. That doesn't bother you, Evangeline?"

I looked him in the eye. "It was uncomfortable for me—this was the private life of someone I know and respect. Not to mention, no one who sees the exhibit can miss the sexual angle of that relationship, and I'll never be one hundred percent okay with the fact that he was a minor when it all started.

"But after I left, it wasn't the nudity—and everything it implied—that I remembered. I was…saddened by what the young man in those pictures didn't know yet. That his forever wouldn't be forever after all. That he'd have his heart broken. That it would be a long time before he looked so trustingly at anyone again."

If ever.

Bennett's father studied me. A long beat of silence passed. "You are a romantic, Evangeline."

"And so are you, I believe," I told him.

One of Zelda's musician friends came up to the appetizers table. "Hey, Evangeline, who did your catering today? Great food."

"Thanks." I set down my wineglass and pulled out my phone. "Hmm, I don't have it on here. Put in your number and I'll text you their contact info—we have it on the fridge somewhere."

Once she'd entered her number, I excused myself and went to the kitchen. After I sent her the text, I turned around and was half startled to see Frances Somerset in the kitchen with me. "You need something, ma'am?"

A word, most probably.

"I hope you won't think me terribly nosy, Evangeline," said Mrs. Somerset, "but would you mind telling me the provenance of your ring?"

A frisson of excitement shot up my spine. Even though I had mixed feelings about the ring, I'd put it on my right index finger as a sign of solidarity. But since I'd had a glass of wine in that hand most of the time, she probably saw it only a minute ago, when I finally set down the wineglass.

"This? It's a present from Bennett."

She inhaled audibly.

"But it's not an engagement ring," I hurried to reassure her. "He just wanted me to have it."

"Right. Of course."

"Is it a family heirloom? If it's meant to stay in the family I'll be happy to return it. I don't wear jewelry in any case—lab protocols and all that."

"Oh, no, absolutely not. Please keep it."

Before I could ask more questions, Mrs. Somerset patted me on the hand and left the kitchen. I looked at the ring for some time. When I returned to the living room, she had disappeared, though her husband was still there, talking to a musician.

Zelda, too, was nowhere to be seen.

The next time I saw Mrs. Somerset was twenty minutes later, right before she and her husband said their good-byes. Bennett not only remained to the end of the party, but stayed on afterward to help us tidy up. Zelda kept glancing at him—and then to my ring—Zelda, who didn't normally pay much attention to accessories. When we'd put everything away she invited Bennett to stay for dinner, but he declined, saying he had to get ready for his shift.

"I'll walk you out," I said.

"What do you think?" he asked, buttoning his coat outside the door.

It was late in the afternoon. A few flakes of snow were again drifting down. One caught in the palm of the glove he was pulling on.

"Your mom doesn't care. You could release a sex tape at this point and it wouldn't faze her."

"I don't have a sex tape—shocking, I know."

"Color me staggered. As for your dad, he might be all right too if he took my advice and saw the exhibit."

Bennett arched a brow. "You recommended that they go see my

bare ass?"

"I recommended that they ignore your bare ass and look at the other pictures."

"You were looking at other pictures? My ass couldn't hold your attention?"

I flicked him on the front of his coat. "You've always known that deep down I'm a pervert who would rather look at your face than your ass."

His expression was one of mock horror. "My God, are the Four Horsemen of the Apocalypse already running loose in Times Square?"

"Would you notice if they were?"

He smiled, kissed me on the cheek, and started down the front steps. But then he turned around. "There's something you want to say to me?"

There were indeed things I wanted to say to him—Bennett was ever perceptive this way. "I worry that you and your dad have come to an impasse. The pattern is becoming clear. Your mom and I arrange these meetings. You and your dad show up—and proceed to make absolutely no progress."

But his making no progress with his father was what kept *us* going, said a part of me. What if he actually took my advice and succeeded? What would happen to us then?

I pressed on. "You can keep meeting like this, but unless one of you comes right out and says those words—'I missed you. I'm sorry. Can we be a family again?'—I'm afraid nothing more will happen."

His scarf whipped in a gust of wind. "And you don't think he'll ever say those words."

"I don't know. I'm not in his confidence. In fact, I can't even be sure whether he meets us because he wants to or because your mom drags him along. I only know that you want this reconciliation. A lot. So you need to ask yourself, if you can't have it on your terms, do you still want it?"

He was silent a long moment, and then he raised the collar of his coat. "Let me think about it."

"I GAVE BENNETT *THE FELLOWSHIP of the Ring* to read," Zelda told me when I came back into the living room.

"Peddling your drug of choice again, I see." I gave her a rub on the shoulder as I passed her on the way to our fireplace. The chill outside had been arctic and I was in need of warmth.

"I told him once he's done with all three books, he can join us for the marathon."

Our annual *The Lord of the Rings* movie marathon fell on Black Friday. We didn't really do Thanksgiving—it wasn't a holiday that Zelda had grown up with. But for the movie marathon we pulled out all the stops: breakfast, second breakfast, elevenses, and so on, in honor of the food-mad hobbits.

"That's planning really far ahead," I said. "Black Friday is nine months away. How do you know Bennett and I will still be going out by then?"

"Well, he gave you a ring."

So she *had* been talking to Frances Somerset, as I'd suspected. I gave the ring a turn. "It's not an engagement ring."

"But it's an important ring—Frances told me a good bit. In the family, it's referred to as the Tremaine ring. Bennett's great-great-grandfather, who was the Marquess of Tremaine before he became the Duke of Fairford, gave it to his fiancée. The marriage didn't begin well—they were separated for ten years. But eventually they reconciled and had a long and happy life together, so the ring is considered lucky.

"For years, Bennett's grandmother had the ring. But after she died, nobody knew where it was. Until now."

"Still, it's just a ring."

But even as I spoke those dismissive words, my heart, which had been everywhere this weekend—blocking my airway, down in my toes, or just plain careening about—settled back in place.

My hypothesis was not wrong. And while Bennett might not have proposed, this was nevertheless a significant pledge on his part.

We were together and we would continue to be together.

"And I still have doubts about the movie marathon." I smiled at Zelda, my heart as light and airy as the world's most perfect soufflé. "After all, you told him he had to finish the books first. That could take him years."

Chapter 15

THE MEDIA STORM STARTED TO taper off a few days into the week—Moira was already dead, Bennett wasn't himself a celebrity, and these days nude pictures were a penny a gross. Bennett reported that his colleagues mostly took it easy on him—it helped that he'd already been at the hospital eight months and proved that he wasn't a flake. He also reported some wackier outcomes, like getting offers to show his junk, to star in actual porn, and to peddle a line of high-end dildos—though not at the same time.

And, of course, proposals and propositions flew in—from both sexes, domestic and abroad.

Such things were more or less to be expected. What took us aback was a legitimate bid from a major fashion label, with very respectable money attached, for him to front a new campaign.

I knew fame had its financial benefits—I failed to realized how much, he texted. *If I were a better businessman, I'd have been posting naked selfies years ago.*

Not too late to start, I texted back.

Same for you.

Given his limited social media presence, online muckrakers scraped other people's accounts for photographs that included him. I was half-afraid that there would be lots of shots floating around of him being young, drunk, and douchebaggy. Instead what had been dug up were largely from various volunteer missions, with a shovel or a stethoscope, rather than a bottle—or a breast—in his hand.

Really? Building houses in third-world countries? What's wrong with young people nowadays? What happened to booze and pussy?

Booze and pussy happened away from cameras—Mrs. Asquith drove the point home when I was a kid.

And it wasn't just his person that did good work; his money, too, hadn't been idle. His charitable foundation had won awards for experimenting with innovative ways to help people, such as buying medical bills from collection agencies for pennies on the dollar, so that uninsured patients could get out from underneath crushing health care–related debts.

If ever a man caught literally with his pants down ended up smelling like roses…

That Thursday I visited MoMA again—partly because I wanted to gauge attendance at the Moira McAllister exhibit, and mostly so that I could see more of his pictures for myself.

The attention of the media might have begun to move on, but the general public was still turning out in droves. The exhibit was far more crowded than it had been the Saturday before. I finished reading several recent research articles before the line finally moved enough to get me into the Bennett room.

Instead of being distracted by the acreage of skin, this time I zoomed in on the smaller pictures, the vast majority of which I'd missed earlier. And what should I see but Bennett sporting a plaid shirt and doing something Vermont farmer–adjacent in every third image: digging up a garden, turning a pile of compost, building a bean trellis from scratch—Moira's backyard must have been fully utilized for urban agriculture.

I held my breath as dozens and dozens of images piled into my head. How would my psyche interpret what I was seeing? Would it link Bennett to my old obsession? Would I then feel a familiar deflation of interest?

Nothing.

Or rather, the only thing I felt was a desire to step over the velvet rope and touch the photographs of my lover. Bennett in the rain, holding an umbrella in one hand and a bag of groceries in the other. Bennett sitting on a picnic blanket, his shades down at the tip of his nose. Bennett, his hair long enough to be tied in a topknot, smiling into the camera, a hen under each arm.

A hen under each arm?

I was about to send him a mercilessly mocking text concerning the chickens when I spied Rowland Somerset. He had just come into the room and I was near the exit. But the velvet rope–barricaded path was in the shape of a horseshoe, and he stood only fifteen feet away.

Recoiling.

There was no other word to describe his reaction. My fingers closed hard around my phone. The young man in the biggest images was a blatantly sexual creature, not at all how any parent would want to see his child, even if they were on the best of terms.

And then Mr. Somerset was looking around, not seeking out the smaller, more ordinary pictures as I'd asked him to, but studying the faces of the hundreds of people who were all there to see a naked Bennett.

The crowd pushed me out of the room. I left the museum in a daze, walking into and out of the nearest train station two times before I remembered where I was headed.

Had I given the worst possible advice? Had I done irreparable damage?

I MIGHT NEED TO APOLOGIZE profusely, I texted Bennett later that day, from my office at the university.

He was at work, but he texted me back within minutes. *What happened?*

Saw your dad at MoMA. I don't think it went well.

I all but gnawed my knuckles as I waited for his response.

Dad is a realist. He'd have gone to the exhibit at some point, whether you suggested it or not, to see what he was dealing with. And it was never going to go well. So don't worry about it.

I exhaled in gratitude. *Thanks.*

I'm going back to my apartment on Saturday. Want to come over?

My answer was short and to the point: *Yes.*

OF COURSE, ONE OF THE reasons I agreed to go to Bennett's apartment was that I wanted to take a good look at his great-great-grandmother's portrait. Yep, the Marchioness of Tremaine had on the exact same ring he had given me.

Needless to say, sex was raunchy and all-consuming. Afterward we showered together, had our dinner, and moved to the masturbation couch.

I pulled out my laptop. I'd texted earlier in the day that I might stay only a short time, because I needed to finish drafting the next paper. He in turn had suggested that I bring work along instead—and I hadn't needed much persuasion.

He made the sign of the cross—which made me laugh—before sitting down at the other end of the masturbation couch. Outside wind howled; rain splattered against the windows. But under the big throw blanket Bennett had spread, we were as snug as two kittens in a basket.

I lost myself in my work. Once I looked up to see my lover typing away on his own laptop. Another time he had a thick volume of medical reference on his lap. But when I was done for the evening, he was reading *The Fellowship of the Ring.*

Not just any old copy—we had at least a dozen different editions—but Zelda's precious, inscribed to her by none other than Professor Tolkien himself. The kind of loan one would make only to a beloved future son-in-law.

"How come you never read it in high school?" I asked.

"I was more into techno-thrillers, when I wasn't busy trying to decide if I wanted to be the next Thoreau." Bennett peered at me over the top of the book. "When did you get started on them?"

"Zelda read them to me when I was little, starting with *The Hobbit.* Instead of playing dolls, we used to play Middle-earth—she was Frodo and I her faithful Sam. And we'd slog our way up Mount Doom to destroy the ring."

He set the book aside, went to the kitchen, and came back with a handful of tangerines. "She told me you surprised her with a trip to New Zealand for the premiere of *The Return of the King.*"

"It was fun—Times Square on New Year's Eve has nothing on that crowd."

He tossed me a tangerine. "So how come you don't love *The Lord of the Rings* as much as she does?"

No one had ever made such an observation, but it was true: Had I been as devoted a fangirl as Zelda, I'd have been the one urging the book on Bennett, not her.

"It's not that I don't love it. I probably have a better grasp of the history of Middle-earth than she does. The map that came with"—I gestured toward the book with the tangerine I was peeling—"I can draw it from memory with ninety-seven percent accuracy and label all the place names in Elvish, Dwarvish, *and* Westron."

"I don't know why, but that's turning me on."

This made me giggle. He popped a tangerine segment into his mouth. I wondered how it would feel to kiss him and taste all that citrusy coolness.

"You were saying?" he reminded me.

"Right." I had to think for a moment to remember what we were talking about. "So it's not the world Tolkien created that I don't love, but the story, I guess. Or maybe the themes. There is such a pervasive sense of loss in his writing—it's all about the end of an age, about those who are leaving and not coming back. At one point Galadriel, the Elvish queen, says to Sam, 'For our spring and our summer are gone by, and they will never be seen on earth again save in memory.'"

Bennett gazed at me thoughtfully. My cheeks warmed. "Sorry. Is that too much geekery?"

"No, keep going."

"There's not much else. Well, not much else without spoiling the whole thing."

"Come on. The books are sixty years old, and I've seen enough Internet memes to know that one does not simply walk into Mordor."

I chortled. "I'll tell you a secret: Actually one does simply walk into Mordor. But carrying the burden of the ring changes Frodo. It damages him so much that he can't stay in Middle-earth anymore. He has to sail away with the last of the High Elves, leaving behind Sam and everything he's ever known, because he can no longer bear the pain."

And Sam, for all his devotion, could not lessen Frodo's torment or heal his wound. Could only stand by and watch as Frodo departed over the vast seas.

Without warning, tears stung the back of my eyes. Hastily I looked up, and then down at my half-peeled tangerine. "I guess you can say I have mixed feelings."

Bennett scooted closer to me, took the tangerine from my hand, and finished peeling it. He divided the segments inside, took half, and gave the other half to me. We ate silently. I watched the storm outside—and his reflection in the window, which watched me.

I felt as transparent as my own reflection. I should have become used to the sensation by now, since we never spent any significant amount of time together without my arriving at this state. But if anything, with repetition the naked vulnerability became more difficult to take, not less.

When we were finished with the tangerine, he said, "Zelda told me you liked arcade games."

I was so grateful for the change of subject, I'd have gone down on him that instant. "Yeah, but I haven't been to an arcade in years."

"Come with me."

He led me upstairs to his man cave, which I hadn't seen before, with a pool table, a card table, and big, deep leather chairs next to two laden bookshelves. I blinked: At the far end of the room stood two old-fashioned arcade video-game machines. Bennett turned them on. The moment the music started blaring, I was swept back to my childhood: sneaking out of the house on Saturday afternoons in a baggy T-shirt, jeans, and a backward baseball cap—so as not to stand out as a girl—and heading to what Pater dismissively called "that dungeon."

"My God, what games are they?"

"Everything," Bennett replied proudly.

For all the machines' retro appearance, they were not actually vintage—and each came loaded with hundreds of different games.

I scrolled through the list of titles, squealing at regular intervals. Many of the games had become available online as browser emulations—but that wasn't the same, was it?

"I brought the machines with me all the way from the West Coast," said Bennett. "Promise me you won't tell my dad."

"I won't tell anybody," I promised, still scrolling down that magnificent list. "And I'll sleep with you for playing time."

"Of course you will."

I played Donkey Kong, Dig Dug, and Bank Panic—the owner of "that dungeon" had a fondness for older games. I was about to start Galaga when Bennett hooked a finger in the waistband of my pajama bottoms. "Okay, Sam. Time to put out."

I caressed the screen of my new best friend before I squeezed Bennett's behind. "All right, you ugly Orc. Take me to your nasty cave and have your way with me."

We did tremendous justice to interspecies captive sex.

As I was on the verge of falling asleep, Bennett said, "I could be wrong, since I'm barely a hundred pages in, but maybe the reason Zelda loves the story is that in the end, no matter his own fate, Frodo left everything better than he found it."

I opened my eyes, but in the dark all I heard was his soft, even breathing.

THE NEXT TWO WEEKS, BENNETT and I spent as much time together as our schedules allowed. We played Cards Against Humanity and laughed ourselves stupid. We gave his arcade machines another workout. One evening, when I had to stay late at the office, he came and read *The Fellowship of the Ring* in a corner. We even met the Material Girls for drinks again, during which Daff and Lara admitted shamefacedly that they'd been to the MoMA exhibit. Carolyn alone abstained from the museum, but not from the online coverage—so Bennett made them all compliment his ass while I choked laughing.

The notable cloud in our silver lining was the lunch with Zelda and his parents. Mr. Somerset didn't recoil at the sight of him, but the meeting turned out to be as sterile as I'd warned Bennett it might be.

"I thought your dad couldn't possibly fail to see the exhibit as both ordinary and beautiful," I said later that day, in his apartment.

We'd been silent for some time, me wondering, with a heavy heart, whether it was possible to recover from this misstep.

"So you think of the exhibit as both ordinary and beautiful?" he asked softly.

Of course I did, but the thought of admitting it outright discomfited me. "Well," I answered, drawing out that syllable, "actually, I always think of the hens. You were cuddling a pair of them in one of the pictures."

"Oh, Lulu and Betty?" At my widened eyes, he grinned. "Did you think our egg hens didn't have names?"

His experience with poultry fascinated me. I had lots of questions, from what the chickens ate to how many eggs they produced to what was done with the chicken poop.

"That went right into the compost."

"Okay, that does it. Come the apocalypse, I'm sticking with you."

A lighthearted conversation followed on how we could bunkerize his house in Cos Cob. By the time that wound down, I was almost entirely out of my gloom concerning his chances with his father.

But Bennett fell quiet again. And didn't say anything else until I'd closed my laptop for good. And then it was only, "Come," as he led me upstairs to bed.

THE FOLLOWING WEDNESDAY, BENNETT TEXTED, *Are you free tonight? I'd like to see you.*

The text reached me at a symposium downtown. I studied the words: They seemed much more formal than was usual for him, almost as if he were arranging a business meeting, rather than a sleepover with his girlfriend.

But that didn't stop me from saying yes. In fact, I was so enthused about seeing him again that on my way back I hopped off at Canal Street and raided Chinatown for takeout.

Bennett had just come out of the shower when I showed up with the loot. "Hmm, what a dilemma," he said, taking the heavy bag from me. "I want to swoop down on both you and the food."

"Let's look at this scientifically: Takeout will be cold after sex, but I'll still be hot after takeout."

He smiled a little and kissed me on my lips. "Food first then, so I can have everything hot."

I rested my hand against his jaw for a moment. He smelled great, his stubble felt marvelous on my palm, and, of course, I still found his eyes, the green of high summer, utterly mesmerizing. My hand slid down to his shoulder—the khaki Henley he wore was made of a soft waffle-weave cotton—and then back to his nape, to play with his still slightly damp hair.

He stared at my parted lips, and then back into my eyes. *You have such hungry eyes*, he'd told me once. Did I look hungry again? Ravenous? Insatiable?

The only remedy to feeling like that was to make him fall victim to the same frenzy of lust, the same avalanche of need.

But before I could slide my hand down his back and lift up his shirt, he moved away from me and walked toward the dining room.

"Come on," he said over his shoulder. "Let's eat."

The food was beyond delicious, but I felt off balance. It wasn't helped by the general silence at the table, our conversation consisting only of variations of, "Try this," and, "This is even better."

Between sips of a clear peppery broth, I observed Bennett surreptitiously. He seemed to be eating with a singular concentration. Did he have something on his mind? I was becoming increasingly convinced that he did. And that he was tense—and had been since I walked in.

I'd barely eyed the soup container before he picked it up. "You want some more?"

"Yeah, thanks. Half a bowl, please."

I loved it when he did little things like that for me. And he was always doing such little things. He was always—

The thought struck me: Was it possible he was going to propose? His formal-ish invitation, his decision to forgo sex, his nerves—everything pointed to a significant decision he had come to, a decision concerning us.

He hadn't wanted an engagement earlier, because the timing would be suspect. But now we'd weathered the storm together. Not to mention, something needed to be done to kick-start his stalled reconciliation with his father. Knowing Bennett, he wasn't going to tell Mr. Somerset outright that he wanted to return to the family. An engagement would be just the thing to get everyone excited and move the process forward.

"I've been meaning to ask you something," said Bennett.

My heart lurched. "Yes?"

"Larry de Villiers got your e-mail address from me a while ago. Did he ever contact you?"

I hadn't felt so deflated since he canceled our previous "engagement." Reaching out, I scooped some stir-fried lotus root into my bowl. "He did. He sent me an e-mail."

"Mind if I ask what he said?"

"He…he thanked me for talking with him that day at Mrs. Asquith's."

"Did you say anything in return?"

I hesitated. "No."

With his chopsticks, Bennett picked up a single peanut from a kung pao dish. "Why not?"

Why did I have the sensation that the ground might be shifting? "No particular reason."

"Did you talk to Zelda about him?"

"Yeah."

"Did you ask her whether she'd consider getting back with him?"

I ate a piece of lotus root, even though my appetite was gone. "She said she didn't know."

"Has he made any overtures?"

"I don't believe so."

Bennett had opened a bottle of Riesling for dinner. He refilled my glass. "Is he holding back because you told him to?"

"I don't know," I said instinctively. Then, forcing myself to be more forthcoming: "Maybe."

He refilled his own glass. "And you're okay with that?"

My conscience might protest once in a while, but since I hadn't done anything about it, it could only mean I was fine with things continuing as they were. But to admit that straight-up was beyond me.

My silence reverberated in every corner of the apartment.

Bennett gave a quarter turn to the base of his wine stem. His expression, as he studied the pale green-gold liquid in the glass, was severe, perhaps the most severe I'd ever seen of him. Yet it was also…unhappy.

I wanted to reach out to him, but I sat exactly where I was, frozen, my chopsticks still gripped in my fingers.

His gaze returned to me. "I've never asked you, have I, why you were wandering the back lanes of Cos Cob in the rain, looking like a character out of *Les Misérables*?"

I quaked inside. "Why are you interested all of a sudden?"

"I've always wanted to know," he said calmly, quietly. "You know that."

Despite the softness of his tone, there was an implacability to his words. "Come on," I said, feeling like a caught fish wriggling on the hook, "you got laid. Aren't you supposed to be happy with that?"

"No."

I laid aside my chopsticks at last. "Why are you asking me so many questions?"

Why won't you let me dodge them, as you've always done before?

"Because you have never told me anything about yourself. Ever."

"You already Googled me up and down before I even knew your last name. What else is there to know?"

He only looked at me. I swallowed, completely rattled. "Look, you're a man who holds his cards close. You have a fake girlfriend, for God's sake. And you can't even tell your parents you want to be their son again. I mean—"

"I know what you mean. You're saying that I, the pot, am asking you, the kettle, why you are such a profoundly sooty shade."

I made no reply: That was exactly what I'd been going for.

"It's a valid point," he said. "You've made other excellent points before on my choices. And I've been thinking about what you said. Today I called my dad and asked him to meet me for a drink Saturday, just the two of us. We already agreed on the time and the place."

This took me aback. "What are you going to say to him?"

"What I should have said long ago."

I was shaken anew. "Why now? Why out of the blue?"

"Is it out of the blue? Maybe it looks that way from the outside, but I've been weighing it for a while. You were right about our reconciliation going nowhere. To go on doing the same thing and hope for different results—that's the definition of insanity, isn't it?"

"I guess. I mean, it's good that you're moving forward with your dad. It's…really good."

"I hope so."

He glanced outside. The weather had been demented lately, swinging from single digits to the forties and back again in forty-eight hours, accompanied by every kind of precipitation imaginable. Now it poured, wind-whipped raindrops pelting the floor-to-ceiling windows like pebbles, the sheets of water cascading down the huge glass panes distorting the buildings across the street into blobs of light and shadow.

Bennett looked back at me—I realized I'd been holding my breath. "When I bowed to the conclusion that continuing along the same path with my dad would be fruitless," he said, "I saw that the same could be said of the two of us."

I stared at him.

He gave his wineglass another quarter turn. "Don't tell me you have no idea. By now somebody must have said something to you about the ring."

"You insisted that it wasn't an engagement ring."

"I didn't ask you to marry me. All the same, it was an unambiguous gesture."

My fingers dug into the seat of my chair. "Tell me, then. What exactly did it signify?"

I couldn't quite believe it, that we were—or he was—going to blow the beautiful, perfect lid off our beautiful, almost perfect relationship.

He was silent for nearly a minute. I was once again reminded of the night we met, his hesitation in the rain.

"Do you remember what I said about the first time I saw you?" he spoke at last.

No more hesitation on his part—and I couldn't hold his gaze. "Central Park. June. My friend's wedding," I answered, looking at the remnants of our dinner. The remnants of my hopes for a wonderful evening.

A wonderful life.

"You forgot the crucial part," he said.

"What crucial part?"

"That I fell in love with you at first sight."

I trembled, even though I did my best to hold still. "I never believed that. It was too outlandish."

"I fell in love with Moira at first sight," he said softly. "I was watching soccer on TV, a match between Real Madrid and FC Barcelona, when I heard a car pull up. I opened the window for a better look. Moira was just coming out of the car, her hair in a ponytail, a bottle of wine in her hand. She saw me, smiled, and said to her boyfriend, '*Mira, el muchacho americano.*' And I knew that instant my life would never be the same.

"After we broke up, I went around and met as many women as I could. I wanted to fall in love again—it seemed that being into someone else would be the best way to forget Moira. Never happened. After a while I realized it was a blessing. Given how our breakup had torn me apart, why would I ever want to fall in love again?

"By the time I moved back east, I was pretty confident that Moira had been a fluke. Which made things easy: I just needed to find a nice woman who'd get me back into my parents' circle and settle down with her.

"I met Julianne my third week in the city. Her mother has served on several boards with my dad. She herself is pretty, outgoing, and personable. Her company does PR for the hospital, she liked me, and she was absolutely perfect for what I had in mind—not as a fake girlfriend, by the way, but a real one."

Julianne must be the friend Damaris Vandermeer kept bringing up. Theirs was exactly the right demographic for Bennett: sociable, well-connected young women who would have loved taking on the challenge of reintegrating him into his family. I drained half my wine, not surprised that he had set his sights on a real relationship, only that I hadn't realized it sooner.

"My plans were all under way when I saw you on that bridge, looking down into the water," he continued, his gaze no longer on me but on the storm that surrounded us. "I remember stopping dead in my tracks, staring at you, and not understanding why—it had been so long since I felt anything of the sort. You had a bouquet of pink peonies in your hand, and you were plucking out the petals and letting them fall. It was the prettiest scene imaginable, your dress almost the same color as the water under the bridge, the petals floating on your reflection—and I was unbelievably pissed off.

"I had plans. Who were you and what the hell was I supposed to do with you? And I hated how it felt to look at you, as if I were standing on my own heart, crushing it with my weight—that kind of romantic shit was fine for a sixteen-year-old, but I was too old, too busy, and too ulterior-motived for it. So I walked away."

"What?" I couldn't help my dismayed exclamation. "You left it to chance whether we'd ever meet again?"

"All weddings in the park need permits—I could find out whose wedding you were attending and track you down that way, if I had to. But you know what I came across on my way out of the park?"

"What?"

"A charcoal drawing of your 'princess' picture, for sale by a street artist. Three days later I saw you in Cos Cob for the first time, walking Biscuit on a Saturday morning."

He studied me, a scowl on his face, as if seeing me again for the very first time. "I tried to proceed with my original plan, but it was hopeless. Julianne thought I was a gentleman for holding off on physical contact, when in fact I wanted nothing to do with her. Beginning of August she went on vacation with her family. I had some time to consider what to do—and guess who called out of the blue, in a panic about a dog.

"At this point I was feeling under siege, but no dog should have to suffer for my problems. So I did what you asked. That Friday, when you texted me and told me you were going back to Cos Cob, I fully intended to stay in Manhattan—away from you. Next thing I knew, I was on the train.

"Still, when I got into my car outside Cos Cob station and started driving, I didn't have any plans besides knocking on your door in the morning and introducing myself. But there you were, trudging along the side of the road, all drenched and miserable-looking.

"To this day I wonder how things would have turned out if I'd kept driving and left you to your own devices."

I was on my feet. The idea that he could have passed me by, that we would have never met…

"It was always a moot point," he said quietly. "There was no way I wouldn't have stopped to make sure you were okay."

Slowly I sank back into my chair. "And then you realized that I was also a pretty good candidate, since I was the one your parents had picked for you in the first place."

He laughed briefly, and without mirth. "No. The moment I saw you wandering around in the dark, in the rain, I knew you had to be completely fucked-up."

My lips moved but I couldn't form a single syllable. Certainly not to defend myself. "Completely fucked-up" was an apt description—except I'd never heard it from anyone but myself. And even I had never said these words out loud.

"But you were also…delightful. When you said, 'Grandma was lying through her teeth. You're just average,' I knew I was in far worse trouble than I'd ever imagined."

He almost smiled. My heart pounded with a searing happiness.

"I parted ways with Julianne. But I couldn't decide what to do about you. For a few weeks I Googled you every day. And then I talked to Mrs. Asquith and she said that I should contact Zelda. So I got in touch.

"All the while I still hesitated—still hoped that I'd wake up and forget about you. Then we ran into each other outside the Met. Do you know how many times you said no to me that day? I lost count. Every time you did, I told myself not to walk away, but run. Instead I kept doubling down. When you refused to be my girlfriend I said how about a fake relationship. When you wouldn't take that I offered money. When even money couldn't move you I…" He took a deep breath. "I think it's fair to say that I begged you to come to the wedding reception with me. I've done some crazy things in my life, but that night was the first time I understood what batshit insane felt like."

We had been in this exact room. I remembered pushing pieces of poached pear around on my plate, freaking out over his escalating offers, and wondering what the hell he actually wanted from me.

Everything. He wanted everything.

He reached for a fortune cookie from the table and broke it in two. An ironic look crossed his face as he scanned the tiny scrap of paper inside. He pushed it my way.

Love is not for the weak of heart.

"I believed then—as I did about my reconciliation with my parents—that time together was all we needed. That the rest would take care of itself. But as you remind me time and again, progress doesn't happen on its own—someone has to speak the truth first. Well, the same applies to us.

"We've also been going around in circles. You are as crazy about me as I am about you, but being in love has done nothing to loosen you up. At this point you're no more likely to open up to me than Gollum would be to the idea of a vacation somewhere nice and sunny.

"So I'm taking your advice. I'm putting all my cards faceup on the table. You can see them for what they are."

I didn't want to. I was happy to have guessed enough of the truth. I was ecstatic with the way things were. But he had to upend my beautiful castle in the sky. "Now what?"

His response was slow to come. "Now I admit that I'd hoped you wouldn't be staring at me with the kind of alarm that borders on horror."

"Sorry," I mumbled, glancing down at my hands. "It's a lot to take in."

"Is it really that frightening to have someone love you?"

No, when I realized that he loved me, it had been one of the best moments of my life. What was frightening was that he wanted to peel back my layers and expose what I'd tried to keep hidden all these years.

I said nothing.

"I don't require that you make the same kind of exhaustive confession, you know," he murmured. "At least not tonight."

"But you will, at some point."

He picked up his wineglass. I had the feeling he wanted to drain the whole thing, but he set it down again without taking a sip. "Do we, as a couple, matter to you?"

I grabbed my wineglass and downed what remained of its contents. "What are you really asking?"

"I'd like to know if you'll make an effort. Will you try to be open, and not change the subject whenever it comes too close to something that hurts or that you're afraid of?"

I felt suspended, above an absolute void. "You want too much. You should have left things alone."

"Believe me, I've thought long and hard about leaving things alone. But then there will always be this wall between us."

"It's all ugly things behind the wall," I said, not looking at him.

"I'm not afraid of what's behind the wall, only the wall itself."

But the wall was my exoskeleton. It was what held me up. Sometimes it was the only thing that held me up.

He lowered his gaze, his lashes shadowing his eyes. "Is not answering your way of letting me know you won't even consider it?"

What was there to consider? Without the wall, would I even exist?

Rain hurtled into the windows, the noise that of a distant barrage of bullets. The silence between us seemed to turn solid, a hard, unmovable entity.

He picked up his wineglass again—and drained it this time. "So between the wall and me, you've made your choice."

I stared down at the table. *Love is not for the weak of heart.* "You knew how this was going to go," I said. "You knew this discussion was never going to end well."

"I knew it would be difficult, yes. I didn't know it would be impossible. I didn't know that your fear is strong enough to crush my hopes."

I reeled, thunder rolling and crashing in my head. "I still have some work to do on my paper. I should go home."

He rose. "Thanks for dinner."

"You're welcome."

I didn't know how I stood up—I'd become as heavy as a monolith from Stonehenge. Back in the living room, as I reached for my purse, I remembered. "Are we still a fake couple? Do you still need me for anything with your parents?"

He leaned against the mantel, looking as worn as I'd ever seen him. "If I tell my dad the truth, I might as well tell him the whole truth."

"So my services are no longer required."

"That's not how I'd put it…." He shrugged. "I'll still honor the financial part of our agreement."

"Don't worry about that. I didn't do it for the money."

"Doesn't matter," he said, as if to himself. "A contract is a contract."

"And ours specified that if I quit before the end of the six months, you won't be out a dime," I reminded him.

"I guess there's that."

I fiddled with the handle of my purse. "So this is good-bye?"

He traced a finger along the chrome candelabra on the mantel. "I'm sure we'll run into each other here and there."

I wished I felt even heavier. I wished I were so massive I'd collapse under my own weight and become part of the floor. "Guess this had to happen, when I finally got used to the idea of a nice fake relationship."

"I'm sorry."

"No, don't apologize."

"I was only stating how I feel. I'll miss you."

I'd miss him too. Desperately. I'd just settled into the rhythm of seeing him regularly, of eagerly anticipating those meetings and relishing every moment of our time together.

I'd just had a taste of not being alone.

Walking up to him, I kissed him on the cheek. Now I should go, leave with some dignity and conviction while I still could.

I didn't move an inch. We stood a bare centimeter apart. I stared at the pulse at the base of his throat; then I was touching it, feeling the erratic beats of his heart. My hand traveled up the column of his neck and trailed along his jawline. I loved touching his face, whether it was freshly shaven or like now, rough with a two-day stubble.

The pad of my thumb traced across his lower lip. He caught my hand, his grip tight. I pulled his hand toward me and rubbed the inside of my lower lip against a knuckle. He sucked in a breath.

"I know why you were walking in the rain, by the way," he said. "I found out from Mrs. Asquith that Zelda wasn't well at the time."

My innards tightened. I turned his hand over and nibbled on his palm. "Then why bother asking me?"

"*You* should be the one telling me. And I shouldn't be brushed aside anytime I ask an important question."

I drew his index finger into my mouth, wanting to shut him up. His eyes darkened. "Why are you so afraid?"

Because life as I know it can end any moment. Because nothing is safe. Because if I don't protect myself, nobody will.

I said nothing, but pressed an openmouthed kiss below his jaw.

"You're not walling yourself off from heartache—there's no possibility of that. You're only walling yourself off from life."

Beneath his pajama trousers he was already thickening and rising. I maneuvered him down onto a nearby armchair and kissed him. But he pushed me away. "You don't want to kiss me. You just want me to stop talking."

"Then why don't you?"

And why couldn't you have left well enough alone?

"Because I care. Because you're stuck. Because there's no coming unstuck for you unless you're willing to change."

I fell to my knees and licked his erection through the pajamas. It flexed under my tongue. "I don't want to change."

"Nobody wants to change, goddammit. But sometimes you have to. Did you think it was easy for me? Did you think I wasn't exactly like you?"

I pulled down his waistband and took him deep into my mouth. He was shower-clean, with a hint of the musk of arousal. I gripped the base of his shaft, and caressed his scrotum with my other hand.

He still persisted—his fingers digging into the arms of the chair. "I never spoke about Moira to anybody. I never spoke about my parents. I could never stand for anyone to know that my life wasn't one hundred percent perfect. But for us to have any chance, I knew I had to be honest with you. And if I could, why can't you?"

I deep-throated him. He emitted a guttural sound. I didn't know what I was trying to do—this went far beyond silencing him. Part of me wanted to punish him, possibly, for everything he was taking away from me.

For the abyss that awaited me outside. And within.

I looked up. His eyes were shut, his teeth clenched together. And then he opened his eyes, and the way he stared at me, with both anger and despair—pain scorched my heart.

I deep-throated him again. He tried to remain quiet and motionless, but couldn't. He thrust into me. His breaths turned harsh and sibilant. Then he plunged his hands into my hair and came in my mouth.

I swallowed and swallowed. When it was all over I wrapped my arms around him and set my cheek against his thigh, unable to let go. He was the one who moved away, leaving me with my head on the chair and no one to embrace.

He returned all too soon. "Your cab will be downstairs in two minutes."

I got up, feeling heavier than ever. Before the private elevator he handed me my coat and my purse. "Maybe you should try to deal with your abandonment issues."

I recoiled. "What do *you* know about abandonment issues?"

"My parents turned their backs on me because they didn't like the person I dated. And the woman for whom I gave up everything sat me down one day and told me that I was too bourgeois for her. What don't I know about abandonment issues?"

Before I could react, he pressed the button on the elevator. "Good-bye, Eva."

I trudged into the elevator. By the time I turned around, the doors were already closing, blocking him from view. And then I was looking at my own reflection in the bright chrome, a wide-eyed, bewildered woman who still couldn't believe that she'd lost the best thing to happen to her in a long, long time.

Chapter 16

IT WAS BARELY PAST NINE o'clock in the evening when I got home. From the living room, Zelda looked up in surprise. "Back so early, darling?"

I managed a smile. "Bennett has a late shift."

White lies were a necessity of life. Yet the moment the fib left my lips, all the lies that I'd ever fed Zelda crashed toward me, an avalanche of falsehood. *No, I never think about my mother. No, I'm not afraid, ever. Of course I already have everything I want in life.*

"Are you all right, darling?"

"I'm fine," I said reflexively. "Well, maybe a bit nervous. Saturday Bennett is meeting his father, the two of them."

It had become second nature, hadn't it, this deflection?

The deflection worked. Zelda's eyes widened. "Are they? I wonder if Frances is on tenterhooks too."

"I'm sure she is."

Zelda reached for her phone. "Let me text her."

"Say hi to her for me. I'm going up."

In my room, I sank down on the edge of the bed. Why couldn't Bennett be happy with us the way we were? Why must he want what wasn't in me to give? Why, if he knew I was fucked-up, did he take up with me in the first place?

You don't hook up with someone crazy unless you're willing to let them be unhinged.

I pulled out my phone and scrolled through the backlog of our texts. Still not that many of them, and mostly of a mundane nature, the discussion of when and where to meet next.

Yet I read them over again and again, this record of my all-too-real fake relationship. I wished now that I hadn't turned him down for Valentine's Day. That I hadn't let weeks and weeks go by between meetings. That I hadn't wasted four months last year not contacting him.

But would anything have made a difference? Or would I still end up sitting alone in my room, my heart in ruins?

I scrolled again through all our texts. So few. Too few. In no time at all I'd arrived at his fatal invitation. *Are you free tonight? I'd like to see you.*

To which I had blithely and innocently replied, *I can be there about 7:15.*

See you then.

We'd seen each other, and everything had fallen apart.

I swiped the screen again. There was one last exchange, from this afternoon.

How's the book coming? I'd asked, regarding his progress on *The Fellowship of the Ring.*

They are about to go into Moria and I'm afraid.

The idea of his joining us for the movie marathon had been incredibly appealing, a wide new vista. But now there would only be Zelda and me.

Until the day I would be left all by myself.

I started tapping, a torrent of geekery on everything there was to know about shuttered, harrowing Moria, which had once been a magnificent city of broad avenues and great carven halls. Until someone dug too carelessly and too deep, and unleashed an ancient demon that caused its untimely destruction.

Only after I'd pressed send on my last text did I realize that what I'd written about was not the end of Moria, but the end of us.

I FELL ASLEEP, PHONE IN hand, waiting for a response.

Any response.

When I woke up there were a dozen new texts, but they were from my grad students, about a problem with our lab machines. Nothing from Bennett.

It was the sanest choice he could have made. But I didn't want him to be sane, logical, or grown-up. I wanted him to engage.

Then at least I wouldn't feel so profoundly alone.

Machine issues took up the whole day. Any moment I wasn't talking to tech support on the phone, technicians in person, or my grad students about how our experiments could be redesigned to bypass the outage, I checked to see whether Bennett had texted me back.

He never did.

Had I been IM'ing into the great digital void? No, I'd broken up my essay on Moria into many separate texts. As I tapped out each new sentence, I'd seen the little notifications that popped up under earlier text bubbles. *Read 10:35. Read 10:37. Read 10:38. Read…*

Read, but not answered.

That night I lay in bed for hours, trying to fall asleep. At some point I made the mistake of reminding myself that he loved me, which only made me curl up in misery. Next thing I knew, I'd gone downstairs and grabbed my purse from the living room couch, where I'd deliberately left it, so I wouldn't have a phone next to me.

Put the phone back. Put the phone back! shouted the still-rational part of me.

But I might as well have been shouting at a pack of zombies to stop advancing.

I crawled back under the covers and started tapping. Munich, the snow, the Englischer Garten, and, at last, him. I described our make-believe encounter in Proustian detail, every course eaten, every drink consumed, every flicker of the light as reflected in his eyes. And then, an entire dissertation on our imaginary lovemaking.

I used to touch myself, weaving this fantasy. But unlike you on your masturbation couch, I didn't want to orgasm right away. I wanted to draw it out for as long as possible.

But I never managed.

Sometimes I came as soon as I got to the part about the two of us returning to your hotel room. Sometimes I didn't even last that long—we'd have barely sat down to coffee. And sometimes all you had to do was say hello, and I'd come to a fiery end, like the Death Star.

Both of them.

Oh, God, now I'd gone and compared myself to a space explosion, the celluloid depiction of which was riddled with scientific inaccuracies. If his phone was ever hacked—or mine—I'd never be able to show my face in public again.

Yet I kept going. I told him exactly where I stroked, rubbed, and sometimes pinched. I told him how I liked to keep the room absolutely dark, and my eyes tightly shut, so that my fantasy took on the greatest clarity and verisimilitude. I told him how afterward, still trembling from my multiple climaxes, I'd peel off my pajamas, feel the sheets against my skin, and imagine instead that it was his hands and his body upon me—and perhaps start the process all over again.

When my shoulders started locking, because I'd held the phone at a strange position for too long, I finally set down the device from hell and groaned into my pillow, dying from mortification.

And imagined him sleeping soundly while my midnight insanity invaded his phone, packet after packet of relentless crazy.

And relentless yearning.

"BENNETT'S WORKING TONIGHT, RIGHT?" ASKED Zelda the next evening, which happened to be the start of the weekend.

I sprinkled some salt into the eggs I'd just finished beating. "His shift is until midnight."

Thank goodness, or I'd have to explain why I was staying home. But what was I going to say tomorrow evening, when he had no shift and I was still hanging around my own house?

"I do admire that boy," said Zelda, checking on the leftover scalloped potatoes she was reheating in the oven. "I'm not sure I'd still work—let alone work so hard—if I had that sort of money sitting in the bank."

I lit the stove, set a pan over the flames, and dropped a pat of butter inside. "He probably knows he'd be up to no good if he didn't stay busy."

"He won't hear any arguments from me about keeping busy. You, darling, on the other hand, could stand to become a little *less* busy."

"Won't be long now before my tenure review."

When's the wedding?

August.

Why August?

'Cause she'll have passed tenure review and I'll have finished with my fellowship. And we can have a nice long honeymoon before her schedule goes crazy again in September.

"Isn't the butter hot enough?" Zelda reminded me.

I started. "Right. Thanks."

The mushroom, spinach, and ham I'd cut up for our dinner omelet went into the pan. Zelda sneaked in with her fork and stole a piece of ham. "Since you're home tonight, how about we stream a movie?"

"Sure."

Anything to keep me from sending deeply humiliating texts that added up to the length of Broadway from end to end.

Of course I hadn't had any replies from him. And that was the most humiliating part of all: He conducted himself with dignity, whereas I behaved like an adolescent in the throes of her first breakup, all self-indulgent misery and hormone-driven drama.

I put half an omelet and one scoop of scalloped potato on the plate for each of us and carried the plates to the living room. Zelda had just sat down next to me, remote in hand, when her phone dinged with the sound of an incoming text. I picked up the phone from the coffee table and handed it to her.

Had Bennett read my texts? Or had their scent of lunacy been too strong for him to do more than scroll through, shaking his head at that endless spew of verbiage?

"My God!" cried Zelda.

I almost dropped my plate. "What's going on?"

"Frances Somerset texted from the hospital. Her husband had a heart attack."

"What?" I clutched the rim of my plate. "Is he okay?"

"They're operating right now, a quadruple bypass."

"Jesus. Does Bennett know?"

"She's been trying to contact him. His hospital says he's in surgery and they don't expect him to come out for at least another two hours."

I turned off the TV. "Which hospital is his dad at? Does his mom need someone to stay with her?"

Zelda exchanged further texts with Mrs. Somerset. Fifteen minutes later we were in a cab, huddled close together on the backseat.

"It can all go away in a heartbeat," murmured Zelda, as the cab glided forward.

I stared out the window. Cones of orange light from street lamps punctuated the night; shadows of still-bare branches swayed back and forth on walls and sidewalks.

At the hospital we found Mrs. Somerset in a nondescript waiting room. Dressed in an incongruously glamorous gown of black cashmere, she rocked back and forth in her chair, her hands over the lower half of her face.

We said hi. She leaped up and hugged both of us. "Thank you so much for coming."

Mrs. Somerset had no further news on her husband's prognosis, and she still hadn't heard back from Bennett. But she'd managed to get in touch with her other children. Imogene would be getting on a red-eye flight that landed early in the morning. Prescott, halfway around the world, wasn't expected to reach New York until late the next evening.

"Have you had any dinner?" I asked. "Can I get you something?"

"No, we were on our way to a fund-raiser when Rowland—when we had to come to the hospital. But please don't trouble yourself. I don't want anything."

I got a coffee for her, tea for Zelda and me, and a couple of muffins—Mrs. Somerset might not want to eat now, but hunger caught up to everyone sooner or later, no matter the circumstances.

We waited. From time to time Mrs. Somerset would give us an update from her far-flung children. *Prescott is at the airport, about to go through security. Imogene has boarded—her boyfriend is coming with her. I hope Prescott doesn't miss his connecting flight—the layover in Taipei is less than two hours.*

Around midnight Zelda moved to a seat in the corner—she was dropping off. I draped both our coats over her and went back to my chair. Two TVs were mounted on opposite walls of the waiting room, their volume muted. The one I happened to face had been set on a cooking channel. Chefs ran about frantically, mopping their foreheads with towels, shouting soundless commands at their underlings.

"Evangeline," came Mrs. Somerset's soft voice.

I glanced toward her. "Yes, ma'am?"

"Do you happen to know why Bennett set up the meeting with his dad, just the two of them?"

After a moment of hesitation, I nodded.

"Did he…Does he want a reconciliation?"

I thought of Mr. Somerset on the operating table, his chest open, his fate in the hands of strangers. "Yes."

Mrs. Somerset covered her face with her hands. "Oh, God. If only he'd made that appointment for one day earlier."

"Maybe Mr. Somerset guessed. Maybe—"

I forgot what I was about to say. Bennett stood in the doorway, looking tired, grim, and more than a little scared. Mrs. Somerset exclaimed and rushed up to him. He enfolded her tightly in his arms and murmured, "It's okay. Everything will be fine."

Since the news of the heart attack, I hadn't thought too much about our breakup or my unfortunate texts. But the moment he looked my way, embarrassment pummeled me.

Especially since I hadn't come clean about my sexual obsession solely because I went a little crazy. There had been an ulterior motive: I'd wanted to turn him on and stick a knife in his heart at the same time, to make an already painful separation even more difficult for him.

To punish him, because he wouldn't let me have my cake and eat it too.

Because he, the one who had made every mistake in the book, had turned out to be the braver, wiser, and more principled of the two of us.

By far.

"Thanks for staying with my mom," he said, and hugged me too.

His strong arms, his wintry scent, the feeling of being safely enclosed—yet another memory to torment me when I was alone again.

He didn't wake up Zelda, but spoke in whispers with his mom. Then they sat down together, her hands holding tightly on to his, her head on his shoulder.

I left and returned with a coffee for Bennett. "There are couple of muffins here, in case you're hungry."

He accepted the coffee. "Thanks. I'm okay for now."

I sat down cattycorner from mother and son and wished I'd taken Zelda home at midnight, before I turned into a pumpkin. Without thinking I reached for my phone, only to feel my face scald. Hurriedly I put it away and looked up at the TV.

On-screen a chef was crying, wiping ineffectually at the corners of his eyes. *I really thought*, read the closed-captioning, *I really thought I had a chance. Not just to go past this round, but to go all the way, win the big prize. My mom thought so too. My friends. Everybody.*

If broken dreams were an actual substance, we could build a six-lane highway to the moon every day of the week.

Something made me glance in Bennett's direction. His mother seemed to have fallen asleep, her eyes closed. His gaze was on me. But I couldn't tell whether he was looking at me or merely happened to be staring in my direction.

"I was at a coronary bypass too," he said.

I remembered that he'd been in surgery, except on the operating end. "How did it go?"

"It went fine. But during the previous major bypass at the hospital, the patient died midprocedure."

My hands tightened around each other. "I'm sure your dad will pull through."

"I hope so," he said, his voice so low I almost couldn't hear. "I really hope so."

I wanted to reassure him. *You'll have time. He'll recover. I can feel it.*

But I'd thought that Pater was going to make it too. I didn't think it was possible for my father to be felled by a random car accident. After all, misanthropes were supposed to last forever, growing more bitter with each passing year.

I got up and sat down next to Bennett, taking his free hand in mine. I didn't say anything. Words were of no use here. One way or the other we would know before the end of the night.

He lifted our clasped hands and kissed the back of my palm.

And then we waited.

I WAS STARTING TO DRIFT off when someone said, "Are you

Rowland Somerset's family?"

Bennett and I both scrambled to our feet. "Yes, we are," he said, giving his mom a small shake.

She jerked and sat up straight. "What's going on? Is he okay?"

The woman in green scrubs was Asian in feature and about forty years old. She shook our hands. "Hi, I'm Dr. Pei. I'm happy to inform you that the surgery was successful. Mr. Somerset is now in recovery and should come out of anesthesia in about an hour or so."

I had tears in my eyes. So did Bennett. Mrs. Somerset wept outright with relief, leaning on her son. The commotion awakened Zelda, who leaped up at the news, which led to many hugs being exchanged. Then we all shook hands with Dr. Pei again, thanking her—and her team—profusely.

"Will we be able to see him?" asked Mrs. Somerset.

"Very briefly," answered Dr. Pei. "He won't be able to speak because he'll still be intubated, and I would ask that you do not excite him, since he needs to rest."

After the surgeon left, we celebrated some more. Bennett and his mother shared a muffin, texted his siblings, and drank a toast with their cold coffees.

"Do you want to go home?" I asked Zelda.

"After Rowland comes out of anesthesia," she said.

Three-quarters of an hour later, a nurse came and told us that Mr. Somerset was awake. Mrs. Somerset and Bennett went into the recovery room; Zelda and I remained just outside.

The recovery room had a window that faced the corridor, its blinds half up. I could see Mr. Somerset on the hospital bed, surrounded by IV stands and various machines, looking incredibly frail. His wife went to him and took his hand. He lifted his other hand a bare inch off the bed. Bennett hesitated, a look of confusion and incredulity on his face. Then he rushed forward and gripped his father's hand in his own.

The nurse was already laying down the law. "Only one family member may remain with the patient. Everyone else must clear out."

"I'll stay," said Bennett. "Mom, you go home and take some rest."

"I love you," said Mrs. Somerset to her husband.

Bennett kissed his father on the forehead. "I love you too, Dad—

and I'm sorry for everything. I'll see the ladies to their cabs and be right back."

We walked out of the hospital. Mrs. Somerset hugged her son. "It's so good to have you back. So very, *very* good."

He kissed her on both cheeks. "It's good to be back."

The prodigal son had returned to the fold. The circle was complete. And I stood outside the circle, looking in.

Zelda felt no such outsider status. She hugged Frances Somerset and then Bennett. "I'm so happy for you. For this entire family."

Mrs. Somerset left waving—and dabbing at the corners of her eyes. The next cab pulled up. Zelda got in first. I looked at Bennett and managed a smile. "Take care."

He kissed me on my lips. "You too. I love you."

My ears rang, as if I'd been to a too-loud concert. "But not enough to take me as I am?" I said, my words barely above a whisper.

His voice dropped just as low. "The other way around. I love you too much to survive being kept at arm's length."

"You want me to be someone I'm not."

"Your work is all about making ceramics conduct electricity. Ceramics are insulators. Why are you wasting your time?"

A hundred rebuttals bounced around in my head, everything from source material and kilning methods to the molecular structure of electroceramics.

"Are you coming or not, lady?" asked the cabdriver, getting impatient.

I grimaced and got in. When we were about to turn the corner and lose sight of the hospital, I looked back. Bennett was still there, watching me leave.

Chapter 17

I WAS ALTERNATELY EXASPERATED WITH Bennett for talking out of his rear end—of course a subset of ceramics conducted electricity, and very well too—and infuriated because, as far as metaphors went, his had been pretty damn seamless.

My work was all about improving properties that the layman might not even know ceramics possessed. And now he wanted me to do the same to my heart, to unearth properties that *I* didn't even know it possessed.

It was midmorning before I walked downstairs. Zelda was putting away groceries in the kitchen. A box of pastries from the 79th Street Greenmarket sat on the counter. Two big "Get well soon" balloons bumped against the ceiling, their ribbons tied to the fridge handle.

"Morning, darling. I had a text from Frances. Rowland is fine. Imogene is already with him. Bennett went home to take a shower but should be back at the hospital in a few minutes. I'm taking the pastry to them, but there's enough for all of us. Do you want to have one now or after we get to the hospital?"

I poured myself a cup of tea from the pot she'd already made. "I have some experiments I need to keep an eye on. Say hi to everybody for me."

"So you're planning to go later in the day?"

It was a grey, drizzly morning. The shopping tote that still lay on the kitchen counter was wet on the outside. I took a dish towel and wiped it down. "No, I'm not going today."

Zelda nudged back the pullout basket where we kept root vegetables and turned around. "I know Rowland is out of danger. But I'm sure

Bennett would appreciate your company. And Frances tells me Imogene is really excited to meet you."

I forced myself to look at her. "There's something you need to know. Bennett and I, we were...we've never been together. He recruited me as his pretend girlfriend, because I offered a means for him to be nearer to his parents without his having to come out and say that he wanted to reconcile. Now they're reconciled and my role is finished."

Zelda stared at me as if I'd told her that all along I'd been a green-skinned alien from a planet that orbited Betelgeuse.

I scraped my fingernail against a balloon ribbon. "I'm sorry I didn't tell you sooner. He wanted to keep it a secret."

Zelda pinched the bridge of her nose. "But I thought he really had a thing for you—and you him. All the times you spent the night at his place—surely you weren't just strategizing about his parents?"

"It was a partnership with...benefits."

"Are the...benefits going to end too?"

"Yeah," I said.

I opened the dishwasher and took out a handful of plates so I wouldn't be just standing there, stupidly saying, "Yeah."

"I don't understand. I mean, I understand the having-a-girlfriend-to-make-reconciliation-easier part. But if the two of you do in fact enjoy each other's company, why stop? And last night, didn't I hear him say that he loved you?"

Had Bennett and I broken up for any other reason, I'd have made something up—or maybe tried to get out of the conversation. But now that he'd shone such a glaring light on the way I lived my life, now that I was exposed for all my tricks and maneuvers, I couldn't bring myself to be business-as-usual with Zelda.

"He wants a real relationship. And I have a problem with that."

"I know you're busy, darling. But surely nobody is too busy for love."

"It's not that. I may be...I may be incapable of a real relationship."

"That's ridiculous." Zelda huffed. Then, less certainly: "Isn't it?"

I kept reaching into the dishwasher. Glasses, mugs, silverware returned to their designated places—anything to prevent me from actually squirming with discomfort. "I don't like to be asked questions. I don't like having to talk about things I don't want to talk about. I'd rather be alone than open myself up to be poked and prodded."

"My God," whispered Zelda.

"I'm sorry."

"No, no, it's just that…I remember a conversation with your father. He stood exactly where you're standing now, and he said more or less the same thing."

I froze, a spatula in hand.

"You know how your father was—great in a crisis, took his responsibilities seriously, and so droll and witty when he was in the right mood. But dear God, a lot of times it was downright impossible to hold a normal conversation with him. I think his father must have been a nasty piece of work, and his mother most likely an alcoholic—so many things touched him off. Absolutely innocent questions on my part would make him snap and tell me it was none of my 'fucking business.'"

The spatula handle dug into my palm. I might not have heard that particular argument, but I very much recognized Pater's emotional volatility.

"It was getting to be too much for me. I wanted our marriage to work, but I also needed him to make a good-faith effort to not be so difficult—and to not keep me always at a distance."

What had Bennett said last night? *I love you too much to survive being kept at arm's length.*

"That was when he told me I could do what I liked but he had no intention of changing. I realized then it would be only a matter of time before we parted ways." She looked at me, her eyes wide with the distress of a doting mother who had just found a stash of coke in her child's room. "But you aren't like him at all. I mean, you're as dependable in a crisis as he was, but the similarities end there. You're the daughter any woman would wish she had. You are…you are…"

I was, in some crucial ways, very much my father's child. But whereas Pater lashed out, I dodged and sidestepped, when I couldn't lie outright.

Zelda covered her mouth. "I should have seen it, shouldn't I? Bennett has known you, what? Seven or eight months at the outside?"

"I'm really good at hiding my deficiencies."

"There have been times when I've asked myself how it is that you're never fazed by anything life throws at you. And then I say to myself, Of course you're that graceful, and of course I'm that lucky to have you." Her voice turned hoarse. "I should have been more observant. I should have realized you were keeping too much to yourself. I should have..."

Tears spilled down her face. And mine. I never wanted Zelda to see that I wasn't as normal and well-adjusted on the inside as I appeared on the outside. She had been the best mother in the world. To be a cause of pain and doubt to her—my heart felt as if it had been scored with a sharp knife.

"Please, *please* don't blame yourself. I've been an adult for a long time now. For better or worse, these have been my own choices."

I wanted to comfort her better. To hug her and tell her that everything would be fine. But at this point, that would be only more lies, wouldn't it?

I dropped the spatula in a stand and went back to unloading the dishwasher. Zelda joined me. Wordlessly we put away the pots and pans that remained on the bottom rack. Then I swept the floor, while she hung up fresh kitchen towels.

We often did household chores side by side—it was one of those little things I treasured. But now I could scarcely breathe against the sense of futility that permeated the air. Against Zelda's bewilderment, sorrow, and guilt.

She broke the silence at last. "Do the Somersets know yet, about you and Bennett?"

"He was going to come clean today—that was the plan, in any case. I don't see why he wouldn't follow through."

"I'll make sure to ask him first before I bring up anything—they should learn from him, not me."

I nodded, dumping the contents of the dustbin into the garbage can, and then tying up the bag and taking it outside.

When I came back, Zelda was biting into a Danish from the box of pastry she'd bought. I grabbed a gooey orange roll from the same box and sank my teeth into it with a vengeance, needing the solace of glucose and refined carbohydrates.

"So what are you going to do?" asked Zelda when only crumbs remained of her Danish. "And I don't mean about Bennett."

About myself then. I thought of my father on his deathbed, asking after Zelda, longing for the lovely woman he'd lost, because he'd been too set in his ways to change.

"I don't know," I said. "I have no idea."

And for once, that was an honest answer.

IMOGENE SOMERSET WAS EVERYTHING A young woman ought to be. Her father's doctors were very pleased with his recovery. And the family was suitably taken aback that there had been no real girlfriend, only an elaborate ruse.

All this Zelda related gingerly over dinner that evening, when I asked how her day had gone. The following week she had further updates. Mr. Somerset was out of ICU and then, a few days later, discharged from the hospital. He insisted that he was well enough, that everyone ought to return home and go back to work so he could recuperate in peace and use the time to try out some reality shows that he didn't want to be caught watching.

Despite my reminder to Bennett that I was in breach of contract and therefore owed nothing, I received effusive thank-you notes from organizations around the city, pouring out their gratitude for the generous donations in my name. A check also arrived at my office, bearing the previously agreed-upon amount for my research, which I voided and sent back.

That night I took my phone in hand, prayed that it could be a force for good, and texted, *How did you deal with your abandonment issues?*

I set the phone aside. I used to know Bennett's schedule, but not anymore, after the disruption of his father's surgery. Even if he wanted to reply, it might be hours before he could.

The phone pinged a few minutes later.

It was easier with Moira. She was right that we wanted different things in life—near the end of our relationship I probably had more in common with Darren, her accountant, than I had with her.

With my parents the anger ran a lot deeper. Relationships end all the time, even for people who once believed themselves soul mates. But family is supposed to be forever, through thick and thin.

Even after I saw them at O'Hare and set the whole moving process into motion, sometimes the resentment still came back. Why was I the one doing this? Why weren't they meeting me at least halfway?

Times like that I had to ask whether I was as blameless in the matter as I preferred to cast myself. And the answer was, of course, no. My dad might have acted out of anger, even pigheadedness, but I was the only one who had retaliated from spite.

Then it was a matter of deciding which was more important: hanging on to my resentment or having my parents back in my life.

I like to think I chose correctly.

I sighed and set the phone on my chest, as if by doing so I could absorb some of the courage and wisdom that had guided him to the right choice.

TEN DAYS AFTER MR. SOMERSET'S heart attack, I received an unexpected call from him, inviting me to lunch at his house.

The address wasn't far from Bennett's apartment. I knocked on the door of the solid four-story brownstone. A smiling housekeeper let me in and took me to an elegant white-and-green living room, where Mr. Somerset was set up comfortably on the couch, with a swing-out table next to him on which sat a phone, a tablet, a laptop, and several books.

He tilted the table out of the way as I came into the room. "Thank you for coming, Evangeline."

I shook his hand and sat down on a chair that had been pulled close. "I thought I'd find you neck-deep in *Real Housewives*."

"If I had it on, my wife might never go to work. Tea, or would you prefer a glass of wine?"

"Tea would be fine."

We chatted for a few minutes. Imogene and Prescott had both reached home safely. Imogene's boyfriend, while he was in Manhattan, had actually asked for Mr. Somerset's permission to propose. But no one thought anything would come of it: Imogene inspired proposals;

she did not accept them.

The housekeeper returned with plates of salad, tea for me, and a tall glass of green smoothie for my host.

"Let me guess," I said. "Kale, green apple, wheatgrass, kiwi, and maybe a few sprigs of basil."

"You forgot ginger, matcha, and chia seeds."

"That's hardcore."

"Tell me about it." Mr. Somerset gave the smoothie a baleful look. "I used to insist I'd never blend my vegetables—I'd ignore them like a man. But it took only one near brush with death for me to change my tune completely."

I raised my glass. "It's a good new tune to sing. Here's to your health."

We talked about this and that as we polished off the salad and the grilled swordfish that followed. From time to time he glanced at the clock, but seemed to be in no hurry to get to what he wanted to see me about.

In fact, it wasn't until we were halfway through the fruit salad served for dessert that he finally said, "Ben tells me I have you to thank for our reconciliation, for pushing him to stop waiting around."

Ben, eh?

"I didn't do anything. He was the one who uprooted his whole life and moved across the country for this one purpose."

"Yes, that was humbling in the best possible way." Mr. Somerset fiddled with a piece of pineapple. "When we came back from Berkeley, the time we severed ties, my wife didn't speak to me for three weeks. Frankly she almost left me again, and might have, if we didn't have Imogene to consider.

"But I'd been brought up to hold that a man's word was his everything. So I believed I had no choice but to follow through with my threats of disownment. I thought he couldn't do it. We knew he'd be getting some paintings when he turned twenty-one, but nobody knew whether they were paintings by actual artists or watercolors by some great-great-aunts that not even their own relatives wanted. Besides, three years is a long time when a boy is eighteen, and has to fend for himself when he's been raised in the lap of luxury."

His gaze strayed to his left. The couch had been placed before a large window. On the windowsill a Siamese cat slept soundly, next to a digital photo frame. The frame was at too oblique an angle for me. But Mr. Somerset caught my line of sight and turned it thirty degrees.

It was a family picture taken on a beach. Since everyone looked about twenty years younger, I had a good idea where they'd been. "Maui?"

"Yes, our last good vacation as a family." He finished the rest of his green juice, and seemed almost to relish it. "Of all my children, Ben was the one who worried me the most. But he surprised us all by becoming far tougher and far more disciplined than I'd thought possible. He dealt fine with having no money. And he dealt pretty well too with all the later windfalls.

"He didn't know it, but we were there at both his college and medical school graduations. I was proud of him, but too proud to admit that, especially after his attempts to take over the family firm.

"When he moved back east, my wife was convinced he wanted a reconciliation. I feared that a reckoning was coming our way instead. We'd walked away from him—*I*'d walked away from him. We weren't there for the bad times or the good. We were just some people he used to know."

Mr. Somerset looked down for a moment at his hands. "I can't tell you how many times I walked past his hospital. A couple of times I even went inside the lobby, pretending that I had a friend who was recovering from something. I never came across him. Then we started seeing the two of you everywhere. But he was so chill that I couldn't read him one way or the other.

"Good thing you convinced me to go to the MoMA exhibit, which I'd thought to avoid like the plague."

My brows shot up. So I hadn't messed things up after all? "I did see you there the Thursday after Zelda's party."

"That was probably my third time at the exhibit. You were right about it being a treasure trove of what we'd been missing all these years."

I exhaled. "Did you see the chickens?"

"There were chickens?" He laughed softly. "No, I didn't see any chickens, but I saw so much else. I saw a full, vibrant life—not a minute wasted. And I can't tell you how much I wished now that we'd been part of it, Ms. McAllister or no Ms. McAllister.

"At the lunch a couple of days later, I wanted to say something to him, but I couldn't in front of everybody. It was frustrating. And I was too…abashed, I guess, to ask my wife or anyone else for his number. So I went to see my lawyer instead, the Wednesday before my heart attack. I thought that if I never managed to say anything to him in person, at least he would learn, when my will was read, what he meant to me—little did I know that would almost happen right away."

"Thank goodness it didn't." Sometimes, thinking back to those moments before we learned of the surgery's success, I still got a little scared.

"Thank goodness," he echoed my sentiment fervently. "But I want to thank you all the same. Because of you, had things gone the other way, he'd still have known it. And that was very important to me."

I smiled at him. "You are very welcome. And I'm really happy for you and Mrs. Somerset. And Bennett too, of course. Everybody."

I half expected him to ask something about Bennett and me, but he didn't. We both had our attention snagged by the next image that scrolled onto the digital photo frame, a young Bennett, seventeen or eighteen, in his Eton uniform—an old-fashioned black tailcoat worn over a black vest and dark grey striped trousers, an outfit one might see in a costume drama set in the Victorian era. He leaned against a brick wall, his arms crossed before his chest, his head turned to his left, his gaze beyond the frame.

There was an impatient look on his face, one not of petulance, but rather a wistful urgency, as if he wished he were anywhere but leaning against that brick wall, next to a rosebush in furious bloom.

"That's the last picture he sent us, when he was still at Eton," said Mr. Somerset. "It's kind of etched on my brain—I used to look at it so much."

"Sorry I'm late," came Bennett's voice. "There was a jam in the subway and—"

I turned around. He stood in the doorway in a slate blue three-piece pin-striped suit, staring at me. My heart thudded painfully.

Into the silence Mr. Somerset joked, "You've become a lawyer now?"

"I was at the free clinic—folks there appreciate it when their doctor puts in some sartorial effort," Bennett answered, his eyes never leaving me. "Hi, Evangeline."

"Hi." Did I sound normal—or did I sound out of breath? "You missed lunch."

"I'll find something in the kitchen."

I rose. "I was just about to leave." I shook Mr. Somerset's hand again. "Thank you for lunch. And I'm so glad to see you're recovering well."

"I'll walk you out," said Bennett.

He waited until we were out of earshot of his father before he added, "I see that he's learned a thing or two about guerrilla tactics from us. If it weren't for the jam I'd have been here twenty minutes earlier."

I'd suspected as much. I'd suspected all along that Mr. Somerset might be trying his hand at matchmaking. It would have been awkward had his plan not been foiled by the subway jam. All the same…

"You didn't miss anything," I said as I shrugged into my coat. "He was just telling me things he must have already told you."

"But it never gets old to hear him admit he was wrong about me." Bennett ran a finger lightly over the piping on the lapel of my coat.

My heart might have stopped briefly. "So they call you Ben. When were you going to tell me?"

"When you told me you're called Eva."

"Huh," I said.

"Exactly." He played with the top button on my coat. "How are you?"

"Fine. Busy. You?"

"Fine. Busy. Reading *The Fellowship of the Ring*. They've made it through Moria."

"But they've lost Gandalf," I reminded him.

"Ten bucks says the old wizard comes back more badass than ever."

My lips curved a little, since he was right on target about that. "Anyway, I'm really happy for you. Your dad told me how proud he is of you—and I'm sure he's told you the same thing. It's everything you hoped for."

"Not everything," he said, his gaze as green as the return of spring. "I still hope for you."

He leaned in and kissed me, a slow, simmering kiss that left me reeling. His hand on my cheek, his lips grazing my jaw, he murmured, "I love you."

I swallowed and left quickly. But that night, as I lay in bed, I reached for my phone.

I love you too, I texted.

His reply came a minute later. *In the immortal words of Han Solo, I know.*

Chapter 18

MRS. ASQUITH PASSED AWAY THE next week.

Zelda immediately purchased a plane ticket for the grand old dame's funeral. I helped her with the packing. When we were finished, I went up to my bedroom, opened my laptop, and pulled up Larry de Villiers's e-mail.

Which made me grimace no less upon rereading. I sighed and began typing.

Dear Larry,

I'm very sorry to learn of Mrs. Asquith's departure. She was tremendous, and I wish she could have lived another twenty years.

Zelda is headed to England tomorrow. I imagine you two will run into each other at the funeral and have much to say. I also imagine that you might hold yourself back, my words of admonition still echoing in your head.

Please allow me to apologize for the more extreme things I said that day in Mrs. Asquith's garden. It is not—nor has it ever been—my place to tell you what to do. The choice belongs to you and Zelda.

I'd be lying if I said that I didn't find the possibility of Zelda embarking upon a new life absolutely nerve-racking. But my role is to love her, not to keep her penned into what little space I consider safe.

I wish you both the very, very best.

Yours,
Evangeline

I hit send before I could change my mind. And then I went downstairs to the kitchen, where Zelda was putting together our dinner, a heated-up, store-bought lasagna alongside a spinach salad.

I helped her carry everything to the dining table, conscious that she peered at me as she handed me the plates and the silverware. My admission that I couldn't handle emotional intimacy had changed things for Zelda and me. Not that it had led to strain or mistrust, but there was a sense of melancholy and regret in the air.

I waited until we had sat down and served ourselves. "I haven't told you this, Zelda, and I don't believe Larry de Villiers has either. When we met in England, he let me know that he'd been debating whether to rekindle your relationship. I told him that he shouldn't even think about it, because of his tendency to make a huge deal of your condition."

Zelda blinked. "And what did he say?"

"He e-mailed me later to say he agreed with my assessment. I e-mailed him back fifteen minutes ago to apologize for overstepping my boundaries." I looked down at my plate. "I should apologize to you too, for meddling in your life."

"Darling." Zelda reached across the table and took my hand. "You expressed an opinion. That's not the same as meddling."

"Maybe not. But I did appoint myself the arbiter of what's good for you, when you're perfectly capable of deciding for yourself."

She shook her head. "Larry isn't the only one who can rekindle this relationship. I could have approached him too. But I've been hesitant. So even if you'd said nothing to him and he everything to me, not much would have happened by this point."

"But now you'll meet in person."

She nodded. "I'm excited—and a bit nervous. It's been a long time."

I gazed at our clasped hands. "I think you'll have a great time together."

"We always do. With your father the challenge was to negotiate the ordinary times. With Larry the ordinary times have never been a problem." She sighed softly. "Don't worry, darling. I'll look out for myself. And I've reached an age when I have no problem telling someone to fuck off."

We both giggled at that.

"It almost makes me wish Larry would do something stupid," I told her, "so I can hear you say those words."

And that made us laugh again.

Zelda took a bite of her lasagna. "But enough about me, darling. How are you?"

I dug a fork into my own serving. "I'm trying to do the right thing. Trying to make good choices."

Trying to understand that I could act *through* fear, and not just out of fear.

She studied me, my beloved Zelda. And slowly she smiled. "You'll do very well, darling. Not all those who wander are lost, remember?"

BEFORE I WENT TO SLEEP that night, I texted Bennett. *I'm very sorry about Mrs. Asquith.*

Me too, he replied. *I fixed her house because she told me she was going to live forever. I believed the old battle-ax.*

I smiled a little, touched his words, and set the phone aside. It promptly pinged again.

She'd enjoy having you at her funeral.

And I really want to go, I answered. *But I've commitments here.*

I did have a number of commitments: several STEM presentations that Lara and I were participating in at middle schools around the city, a grad student's mock defense that I'd agreed to attend, plus a conference in Montreal. But by far the most important appointment on my calendar was to take place after the conference.

The Vermont farmer lived in the Northeast Kingdom. The farm had been and still was a dairy operation, but now there was also a B and B. I was booked for a one-night stay, to break my return journey from Montreal.

I left Montreal late and didn't reach the farm until after midnight. It was difficult to see anything in the dark. Even the B and B, which according to the website was a white-clapboard, picture-perfect restored farmhouse, was nothing but bulk and shadows.

When I came out of the car, the cold night air was piercingly clear, and carried with it a whiff of manure. I inhaled deeply and could almost smell spring, the loamy scent that comes when soil wakes up after the long freeze of winter.

The innkeeper had gone to bed. I let myself in with a key that had been left in a digital lockbox outside the front door. My room was on the top floor, snuggled beneath a slanting roof. The walls were a thick, creamy white, the floor light planks of ash. On the wrought-iron bed was a contemporary quilt that resembled a pixelated forest.

I shook my head. The place was more chic than my own and bore little resemblance to my impression of the farm from more than twenty years ago. And I could see no trace of my mother. It had been a generation since she'd died—not to mention that she'd moved out of the farm even before that.

Deep down, I always knew that the origin of my fear was not Zelda's illness, but my mother's abrupt disappearance from my life. I couldn't remember her or those days when I must have cried for her after she was gone. But she was the reason I'd clung to Zelda from the very beginning, long before her first episode in Manhattan.

I hadn't wanted to lose another mother.

And now I was here, at last, in the one place that was inextricably bound up with her. Her home, her refuge, the rustic backdrop against which I'd spun the first great escapist fantasy of my life.

I took a picture of my room and sent it to Bennett. *I thought abandonment issues usually don't look so pretty up close.*

It must be the crack of dawn in England, but he replied only minutes later. *No, they always look so pretty up close.*

The image that accompanied his text was a scanned photograph of a beautiful young man sitting on a set of wide, shallow steps—I recognized the back of Mrs. Asquith's house. His shirt was rumpled, his hand covered his eyes, and in the slump of his shoulders there was so much fatigue and despair that my heart trembled.

23? I asked.

Thereabout.

As I thought. Not long after the breakup with Moira.

In his other hand was a lit cigarette and at his feet an ashtray stuffed with cigarette butts. I wasn't sure why, but I tapped, *Are you smoking again, btw?*

This time his answer took a while. But eventually it came. *Yes.*

IN THE MORNING I WENT down to breakfast and took a seat by the window. The dining room overlooked a small lake, its water rippling in the light of the rising sun. Mother had sent some photographs of herself and her husband in rowboats. Had that been on this lake?

"Evangeline?"

I looked up. A man in a Fair Isle sweater and brown corduroys stood by my table. He was in his fifties and looked like a member of a local council. "Yes?"

He extended his hand. "Doug Tipton. Nice to meet you at last."

Mother's husband. I scrambled to my feet and shook his hand. "Hi. I didn't recognize you without the beard."

He laughed. "Haven't had it for at least ten years. But I guess that's what I looked like in all the pictures your mother used to send you. Mind if I join you?"

"No, not at all. Please."

He sat down. "When I came across your name on the reservation list, I thought to myself, Is that possible? But as soon as I saw you, I knew it. You look just like your mother."

Not something I heard every day, since most people I knew had never met my mother.

"I'm glad you recognized me. I'd have passed you right by."

For the rest of breakfast, we chatted about our lives, filling each other in on the twenty-plus years since Mother died. At the end of the meal, he asked whether I had any particular plans, and when I said no, he offered to give me a tour of the farm.

Half an hour later we found ourselves standing in a pasture that still had thin scabs of snow, looking toward a line of purple hills in the distance.

"To think, this is where you might have grown up, had things been different," said Doug.

The thought was shocking—I couldn't imagine growing up with anyone except Zelda.

"Your mother never thought she wouldn't be granted full or at least joint custody of you. So your father had documented evidence that she was seeing me behind his back; that didn't mean she was an unfit mother. She made it clear that she had every intention of marrying me and raising you on this farm. No judge was going to deny a girl a chance to grow up where there's clean air, open space, a stretch of white picket fence, and even a small apple orchard—it doesn't get any more wholesome, quintessentially American than that.

"But your father, he was…determined. He found out that apples and dairy cows weren't the only things we grew here."

My eyes popped. Mother's Vermont Farmer cultivated marijuana? "Pot?"

"Pot. Shrooms. Opium poppies."

My eyes bulged further. My former stepfather was a minor kingpin?

"Nothing on a serious scale, of course!" He laughed ruefully. "I was young and I was more curious than anything else. Unfortunately my curiosity extended to extracting sap from P. somniferum to make opium. I wanted to see whether it could be done—and your father had evidence that I managed it.

"You must understand, those were the days of Just Say No and very zealous drug-law enforcement. I'd have been looking at forfeiture of house and land and a huge fine, not to mention a mandatory jail sentence, if he were to turn the evidence over to the police. Your mother had no choice but to agree to give up custody, so that he wouldn't do exactly that.

"She was one for holding a grudge, your mother. She was so pissed off at your father that for years she refused to exercise her visitation rights, because he had it mandated in the divorce documents that he had to be present when she saw you."

I sighed inwardly. I'd always known there had been a sea of bad blood between my parents. But this was even worse than I'd imagined: It was all so ordinary, everyday spite that had somehow swollen to monumental proportions.

"And then she came to her senses one day and drove down. But when she came back and I asked her how it had gone, she kept shaking her head. Several days later she told me that she'd seen you in the park with your stepmother. And you were so happy that she felt completely unnecessary.

"But the real blow came when your stepmother contacted her and asked whether it was all right for her to bring you up for a visit. Your mother was so excited. We cleaned and painted and baked, and I just about gave a bath to every cow on the farm. But you never came. When your mother called, she got your father, who barked that there had never been any plan for you to visit her."

I didn't know about the phone call, but I did remember the plan. "He didn't know. We were going to come when he was on a business trip to Europe. But then my stepmother had some health issues."

It was Zelda's first episode after she came into our lives. That entire autumn had been a dark time for all of us.

"We got a call from her the next spring," said Doug. "She told us that she'd been sick and apologized for the bad timing of everything. But the main thrust was that you didn't want to come up and see your mother anymore."

I couldn't remember what exactly had made me change my mind—it was so long ago. Had I feared that it had been my demands to see my mother that had led to Zelda's episode? Or had it been a bargain I'd made with God—*Keep Zelda safe and I won't ask to see my mother again*?

Doug rubbed his palm on his clean-shaven chin. "I kept telling her that she shouldn't let any of that stop her. It didn't matter what your father did, or what you said you did or didn't want: It was up to her to make the effort and build a relationship. But she was convinced that she'd already failed. That your father, and your stepmother too, possibly, had poisoned you against her."

"My father never talked about her at all."

"The whole thing was screwed up, wasn't it?" Doug sighed. "She thought the only way you two could have a relationship would be after you grew up. But she didn't live long enough for it."

The day after Bennett had retorted, *What don't I know about abandonment issues?*, I'd had a flash of insight. His attempts to take over the family firm hadn't been only about Moira. There had also been a deep anger against his parents—for leaving and never coming back.

I'd expected to deal with a similar anger. My mother had failed in many ways: She'd been too obdurate at the beginning and too much of a quitter at the end.

But there had been no malice in her failure, only a lot of fucked-upness.

And with everything I now knew, the pictures she'd sent took on a whole new light. Instead of a glamorous showcase, as I'd always taken them to be, they were actually desperate appeals from a woman who didn't know how else to be a part of my life. *Look at this*, said her pictures. *Don't you want to be here? Don't you want to join us in our rustic idyll? Come. Do come.*

We were all fucked-up. And we were all fuckups by choice. My father chose not to change. My mother chose not to engage. And I chose to pretend that nothing was the matter, that I was—and had always been—the most perfect girl living the most perfect life.

FOUR HOURS LATER, I PULLED into a rest stop somewhere in Massachusetts, to stretch my legs and check my phone for messages.

There was an e-mail from Zelda, who had reunited with quite a few friends and relatives at Mrs. Asquith's funeral the previous day and gone out for dinner afterward. The first attachment showed a large group around a dinner table. Larry was there, a few seats down from her.

I thought the other attachment would also be a shot of dinner. Instead it was a shot of Bennett, standing before the still-open grave, looking somber and thoughtful in a long black overcoat.

The phone dinged—Zelda had e-mailed again.

I forgot to tell you, darling. Bennett found an earlier flight and left yesterday evening. He must already be back in the city.

With the time difference, he'd have landed late last night. I didn't hesitate long before I texted him. *You didn't tell me you're already back.*

I thought you knew.

You're not working today, are you?

No. Headed for Cos Cob now. And I have your tiara.

What?

Mrs. Asquith left you her tiara, the one you wore in that picture. Now you're a real princess. When are you coming to rescue me? From lung cancer, if nothing else.

He was joking, of course, but not entirely. I was the only one who could rescue him from his heartache and disappointment, I who loved him, but didn't have the courage of my conviction.

I resumed driving, but at the next rest stop I again pulled off the highway.

It was a sunny day. A family of four were having chips and sandwiches on a nearby picnic table. I opened my windows a crack, and in came the noise of a car zooming by.

My phone sat on the passenger seat, waiting.

One does not simply walk into Mordor.

Except, as I'd told Bennett, that was exactly what one did, one foot before the other, for thousands of miles.

I picked up the phone, my heart thumping hard against my rib cage. I'd never known anything but this pretense of strength and serenity. Never known what it was like to voluntarily expose the rawness underneath. Never known how life was to be lived, except behind all the closed doors in the world, and with a high wall thrown in too.

I'm fragile, I typed as quickly as my fingers could move, *the fragility of a hopeless romantic trapped in a reality in which there is no happily ever after.*

I hit send—and covered my mouth as the phone made the tiny whooshing sound of bytes being delivered at the speed of electrons. The muscles of my right calf twitched. Tiny involuntary whimpers escaped my throat. The tips of my fingers tingled, as if their circulation had been cut off.

But it had happened: I had taken the first step toward destroying the ring in the fires of Mount Doom.

Some people outgrow their fragility. I never did. Instead I became proficient at packaging it. Have you ever encountered a product that comes in a box covered with duct tape, which opens to an explosion of packing peanuts, and then you are faced with layers of tightly taped bubble wrap, only to find after that there's :still: a hard plastic shell that's a pain in the ass to pry apart?

That's me. Except I never let anyone get past the duct-tape stage. Okay, maybe occasionally Zelda saw the packing peanuts, but no further, no deeper.

I read over what I'd written and felt like an underground creature suddenly exposed to air and sunlight, wriggling desperately to get back to the stale darkness I knew so well.

Too late.

So what's underneath it all? Fear, yes. Need, so much of it. More wishful thinking than there is in the entire country on a Powerball weekend. Maybe greed too, a greed for happiness that's matched only by the fear of losing it.

I exhaled, every last one of my muscles tight and knotty. But I was almost done. Almost.

You told me you're not afraid of the baggage I bring. You might be the only one. I believe that if I were sitting on a mountain of pure gold, most dragons, including Smaug himself, would prefer to hire themselves out as furnaces, rather than face the trouble of dealing with me.

That said, I'm coming to rescue you. Brace yourself.

I PARKED MY RENTAL CAR outside Bennett's house and rang the bell.

The door opened quickly.

"Evangeline!" said Mrs. Somerset. Her eyes widened as she took in the bouquet of gladioluses I had in one arm, the bag of takeout in my other arm, two large heart-shaped Mylar balloons, the ribbons of which had been wound around my wrist, *and* the big princess gown I'd rented from a Greenwich costume shop. "What a lovely surprise! Come in! Come in!"

Shit. I never thought to ask whether his parents had come with him to Cos Cob.

Mrs. Somerset took the flowers from me and called toward the interior of the house, "Bennett, Rowland, Evangeline is here."

I followed, my face as red as the balloons, only because I couldn't run. Where was I going to go, looking like a huge blue meringue?

"They're still outside," explained Mrs. Somerset. "I came in to get a drink of water; that's how I heard the doorbell. Let me take you to the kitchen so you can put everything down."

Maybe there was time for me to sneak away to my car and change out of the stupid costume. Maybe—

As we entered the kitchen, so did Bennett and his dad from the door leading in from the backyard. Mr. Somerset grinned at my surfeit of romantic gestures. Bennett, after a moment of stunned stillness, was trying not to laugh out loud.

I narrowed my eyes at him, as I set down the stuff I'd brought.

"Wonderful to see you again, Evangeline," said Mr. Somerset. "It's really too bad that my wife and I must head back to the city now. We're having dinner with friends."

"Oh, right," said his wife. "I almost forgot. Let me grab my handbag."

"Take my car," said Bennett. "I can get it back from the station later."

We saw his parents off and Bennett burst out laughing, collapsing against the doorjamb.

"Oh, shut up."

He tried, only to succumb again. I rolled my eyes, went back to the kitchen, and found a vase for the gladioluses.

When I set down the bouquet on the kitchen island, I saw a hardcover notebook exactly like the one Mrs. Asquith had given to Bennett when we visited her. I flipped it open, thinking it was the same one.

But on the inside cover was the image of Bennett that I'd seen at his parents' house, the one with him in his Eton uniform, looking to his left. Except here, on the opposite page, was a picture of Mrs. Asquith, her lips pursed, her cane raised in mock threat toward him.

An inscription read, *To my young hooligan. What a shame you never gave me a reason to use that cane on you. Your favorite old lady, bar none.*

I smiled, my heart melting like ice cream on a hot sidewalk. The notebook was actually a custom photo book, with pictures of them together throughout the years, in her house and all over the world. The last image made me suck in a breath in surprise. It was the three of us at lunch that day—I remembered now that she'd asked Larry to take a photo.

Bennett stood between us, one hand on Mrs. Asquith's shoulder, the other on mine. And on this page Mrs. Asquith had written, *Have faith, my dear, it will happen. I wish the two of you a wonderful life together.*

My phone pinged with an incoming text. Bennett.

I've known, since the moment I first saw you in Central Park, that you're fragile. When I came across your princess picture within minutes, that impression was only further reinforced.

But sometimes people forget that there is no strength greater than that of the fragile who carry on in spite of their fragility. You are strong. You have always been. And I hope today you proved it to yourself beyond a shadow of a doubt.

I've missed you. And there are no words to tell you how much I love being rescued with food, flowers, and balloons. But did you forget the chocolates in the car?

I snorted. He was already behind me, lifting my hair and kissing my neck. "I saw your texts only after my parents left. Or I'd have booted them out much sooner."

"I'll never live down the big poufy dress."

"Don't. It's already one of my favorite memories of you."

He unzipped the costume and disentangled me from the enormous skirt. Underneath I had on my camisole and my jeans—the weather was still too cool for going around in nothing but crinkly tulle.

Wrapping his arms around me from behind, he sighed and held me against him. The sweetness in my heart rivaled that of all the maple syrup in Vermont. I reached back and looped an arm about his neck. "I actually bought some chocolates in Montreal for my friends. I'll totally shortchange them for you."

"If that's not true love," he murmured against my ear, "then I don't have one of the most viewed asses on the Upper East Side."

I giggled and turned around.

He cupped my face. "Can I tell you again how much I love being rescued?"

I tugged his earlobe. "Anytime. But you know, rescuing you is hard work. Do you have a bed I can lie down on for a few minutes?"

He laughed softly. "Of course. This way, Your Highness."

We stopped a few times to kiss along the way, but finally arrived in his bedroom. "Hey, it's that drawing!" I exclaimed. The framed charcoal rendering of my 'princess' picture, a good eighteen by twenty-four inches, took up his entire nightstand. "I've been wondering whether you ever bought it."

He scooped me up and laid me down on the bed. "Of course I bought it."

"Has it been in this house all along?"

He pulled off my boots. "Why do you think we did it in the kitchen that first time? I was terrified you'd see it if I brought you in here, even if I hid it under the bed."

"Aww."

"I know. But what we did that night was so hot, I might have developed a taste for kitchen sex." He stretched out beside me. "Can you stand naked against that wall again tonight?"

"Sure. And I'll look at you with extra hungry eyes."

He caressed the entire length of my arm. "Now *that* is everything I hoped for."

I pulled him close and kissed him. "If…if ever you ask me a question and I find it difficult to answer, will you give me some time?"

"Of course," he said, his gaze deep and clear. "Let me know that it's difficult and I'll wait."

My heart overflowed with sunshine and tenderness. "Thank you for being so easy to rescue. And thank you for giving a damn that I was stuck and couldn't see my way out."

"I'll always give a damn." Gently, he traced his thumb over my cheekbone. "I love you. I love everything about you."

I kissed him again, my agent of chaos who had brought so many wonderful and necessary changes to my life. "I love everything about you too. *Everything.*"

Epilogue

"WOW," SAID BENNETT AS WE walked into the house on 81st Street. "Nice."

Life-size cardboard cutouts of Aragorn, Legolas, and Boromir stood in the corners of the living room. A banner with the white tree of Gondor hung from the rafters. And a large, detailed map of Middle-earth was spread on an ottoman, in case our newbie needed to consult it.

We bustled in and out of the kitchen, loading the coffee table with our marathon-watching feast—although it was a slightly less copious feast than usual, as we'd spent the previous day at Bennett's parents' place. The Somersets were serious about Thanksgiving. And dinner had been extra plentiful, since it was Bennett's first one back in the fold, Mr. Somerset's first after the heart attack, and my first as the newest member of the family—Bennett and I did get married in August after all, after he finished his fellowship and I earned my tenure.

It was a lovely wedding, but my favorite part might have been the invitations, which, inspired by Mrs. Asquith's photo book, had my princess picture on the right side, his Eton image on the left, and the two of us looking toward each other. In the middle was written, *At the time these photographs were taken, Evangeline and Bennett each had someone else in mind. But from now on they will always be thinking of each other.*

When all the food and drinks were in place, Zelda's phone pinged with an incoming text. "It's Larry," she said, "wishing us a great movie marathon."

Larry and Zelda had been taking things slowly. But she was going to England next month and they'd probably spend a good bit of time together.

We settled down to start the first movie. "Make sure you point out Rosie to me," said Bennett, reaching for a cream scone.

"What's that?" asked Zelda.

"Since you're Frodo, and I'm Sam," I answered, nudging a jar of clotted cream toward my husband, "that makes Bennett Rosie, the one Sam married."

Bennett had finished the books—and quit smoking—a month before we exchanged vows. On the day of the wedding, as I was getting dressed, a note had come from him. *Dear Sam, Good luck on the quest with Frodo. I will always be here. Your Rosie.*

And I knew then that I had made the best choice of my whole life.

Zelda pressed play. Bennett took my hand in his. I kissed his cheek and laid my head on his shoulder.

Before our eyes, the epic adventure unspooled.

Thank you for reading *The One in My Heart.*

- Want to know when the next Sherry Thomas novel will be released? Sign up for her newsletter at www.sherrythomas.com. You can also follow her on twitter at @sherrythomas and like her Facebook page at http://facebook.com/authorsherrythomas.
- A review at Goodreads or at a venue of your choice would be greatly appreciated.
- *The One in My Heart* is Sherry's first—and so far, only—contemporary romance. But if Bennett's almost divorced great-great-grandparents sound like interesting characters, their story is told in her book *Private Arrangements*, a historical romance set in the 1890s.

Acknowledgments

Tiffany Yates Martin, for being the awesome editor she is.

Janine Ballard, for always demanding my best.

Kristin Nelson, for rejecting the first draft in 2010—or thereabouts. And Meredith Duran, for providing the concurring opinion that it really did suck.

Shellee Roberts, for making me get off my ass and rework the opening.

Dr. Pei-Lee Ee, for being a fantastic expert medical consultant.

Emily McKay, for sharing her knowledge on backyard poultry.

Kristan Higgins, for serving as my reservoir of knowledge on all things New England. And for the lovely cover quote.

Mike Ruprich, for recommending Salamanca as a good locale for a fictional exchange student.

My friends in the ARWA NaNoWriMo group, for providing a fun, supportive environment, and for double-checking my Spanish and Italian phrases.

And as always, if you are reading this, thank you. Thank you for everything.

More Books by Sherry Thomas

Heart of Blade Series

The Hidden Blade

My Beautiful Enemy

The London Series

The Luckiest Lady in London

Private Arrangements

His at Night

The Fitzhugh Trilogy

Claiming the Duchess (short story)

Beguiling the Beauty

Ravishing the Heiress

A Dance in Moonlight (novella)

Tempting the Bride

The Bride of Larkspear (novella)

The Marsden Brothers Series

Delicious

Not Quite a Husband

The Elemental Trilogy (Young Adult Fantasy)

The Burning Sky

The Perilous Sea

The Immortal Heights

Contemporary Romance

The One in My Heart

Printed in Great Britain
by Amazon

57675922R00148